Praise for L

P9-CFG-533

Praise for *The Marriage Pact*
by #1 *New York Times* bestselling author
Linda Lael Miller

"Miller has found a perfect niche with charming western romances and cowboys who will set readers' hearts aflutter. Funny and heartwarming, *The Marriage Pact* will intrigue readers by the first few pages. Unforgettable characters with endless spunk and desire make this a must-read."

—*RT Book Reviews*

"This is a solid foundation for this new series by one of my favorite authors. The secondary characters rounded out the story with humor and give the reader an introduction to characters we are sure to meet again in the future."

—*Romancing the Book*

"Miller treads familiar ground with her detailing of close-knit small town life, developed characters, sweet romance, and a hint of cowboy excitement."

—*Publishers Weekly*

"I really loved this story. I laughed, cried and had several *aww* moments."

—*Book Reads and Reviews*

"With her signature complex and well-developed characters, breathtaking scenery and well-written and told stories, she transports me to each locale and event. Her characters are true to life and could easily be your own neighbors and friends."

—*Love Romances and More*

"Fans of Linda Lael Miller will fall in love with *The Marriage Pact* and without a doubt be waiting for the next installments, which will feature Hadleigh's friends. Miller gives a little hint, just enough to whet my appetite, as to where one of the next storylines will go. There are the requisite pets, for without them this would not qualify as a true Linda Lael Miller book. Her ranch-based westerns have always entertained and stayed with me long after reading them."

—*Idaho Statesman*

Also available from

LINDA·LAEL
MILLER

and HQN Books

The Brides of Bliss County

The Marriage Pact

The Parable Series

Big Sky Secrets
Big Sky Wedding
Big Sky Summer
Big Sky River
Big Sky Mountain
Big Sky Country

McKettricks of Texas

An Outlaw's Christmas
A Lawman's Christmas
McKettricks of Texas: Austin
McKettricks of Texas: Garrett
McKettricks of Texas: Tate

The Creed Cowboys

The Creed Legacy
Creed's Honor
A Creed in Stone Creek

Stone Creek

The Bridegroom
The Rustler
A Wanted Man
The Man from Stone Creek

The McKettricks

A McKettrick Christmas
McKettrick's Heart
McKettrick's Pride
McKettrick's Luck
McKettrick's Choice

The Mojo Sheepshanks Series

Deadly Deceptions
Deadly Gamble

The Montana Creeds

A Creed Country Christmas
Montana Creeds: Tyler
Montana Creeds: Dylan
Montana Creeds: Logan

Coming Soon

The Marriage Season

LINDA LAEL MILLER

THE Marriage CHARM

HQN™

ISBN-13: 978-0-373-77892-8

Recycling programs
for this product may
not exist in your area.

The Marriage Charm

Copyright © 2015 by Hometown Girl Makes Good, Inc.

www.HQNBooks.com

Printed in U.S.A.

Dear Reader,

I want to welcome you back to Bliss County, Wyoming!
Mustang Creek, the heart of this county, is the kind of
small town that appeals to people everywhere—with the
kinds of friends and neighbors we all want. And, like most
towns in Wyoming, it's surrounded by some of the most
beautiful country anywhere. The mountains and forests
and rivers of Wyoming are still pristine, still wild, always
majestic. It's a landscape that defines people, becomes
part of them.

That's how it is with the characters in this trilogy.
The Marriage Pact introduced the three friends
(Hadleigh, Becca—known as Bex—and Melody). Over
the course of these stories, each woman finds the man
she's meant to be with. In the first two stories she has
a history with him that sometimes gets in the way. For
Hadleigh, that man is Tripp Galloway, and for Melody it's
Spencer Hogan. (And as far as Bex goes, you'll have to
wait and see!)

The West and romance are two of my favorite themes,
especially when I can bring them together. And friendship,
which I've explored in all three stories, is another one.
Needless to say, the role of animals in my characters'
lives (and in my life and maybe yours) is also of huge
importance to me. There's nothing like the unconditional
love of an animal. You'll see that with Spence and his
dog, Harley, as well as his horse, Reb. Then there's
Melody and her cats, Ralph, Waldo and Emerson. Neither
of these people would be who they are, *what* they are,
without the animals who share their households and their
lives.

Oh, I should mention that I'm also interested in art—
appreciating it and making it—just like Melody. Jewelry

especially. Among many other things, Melody created the charms that commemorate the marriage pact these three friends entered into in the previous book.

I hope you'll enjoy Melody's story as she comes to realize that her first instincts about Spence Hogan were right all along. Spence is now the police chief of Mustang Creek, and he typifies everything that's most admirable about the men and women who protect us and keep us safe.

Please visit my website, LindaLaelMiller.com, to check out my upcoming books, read my blog and, of course, leave your own comments.

Happy reading! And happy trails to you. (This will make sense later in the book…)

With love,

Linda Lael Miller

For Bill Francis and Renae Kinsey,
two of the best friends I've ever had, with love and thanks.

CHAPTER ONE

After the wedding...

MOST OF HIS duties as his buddy Tripp's best man complete, Spencer "Spence" Hogan ducked out of the reception, held in the library's community room, as soon as the bride and groom left the scene, both of them beaming with just-married joy and understandably eager to get the honeymoon underway.

It was a five-minute drive to the police station. Once there, Spence strode through the small lobby without sparing more than a nod of greeting for Junie McFarlane, the second-shift dispatcher, or either of the two duty officers chatting her up.

Inside his modest office, he wasted no time swapping out the rented tux and shiny lace-up shoes for the well-worn jeans, blue cotton shirt and everyday boots he'd stashed there earlier in the day. He took his hat from the hook next to the door, put it on and then, feeling like his normal self instead of somebody's pet monkey, Spence allowed himself a sigh of pure relief.

Out front again, he surveyed the goings-on.

The deputies, Nick Estes and Moe Radner, were back at their desks, focusing intently on pretty much nothing in particular and fairly radiating the Protestant work ethic. Both were rookies, their hair buzz-cut, their uniforms so starched that the fold lines still showed, their badges buffed to a high shine.

Junie caught Spence's gaze and smiled slightly. She was just this side of forty and beautiful, in a country-music diva way. Mercifully, though, she went easy on the makeup, at least when she was on the job, saving the big hair, false eyelashes, sprayed-on jeans and rhinestones for her nights off. "How'd the wedding go, Chief?" she asked, with a twinkle in her green eyes. "Did Hadleigh Stevens manage to get herself married for real this time around, or did some yahoo show up and derail the whole shindig?"

Like Spence, Junie had attended the *other* ceremony, by now a local legend, right up there with the bank robbery back in 1894 and the time Elvis and his entourage breezed through town in a convoy of limos, somewhere in the mid-1950s, reportedly on their way to Yellowstone.

Spence chuckled. "Yep," he confirmed, recalling the almost-wedding, just over a decade before. Tripp Galloway had been the yahoo-of-record, and Hadleigh had been the bride, eighteen, storybook-beautiful, naive as hell and in dire need of rescue, although she'd raised some spirited objections that sunny September afternoon. The ousted groom, well, he'd been the personification of Mr. Wrong. Otherwise known as Oakley Smyth.

Tripp, a man on a mission, had blown into that little redbrick church like a dust devil working itself up into a full-scale tornado, moments before the *I do*s would've been exchanged, calmly announced that he could give the proverbial just cause why these two could not be joined in holy matrimony and proceeded to do so.

Understandably, Hadleigh hadn't taken Tripp's interference at all well; in fact, she'd pitched a memorable fit and whacked him hard with her bridal bouquet, not once, but repeatedly, scattering flower petals every time she made contact.

There was no reasoning with her.

Finally, Tripp had lifted Hadleigh off her feet, slung her over one shoulder like a feed sack and carried her out of the sanctuary.

At that point, Hadleigh's protests had escalated considerably, of course, and she'd kicked and squirmed and yelled all the way back down the aisle, through the main doors and outside, into a world of much wider possibilities. Most likely, she hadn't been aware of that last part, being in a royal tizzy and everything.

For all Hadleigh's outrage, no one had interceded— not the preacher, not Alice Stevens, Hadleigh's grandmother and last living relative, not the stunned guests jamming the pews. Nobody moved a muscle, and nobody spoke up, either.

And that was a peculiar thing in itself, given the nature of small towns in general and Mustang Creek in particular. There, folks didn't hesitate to get involved when there was a ruckus, the way they might in a big city. No, sir. These were country people; the men were cowboys and farmers, carpenters and electricians, truck drivers and garage mechanics, sure to wade in and fight if the need arose—and the women, when sufficiently riled, could be fierce, with or without their men to back them up, alone or running in a pack.

This time, though, they'd all stood by and watched, the whole bunch of them, male *and* female, while

Hadleigh was being, as she'd put it, "abducted, damn it!"

After all, the collective reasoning went, it wasn't as if Tripp was some stranger with dubious intentions. Like the indignant bride slung over his shoulder, he was one of their own, a hard worker, decent to the core—even if he *had* been a little wild in his youth and not much of a churchgoer.

He'd served his country, honorably and in a time of war, too, when the stakes were high. In places like Mustang Creek, things like that mattered.

Oakley, on the other hand, hometown boy though he was and from a prominent family into the bargain, barely registered a blip on the public-opinion meter, one way or the other. Still more kid than man, he'd never exhibited signs of even modest ambition, partied all through college and, most damning of all, forged himself a reputation for always taking the easy route.

He wasn't hated, but he wasn't liked, either.

When the locals thought about Oakley at all, it was usually to wonder what in creation the Stevens girl, an otherwise intelligent and exceptionally pretty one at that, saw in the guy. She was nice, in addition to her other favorable qualities and, in the town's opinion, could've had just about any eligible man she took a liking to.

At that point in his mental wanderings, Junie snapped Spence back to the here and now with a soft, wistful "Isn't it romantic? How Tripp and Hadleigh finally ended up together, even after everything that happened way back when?"

Spence adjusted his hat, frowning. "Romantic?" Just hearing the word, let alone saying it aloud, made him a little nervous, although he wouldn't have admitted as much. Sure, okay, he was glad for the newlyweds— Tripp and Hadleigh *wanted* to spend the rest of their lives together, and they were obviously meant for each other. They'd traveled separate trails, long and lonely ones mostly, before their paths finally crossed again and, after some fuss and fury, decided to buckle down and forge the kind of relationship that can ride out practically anything.

And if anybody, anywhere, deserved happily-ever-after, it was those two.

Still, as far as Spence was concerned, Tripp and Hadleigh were the exception, not the rule. He felt what he always did when a buddy got married—a certain bittersweet relief that *he* hadn't been the groom, standing up in front of God and everybody, vowing to hang in there, for better or for worse and all the rest of it.

In the event that things wound up on the "for better" side of the equation, great. Bring on the house with the picket fence, the regular sex and the crop of kids that usually followed.

But what if "for worse" was the name of the game? And let's face it, the statistics definitely indicated that the odds of success were somewhere around 50/50. For Spence's money, a man might as well make advance reservations at the Heartbreak Hotel—at least that way, he'd have someplace to go when the glow wore off and the crap hit the fan.

Room for one, please, and no definite checkout date.

He liked women and made no bones about it, but his reputation had gotten out of control because he didn't typically stick around after a date or two. There were reasons—one reason, actually, and she had a name—but whose business was that, anyway?

Clearly no optimist when it came to matters of the heart, Spence didn't make commitments if he could avoid it. He was considered a ladies' man, even a womanizer, and if that perception wasn't entirely accurate, so be it. Nobody needed to know about the side of himself he went to great lengths to hide—or that he was essentially incapable of breaking a promise, no matter how stupid that promise might be farther down the road. Come hell or high water, he wouldn't—*couldn't*—be the one to call it quits.

His own father had bailed on the family early on, when things got rocky, and the last thing Spence wanted was to follow in the old man's footsteps. He couldn't help sharing Judd Hogan's DNA, obviously, but the rest of it was a matter of choice.

If the woman he'd married ever wanted a divorce, he wouldn't try to stop her, wouldn't harass her or anything like that. But he knew this much about himself: he'd be half again as stubborn to make the first move. Not only that, but he'd know, deep down, that forcing somebody's hand was bound to leave him feeling like a coward.

He was almost grateful when Junie brought him up short again. She touched his arm, and there was an impish sparkle in her eyes and a got-your-number slant to her mouth.

"What?" Spence asked, looking and sounding more irritated than he really felt and taking care to keep his voice down. On the other side of the room, Estes and Radner sat with their thick noggins bent over their keyboards, fingers tapping industriously away. Spence figured they were probably playing shoot-'em-up video games or updating their profiles on some social-media website rather than checking law-enforcement sites for all-points bulletins and other information of interest to dedicated cops everywhere, as they no doubt wanted him to believe.

Neither scenario, of course, meant their ears weren't pitched in his and Junie's direction, in case a tidbit of gossip drifted their way, something they could take home to their young and talkative wives. Although there was no truth to the rumor that he and Junie had been having an on-again, off-again love affair for years, it was out there and circulating, just the same.

Junie's smile turned downright mischievous. They'd been friends, the two of them, long before they'd become coworkers, and she could read him like a road sign. She liked to remind him of this often.

They'd buddied up, he and Junie, way back when Spence's mother had dumped him on her sister-in-law's doorstep when he was nine, loudly declaring that enough was enough, by God, and she was through being a parent, through being the responsible one, through making all the decisions and all the sacrifices. Done, kaput, over it, fed up, *finished*.

Kathy Hogan was never the same after Spence's dad ditched her for another woman—younger and thinner, of course—though the truth was, she hadn't exactly been the nurturing type even before the divorce. To her credit, Kathy had made a few half-hearted attempts at parenting after that initial drop-off at his aunt Libby's place, reappearing periodically to gather up her young son and haul him, over Libby's protests and his own, "home" to Virginia. But she'd never really gotten the hang of mothering, for all her fretful efforts, and sooner rather than later, Spence always ended up back in Mustang Creek.

When Judd and the new wife were killed in a boating accident three years after they got married, something in Spence's mom had evidently died right along with them. At Libby's insistence, she'd stopped hauling him from one place to another, the only bright spot in an otherwise dark time.

With a sigh, he pushed away the memories of that initial parting, although he knew they'd be back, soon and with a vengeance. Just when he thought he had it handled, squared it all away in his mind, the whole sad scenario would ambush him again.

If it hadn't been for Libby, his father's oldest sister, and for Junie, who'd lived down the block and appointed herself Spence's new best friend, he might have run off in his teens. It wasn't like it hadn't crossed his mind.

End result: he didn't have a whole lot of faith in marriage. He liked women, no question, but maybe his trust in them was more than a little compromised.

Ya think, Einstein?

He set his jaw briefly before meeting Junie's silent challenge with a glare. "I'm out of here," he told her gruffly. "If you need me—do your best not to—I'll be over at the Moose Jaw. After that I plan to go straight home, do the chores, rustle up some grub and then sleep until I damn well feel like waking up." He turned, adjusting his hat again as he moved, and stopped long enough to fling a narrow-eyed glance at the pair of deputies. "There's a town out there," he reminded them, indicating its presence with a motion of one hand. "If you two can work a little patrol time into your busy schedules, I would appreciate the effort and so would the taxpayers. We've had those robberies lately. I think some visibility would not hurt this department."

Instantly flustered, Radner and Estes clattered and jingled into action, grabbing keys and gear and beating feet for the exit. Chorusing a hurried "yes, sir," they nearly collided with each other in the rush to get out there and protect truth, justice and the American way.

Presto, they were invisible, which was how Spence preferred them to be, at least most of the time.

"You *enjoy* watching those poor guys scramble like a pair of idiots," Junie observed, amused, from her post behind the desk.

Spence smiled, looked back at his friend. "Yeah," he agreed affably. "I do. Guess all this power goes to my head." A pause. "See you around."

Junie's stock response was *not if I see you first,* but the phone rang just then, so her reply was a distracted, "See you," instead, followed by a business-like, "Mustang Creek Police Department. How can I help you?"

Spence didn't wait for a rundown, since anything he really needed to know could be relayed to him in nanoseconds via his cell phone or the state-of-the-art communications system wired into his truck. Anyhow, genuine emergencies were blessedly rare in this neck of the woods; most incoming calls had to do with stranded cats, scary noises coming from an attic or a basement, routine fender benders, inconsiderate neighbors blocking somebody else's driveway or playing their music too loudly, sometimes parents fretting about teenagers who should've been home hours before and weren't.

The duty officers ought to be up to handling any of the normal problems.

But the robberies had him mightily bothered. They were definitely not business as usual in this quiet town. It disturbed him that the thieves seemed to know exactly where to go. When he reached the police station parking lot, said deputies were already pulling out in their spiffy city-owned SUVs, one headed east, one west.

Spence grinned. He'd handpicked both Radner and Estes from a whole passel of fresh-from-the-academy applicants, six months before, when the mayor and the town council increased his budget. They were good cops, he reflected, arriving at his blue extended-cab pickup, and they'd be even better ones in time, when they'd logged in more hours on the job. They certainly had potential.

He got into his truck, flipped on the headlights, started the engine, glanced ruefully at the glowing blue screen of the computer affixed to the dashboard and then rolled toward the Moose Jaw Tavern, out on the edge of town. Yep, he would have preferred to go straight home, do what needed doing, and crash for the night. After all, he was officially off duty for the rest of the weekend, and he'd earned some downtime.

Still, as best man, he'd be expected to put in an appearance, however brief, at the after-wedding party. Spence knew Tripp wouldn't have cared if he skipped the festivities—by now, the brand-new husband would be making red-hot love to his red-hot wife, the lucky SOB. Mustang Creek's long-standing post-nuptial traditions had to be the furthest thing from the man's mind right now, and who could blame him?

Spence felt a nebulous pang of—whatever—in the pit of his stomach, but he didn't explore it.

Passing the Moose Jaw without stopping wasn't an option, he decided glumly. If he didn't show up, some of the gossips might invent a few fanciful reasons to explain his absence. That he, Spence, had been in love with Hadleigh, for instance, his friendship with Tripp notwithstanding. That he'd kept it together during the ceremony, and put up a good front at the reception afterward, too, but now that the deed was done, he'd made himself scarce. Gone home to lick his wounds.

All bullshit, of course. He liked Hadleigh, liked her a lot. And she was certainly easy on the eyes, no denying that.

There'd never been any kind of spark between them, though. Not on either side. When that rumor had emerged, he'd been extremely annoyed. It was even more ridiculous than the one about Junie. At one time, he'd played fast and loose with the ladies, but if anyone looked closely, maybe they'd realize that the reason there'd been so many was that he hadn't really been *involved* with any of them. Even his friendship with Trudy Reinholt was exactly that, a friendship. Until she'd begun to expect more than he was willing to offer. More than he *could* offer...

So yes, he'd show his face at the Moose Jaw, make it clear that he wasn't pining for a lost love.

Besides, he *was* the chief of police, off duty or not. It was his job to keep the peace, and to do that, he needed to get a read on the crowd. The wedding guests, well, they were sensible people for the most part, all of them friends of the bride or groom or both. But this was Saturday night, so the regulars were sure to be around, along with a few tourists. In Spence's experience, emotions ran higher on sentimental occasions like weddings or holidays or funerals—any event with a lot of symbolism attached. Throw in a little alcohol and just about anything could happen.

Soon enough, the Moose Jaw was in sight, and it was definitely jumping. Cars, pickups, motorcycles, ten-speed bikes, any rig with wheels, short of little red wagons and skateboards, crowded the gravel lot. There was no evident method to the madness, either—the vehicles were parked at odd angles, as though drivers and passengers alike had abandoned them in a sudden panic. The overall effect was chaotic, like a mess of dominoes dumped out of the box.

If the patrons inside had been in that much of a rush to start swilling beer, Spence speculated wearily, what kind of shape would they be in by closing time?

He sighed as he got out of the truck, locking it behind him. By now, he'd been up just shy of twenty-four hours, having put in a double shift on Friday, before attending Tripp's bachelor party. He was bone-weary and ravenous, too, since he'd had nothing but wedding food since last night's pizza—a slice of cake, a handful of those dainty pastel mints, and a smoked salmon "sandwich" about the size of a silver dollar.

He needed protein, preferably in the form of a thick steak, medium rare, and after feeding a couple of critters—one horse, one dog—a long, hot shower. After that, God willing, he could fall facedown on his bed and *sleep*.

Even with a plan in place, such as it was, Spence felt faintly anxious.

His black-and-white mutt, Harley, in whom a number of mysterious breeds converged, would be watching the road for him, perched vulture-style on the back of the living room couch, peering through the picture window and fogging up the glass with dog breath while he kept his vigil.

The stone-gray gelding, called Reb in deference to Spence's Southern heritage, was content enough, he figured, grazing in the pasture beside the barn, enjoying the pleasures of summer. Still, horses were social creatures by nature, whether they were wild or tame, and all of them needed company.

With these things occupying his mind, Spence was tempted to breeze right out of town, back to his ranch, pretending he'd never planned to stop in at the Moose Jaw in the first place.

Instead, and with considerable resignation, he walked across the parking lot. The bar had been in business since frontier days, when it was a bona fide Old West saloon, and the building listed slightly to one side, like a drunk trying to look sober. The roof sloped, streaks of rust marked the presence of every nail, and the never-painted wall boards had weathered to a grungy gray.

He'd stay for ten minutes, max, Spence told himself, resolute. He'd see and be seen, say howdy where a verbal exchange was required, size things up and, finally, hit the road.

Dutifully, he opened the door.

I'll stay for ten minutes, he promised himself again. No more.

THE MUSIC ROARING out of the jukebox was too loud, and the Moose Jaw was too crowded.

In Melody Nolan's opinion, that is. Everyone else seemed to be having a grand old time, whooping it up, laughing and dancing and consuming plenty of cold beer.

Oh, there was reason to celebrate, all right. Hadleigh and Tripp were *finally* married, and that was practically a miracle, given how stubborn those two were. And Melody could comfort herself with the knowledge that the marriage pact, a secret plan that she and Hadleigh and Bex had agreed upon and set in motion a few months before was actually working—one wedding down, two to go.

Melody fingered the tiny gold horsehead on her bracelet, a symbol of triumph, not just for Hadleigh, the first bride, but for herself and Bex, as well. She'd personally designed and crafted the sparkling talismans, one for each of the three friends, and this initial charm represented Hadleigh's relationship with Tripp, a rancher and born cowboy.

So far, so good.

Melody was wildly happy for Hadleigh, BFF extraordinaire. It was probably just fatigue—along with her very sore feet—that made her feel forlorn at the moment, unusually fractious and on the verge of tears.

Physical discomfort exacerbated this sorry state of affairs, but Melody didn't dare kick off the spiked heels she'd been wearing for six-plus hours as one of Hadleigh's two bridesmaids.

If she did, regret would soon overshadow relief, because her poor tootsies would puff up to three times their normal size, in which case it would be impossible to get those wretched shoes on again. Furthermore, Melody had no intention of going barefoot for the rest of the evening, since the Moose Jaw's sawdust floor was filthy and, besides, some overenthusiastic dancer might step on her toes.

So she suffered, though not in silence.

When her *other* best friend forever, Bex, short for Becca, Stuart came back to their sticky-topped table, laughing and breathless after yet another Texas two-step with yet another cowboy, Melody glowered at her.

Bex, clad in an elegant yellow dress, identical to the one Melody wore, registered the look and made a face in response.

"Why aren't you dancing?" Bex half shouted in order to be heard over the blare of the music and the general hoot and holler of the crowd packing the seediest watering hole in Mustang Creek, Wyoming.

"Why aren't *you* limping?" Melody countered. Bex's shoes, like her dress, were duplicates of her own. Yellow, pointed at the toes and stilt-like. They were definitely out of place in their surroundings. Cowboy boots were the footwear du jour.

Bex's sigh was visible rather than audible, because of the din, and the horsehead charm on her bracelet winked in the light when she lifted one hand to push a lock of artfully streaked hair from her forehead. "Honestly, Mel," she said. Melody was reading her lips. "Do you have to be such a party pooper?"

Mildly chagrined, Melody once again touched the charm on her own bracelet. "I'm happy," she retorted unhappily. "Okay?"

Bex merely shook her head. The woman was a fitness guru, for heaven's sake, and she *lived* in athletic shoes, not three-inch heels. So why wasn't *she* in pain? Those toned calves, no doubt, gained from giving classes at one of her fitness centers. "That's not exactly convincing."

Just let me welter in my self-pity. In the midst of that unbecoming thought, Melody felt an odd, heated charge tingle between the tips of her fingers and shoot up her arm, as if from the charm itself. Startled, she released it quickly, forgetting all about the exchange with Bex, sitting up a little straighter and glancing instinctively toward the bar's entrance.

And there he was. Spence Hogan, the only man who had ever broken her heart.

Not just hers, of course. Pretty much any attractive female he came into contact with fell into that category. He should have a sign around his neck—Ol' Love 'em and Leave 'em. Apparently you weren't breathing if you were female and lived in this town and *didn't* want to snag a date with him. By all accounts, many had. But she tried hard to plug her gossip ears when it came to him.

Spence was crossing the threshold, hat in one hand, standing so tall he almost had to duck to keep from bumping his head on the door frame.

It shouldn't have been possible, but he looked even better in regular clothes than he had in the elegantly fitted tux he'd worn to the wedding. The guy gave a new meaning to the term "best man," Melody thought peevishly. Her rising irritation was due to being constantly thrown into his company for the past two days. Hell, she'd had to sit next to him at the rehearsal dinner! If Tripp's father, Jim, and his new wife hadn't arranged that particular event, she might've been really annoyed at that seating snafu, but Jim was a sweetheart, and his wife probably didn't realize she and Spence had a past.

Besides, it was logical, since she was a bridesmaid and he was the best man.

Best man.

Best at *what*? Looking good? Making love? Shattering dreams?

Melody was thrown by the mere sight of Spence, which was weird because not only had they been forced into close proximity by the wedding ceremony, they'd also lived in the same small community for most of their lives. Inevitably, they ran into each other fairly often, despite her efforts to steer clear.

Nonetheless, her nerves shorted out, like an electrical circuit on overload.

Why, she wondered, silently frantic, couldn't she just look away, render Spencer Hogan invisible, pretend he didn't exist, as she usually managed to do?

No answer came to mind—and this development alone was maddening, since Melody *always* had a ready supply of answers. Except when it concerned Spence. Spence, with that easy, confident cowboy's stride of his, and the vivid, new-denim blue of his eyes; if she hadn't known better, she would've sworn he wore tinted contacts. The color was striking even from the far side of a crowded bar. So were his dark hair and his broad shoulders, the way his jeans fit his lean hips and long legs… Somehow, these familiar elements never failed to take her by surprise.

Spence had been about thirteen years old that memorable summer, when he first appeared on Melody's personal radar, although he'd been around for a while. She'd been just six at the time, already thick as thieves with Bex and Hadleigh, all of them due to enter first grade in the fall.

Friends with Hadleigh's big brother, Will, and Tripp Galloway, Spence hung around the Stevenses' house a lot in those days, shooting hoops in the driveway with other boys from the neighborhood, playing rhythm guitar in Will and Tripp's garage band.

One day that summer, though, he'd definitely caught her attention, which started a serious case of hero worship.

It wasn't anything more complicated than the chain coming off her bicycle, causing her to wipe out in the street. He happened to be arriving at Will's just then and jumped off his own battered bike. He dashed over, helping her up and examining her scraped knee and elbow, not one teasing word about the tears rolling down her face. Instead, he used the edge of his T-shirt to wipe them away. Then he brought her inside and delivered her into the caring hands of Hadleigh's grandmother. When Melody came back out, the damage duly cleaned and bandaged, her bike was fixed and sitting by the garage.

"Hey, you okay?" he'd asked, as if he actually cared about the answer.

When she nodded, Tripp said, "I adjusted your chain. It was really loose."

Will added, "The last time I wrecked like that, I'm pretty sure I cried, too. Don't feel like a baby or anything."

Then they went back to their basketball game.

That was it.

But both Hadleigh and Bex were impressed. Normally, in their experience, the boys didn't even notice their existence.

Outwardly, nothing had changed after that day. Will

and Tripp tolerated Hadleigh and her two sidekicks with benign indifference, and Spence followed their lead.

Hadleigh, Bex and Melody, on the other hand, shared a secret new awareness that nothing would ever be quite the same. They giggled and whispered among themselves, trying to unravel the mystery of this new fascination, but years passed before they finally succeeded.

Now, after all these years, Hadleigh and Tripp were deeply in love, the forever kind, and as of that very afternoon, joined in holy wedlock.

Coincidence? *Probably not*, Melody mused with a sense of philosophical awareness—undoubtedly brought on by the events of the day—as she took a sip of the beer some cowboy had bought her. She really believed this wedding was the culmination of something that had started when they were just kids.

The fairy-tale aspects of their shared history might have fostered legends if Bex and Will had grown up and fallen for each other, like Hadleigh and Tripp, but Will had been killed in Afghanistan and, while Bex had dated a lot, especially in college, she'd never met The One.

As for Melody and Spence, they'd had a summer fling once upon a time before she realized he wasn't interested in permanence, and she'd been starry-eyed with dreams of a future together—a cozy house, children and all the rest. In the end, though, she'd made a complete fool of herself by blurting out a marriage proposal, one perfect night in July, with the last of the Independence Day fireworks still dribbling from the sky. And she would never forget—God knew, she'd *tried*—the expression on Spence's face as he prepared his answer.

Instead of flashing that patented grin of his, instead of saying "yes, let's do it," the way Melody had expected him to, Spence had given her a figurative pat on the head and then, very gently, explained that he wasn't ready to make that kind of commitment, and neither was she. She wasn't even through college yet, Spence had reminded her, wounding her with kindness.

It had taken her years to recover. She took another sip of tepid beer as she grimly remembered that night.

Yes, he'd claimed, when she'd tearfully demanded whether he loved her, he *did* care for her, very much as a matter of fact. And that was one *more* reason he wasn't going to be the one to derail her career, maybe even her whole life, before she'd had a chance to go places, figure things out, decide what she really wanted.

Before Melody's personal universe disappeared into a black hole, she and Spence had spent virtually every spare moment together. Gradually, they'd grown closer and then closer still, until they'd finally made love, sweet and slow, under a star-spangled sky the first time, and in every private place they could find after that.

Oh, yes. Melody had loved Spencer Hogan with all that she had and all that she was.

Silly girl. She'd actually believed he loved her right back.

Until the breakup, of course. Spence had immediately consoled himself with Junie McFarlane, and Melody had moped around the house until it was time to go back to college in late August. There she was like a sleepwalker, distracted and depressed. Aware that things had to change, she'd switched her major from pre-law to fine arts, since she'd always loved shape and texture and color, and when that didn't help, she hid out in the dorm, skipping classes and meals, rarely sleeping through the night.

Melody's mother was beside herself with worry. After years of widowhood, she'd just remarried and was planning a move to Casper. Realizing she was causing distress to someone she loved—even knowing that she was keeping her mother from enjoying her newfound happiness—couldn't cure the blues, apparently.

Left to her own devices, she would surely have crashed and burned.

Fortunately for her, however, Bex and Hadleigh had refused to let her self-destruct. They'd improvised an amateur intervention, the two of them, confronting Melody in the cramped little room the three of them shared all through college. Melody had balked at first, demanding that they leave her alone, but they were as stubborn as she was and simply wouldn't give up.

They'd badgered her all one Saturday, until she would've agreed to practically anything just to get five minutes of peace and quiet. Knowing they'd finally cracked her armor, they'd pestered her to get out of the pajamas she'd been wearing for days on end, take a hot shower and put on her favorite outfit.

After that, Hadleigh and Bex had dragged Melody out of the dorm and off campus, winding up at the nearest mall, in one of those snip-and-dash salons, where a very gay guy with a pink Mohawk and a disturbing number of body piercings ordered her into a chair and proceeded to trim and fluff and spray her unkempt hair until she looked almost like her old self again.

Miraculous as it seemed, that was only the beginning of the Save Melody from Herself campaign.

Next, Hadleigh and Bex had declared that they were starving, and all three of them trooped over to the food court, with its plethora of unhealthy dining choices, and agreed, after some discussion, to share orders of yakisoba, chicken teriyaki and egg rolls.

Then, since the multiscreen theater was right there, and they'd all been fortified by a hot meal, they decided to take in a movie or two.

In the end, the total was three—two chick flicks and an apocalyptic action film.

The next day, she'd gone back to class, and for weeks afterward, Bex and Hadleigh had helped her catch up on the work she'd let slide.

Remembering all that in mere moments, Melody smiled to herself, there at the grubby table in the Moose Jaw Tavern, despite her aching feet and admittedly bad attitude.

The whole experience was ancient history now, she reflected, still watching Spence, still unable to *stop* watching him, as he made his way across the sawdust floor, pausing here and there to exchange a friendly word or a handshake with somebody or to laugh at some joke.

He approached the bar, spoke to the man behind it, but came away without a drink. Spence rarely indulged in alcohol; he'd told her once that it smoothed away the rough edges a little too well, whatever that meant.

At last, and with enormous effort, Melody finally managed to tear her eyes away from him, her face burning at the difficulty, and when she shifted her gaze in the opposite direction, it was to catch Bex grinning in that knowing way best friends have.

Melody grimaced at her.

Bex, unruffled as usual, laughed and shook her head, rising when yet another cowboy asked her to dance.

"Don't be surprised if I'm not here when you get back," Melody yelled over the music.

"Suit yourself," Bex yelled back, good-natured to the end.

Melody was beginning to feel like a real wallflower, which was a stretch, considering how often she'd been invited to dance since she and Bex had arrived an hour or so before. After a few polite refusals, the invitations had stopped coming, and that had been okay with her *and* with her screaming feet.

She'd had, as her grandfather liked to say, all the fun she could stand.

Time to vamoose.

The waitress had been running a tab, and Melody wanted to pay her share, so she elbowed her way through to the cash register at the far end of the bar, searching her little yellow purse—part of the bridesmaids' outfit—for her credit card.

She settled up and then limped toward the door, propped open to admit the summer breezes, and scanned the demolition derby in the parking lot for her car.

It was blocked in on all sides.

"Oh, hell," she muttered, faced with two equally unappealing choices—go back inside the Moose Jaw, hunt down the bar owner and convince him to find the patrons responsible for the dilemma and get them to move their vehicles—or she could walk home.

"Is there a problem?" The voice, all too familiar, took her off guard.

She turned her head and, sure enough, Spence was standing there, watching her, his face in shadow and his expression, therefore, unreadable. Well, not completely. Was that a grin just barely tugging at one corner of his mouth?

"Yes," Melody said stiffly. "There *is* a problem." She sucked in a breath and continued in a rush of words. "In fact, there are *several* problems. First of all, I want to go home, and I can't because my car is literally *surrounded*. Furthermore, my feet are killing me—"

Melody put on the brakes, stopped talking.

Spence, frowning as he listened, surveyed the lot full of rigs that might have been parked by half-trained baboons, and sighed. She was unprepared for the impact of his blue eyes when he looked back at her face then slid a leisurely glance down the length of her body to her shoes, which weren't suitable for walking through gravel, let alone making the long hike home. The grin he'd probably been trying to suppress broke loose at last.

"I don't know how you can walk in those things," he remarked. "And, no offense, but that dress makes you look like an inverted daffodil. A wilted one. I'll bet it's stylish or something, but I'm not positive yellow is your color. The only good point is that it shows off one leg. I like that. You have nice legs."

Melody rolled her eyes then snapped, "Well, thanks a whole heap for nothing."

"Just my opinion," Spence said. "I wasn't kidding about the leg part."

"I don't remember *asking* for your opinion of my dress *or* my shoes *or* my legs," she said, more than cranky now. When would this damnable night be over?

Spence's response was a low chuckle, and the sound was so thoroughly masculine it made her heart pound. "Come to think of it," he drawled, "you didn't." He paused, and in an instant, his expression changed. He seemed tired, no longer amused. "I'm headed for home myself, and I'd be glad to drop you off at your place." A beat of silence. "Your car will be all right here till morning, if that's what you're worried about."

By then, Melody's heart had shinnied up into the back of her throat, but she managed to croak out a reply, anyway. "I don't think—I wouldn't—I mean—"

Spence's mouth twitched again, and his eyes twinkled as he watched her.

Melody wanted to punch him.

She also wanted, perversely, to kiss him.

She wanted to…

Damn it all to hell, she didn't know *what* she wanted.

Typically, Spence didn't ask. Instead, without any warning at all, he swept Melody up into his arms and proceeded to carry her across the parking lot, his strides purposeful.

"What," Melody gasped, after a considerable delay and with significant effort, "are you doing?"

"That ought to be obvious," Spence replied reasonably. "I'm hauling you to my truck so I can drive you home. It's not as if you could cover much ground under your own power—not in those ridiculous shoes, anyhow."

"*Hauling* me?"

He nodded matter-of-factly. "You *look* thin enough, but I'd say you're on the hefty side. I've lugged around calves that weighed less."

Melody seethed, stung, even as something primitive and hungry unfurled inside her. "That was a terrible thing to say!" she protested. *"Hefty?"*

They'd reached Spence's truck, and he set her on the passenger-side running board, holding her in place with one hand while he extracted his keys from the pocket of his jeans. After easing her to one side, he opened the door and gestured for her to get in.

"Sorry," he finally said, without conviction. When she didn't move, he just put her in the truck's cab.

Melody's backside landed hard on the seat, and she was too stunned by his audacity to say another word. *Or* to climb right out of the truck.

Spence paused to consider some passing thought, rubbing his chin as he apparently pondered. His beard was already coming in, Melody noticed, oddly distracted.

"I guess I can be fairly tactless," he conceded. "*Hefty* might have been the wrong word. But I *did* apologize, didn't I?"

Melody found some remnant of her voice, enough to call him a name.

Spence shook his head in apparent amazement, but Melody knew that lethal grin of his was lurking just out of sight and might reappear at any moment, a dazzling flash that would leave her temporarily blinded.

"I should've known better than to try and do you a favor," he said with a long-suffering sigh. Before Melody could react, he added a brusque, "Fasten your seat belt." With that, he slammed the door, came around to the driver's side and got behind the wheel.

If she hadn't been fresh out of steam and in no mood to cripple herself for life by trying to walk home in the heels from hell, she would've told Spence Hogan what he could do with his *favor*. After that, she would have pushed the door open again and left him sitting there in his gas-guzzling phallic symbol of a truck to think what he liked.

It was a nice fantasy.

Melody folded her arms and fumed until they were out of the parking lot and on the highway. Then—she just couldn't help it—she muttered, "*You* started it."

Spence threw back his head and gave a shout of laughter.

"Well, you *did,"* Melody insisted. Why couldn't she shut up, leave well enough alone? After all, her house was less than five minutes away. Surely she could have held her tongue *that* long.

But no.

Grinning, Spence turned to look at her. "What's so funny?" Melody asked.

"You," he answered succinctly. "It's really true what they say."

"Which *is?*"

"Some things never change. Neither do some people."

CHAPTER TWO

By Spence's rueful calculations, the whole fiasco took less than ten minutes to unfold, from start to finish.

The instant he'd brought the truck to a stop at the curb in front of Melody's house, and before he could get out of the rig and walk around to open her door, she'd bolted, making her gimpy way across the sidewalk without a wave of the hand or even a backward glance—never mind saying goodbye or thank you.

Since no self-respecting man drove a woman home after dark and then just sat behind the wheel like a lump and watched while she hiked to her door, Spence was on the move in a heartbeat.

He'd caught up to Melody at the gate, when the pain in her feet finally reined her in. She'd paused, resting her right hand on one of the newel posts to keep her balance while she used her left to pry off her shoes, one and then the other, grimacing with relief. For a moment, Spence thought she might pitch the things into the nearby bushes, but in the end, she didn't.

Instead, she tilted her chin upward, met Spence's gaze straight on, and said tersely, "You can leave anytime now." She gestured in the direction of the house, the offending stilettos waggling with the motion. "I hardly think I need a police escort to get to my own front door."

Stubbornly silent, Spence had opened the gate, taken Melody by the elbow and squired her onto the porch. She hadn't objected, not verbally, anyway, but she'd looked mad enough to bite off the business end of a shovel.

Spence had waited, without comment, until she'd fished a key from her impossibly small handbag and thrust it into the lock with so much force that he wouldn't have been surprised if the thing snapped in two.

Fortunately, that didn't happen.

As soon as Melody was over the threshold, she'd favored Spence with one last glare and slammed the door in his face.

At the memory, a muscle bunched in Spence's jaw, and he ground the truck's gears as he left the town behind, speeding up the second he hit the open road. With a conscious effort, he unclamped his molars and relaxed his rigid shoulders.

All right, yeah. He'd put his foot in his mouth a couple of times, back there at the Moose Jaw—he'd never been able to think straight in close proximity to Melody—but he'd said he was sorry, after all, and he'd meant it. Mostly.

Shouldn't his apology, however halfhearted, have counted for something?

If the woman hadn't been contrary to the marrow of her bones, she'd have met him halfway, or at least made a stab at civility, if only because he'd obviously been trying to help her out. Anybody else would've cut him some slack for his good intentions.

Of course, Melody wasn't *anybody else*, she was her usual hardheaded, cussed self. A casual observer might have thought he was fixing to kidnap her, the way she'd carried on.

Irritated beyond all common sense—Spence was tired and he was hungry and that combination virtually guaranteed a bad attitude—he flung his hat onto the passenger seat and shoved splayed fingers through his hair.

He hadn't improved matters, he reflected, by tossing the little hellcat over his shoulder and lugging her to his truck, either. This was real life, present tense, complete with new and often puzzling rules for any male-female interaction—not some vintage John Wayne-Maureen O'Hara movie.

No question, Spence reasoned grimly; he'd acted in haste, and he would surely repent at leisure.

And yet he'd had to do *something* to break the stand-off, didn't he? Otherwise, he and Melody would probably still be standing in that parking lot, bickering like a couple of damn fools, with no end in sight.

Just when Spence was beginning to think he might be getting some adult perspective on the events of the evening, another rush of frustration came over him, and he was right back at square one.

He simmered for at least five more minutes then put a foot to the clutch and shifted again. By degrees, he began to calm down. He recalled the way Melody had looked, standing in the bug-specked yellow glow of her porch light, with her makeup worn away in some places and smudged in others. He remembered how she'd bitten down on her lower lip like she did whenever she was stressed out. And how her hair, her gorgeous honey-colored hair, seemed ready to come unpinned of its own accord and tumble down around her shoulders.

Just picturing that made his groin tighten.

He sighed.

Melody was always beautiful, no matter what, Spence admitted silently, with a sad twitch of his mouth that didn't stretch far enough to classify as a smile.

The ache between his legs migrated upward, nestling in the uncharted territory hidden somewhere behind his heart, a slow, familiar throb of sorrow and regret.

He'd lost her.

That wasn't exactly breaking news. Whatever he and Melody had had together—or *almost* had—was part of the distant past. At times, though, it rose up out of nowhere and seared him.

Like tonight.

Spence clenched his back teeth, determined to tough out the rush of emotion that had ambushed him, partly because he knew he didn't have a choice and partly because that was what he did. He endured, knowing all too well that resisting these particular feelings was futile and would merely deepen and prolong the misery.

Again, he sighed.

Since both Spence and Melody made every effort to avoid each other, the figurative bodies stayed buried. Invariably, though, some special occasion rolled around, like their friends' wedding that afternoon, and all the tattered specters rose like howls riding a night wind, reminding him that the dreams and plans he'd once cherished were over for good.

This, too, he reminded himself grimly, would pass.

Sooner or later.

So he just drove.

Mercifully, his mood improved a notch or two when the outlines of his house and barn came into sight. They weren't anything fancy, those structures, but they had good, solid bones and so much history they'd probably grown roots over the years. Deep ones, too, stretching far into the earth, gnarled and sturdy, anchoring themselves to the land.

Spence parked behind the dark house then reclaimed his hat from the passenger seat and got out. The instant the soles of his boots struck the fine Wyoming dirt, he felt the familiar mantle of peace settle over him.

He was home.

He smiled at the sounds heralding his return from the outside world—his gelding, Reb, nickered a greeting from the nearby pasture, all but invisible in the darkness, while Harley tuned up a one-dog orchestra, yipping with joyful anticipation behind the kitchen door a few yards away.

"Hold on," Spence called out to both critters. "I'm on my way."

MELODY'S THREE CATS, Ralph, Waldo and Emerson, were sitting in a tidy row when she hobbled into the kitchen, barefoot and vowing never to put on high heels again, no matter *who* was getting married, herself included.

Not that there was much danger of that, considering the state of her love life.

"Reoooow," the cats chorused in perfect unison.

Despite appearances, Melody knew the animals hadn't formed a welcoming committee—this was a protest.

She laughed, still shaken from her most recent encounter with Spence but recovering fast, now that he'd gone and her shoeless feet were free to swell as they liked. "Spare me the drama," she chided her pets, padding over to the counter, taking a favorite mug from the wooden rack on the wall next to the sink. "I know I'm late serving your supper, but I don't feel guilty about it, okay? One of my best friends tied the knot today." Melody paused to smile, happy because *Hadleigh* was happy, and wasn't that proof things worked out, at least some of the time?

Melody filled the mug with water, dropped in an herbal tea bag—electric raspberry—and fired up the microwave.

The furry trio didn't break rank, merely turning their heads her way instead, watching accusingly as Melody opened a can of cat food, took three small plates from the appropriate stack in the cupboard and divided the grub evenly.

In the meantime, the microwave whirred companionably.

The cats remained in formation while Melody, carrying their feast with the deftness of a veteran truck-stop waitress, delivered their evening meal.

They *were* an odd bunch, her regal and totally opinionated fuzz balls. Hadleigh and Bex said so often, and Melody had to agree. Littermates adopted from the local shelter a few years ago, they looked so much alike, right down to the last splotch of calico, that even she couldn't tell them apart.

Interchangeable as they were, she reasoned, she might as well have named them all Bob. It would've been simpler.

Leaving the felines to their banquet, Melody walked

out of the kitchen, down the nearby hallway and into her bedroom.

There, full of sleepy relief, she took off the dress, the snagged pantyhose and the scratchy slip, letting them fall in a heap on the floor. Then, in her bra and panties, she got a clean and well-worn nightshirt from a dresser drawer and headed for the shower.

She turned on the spigots, adjusted them until the water temperature was exactly right and stepped under the spray. Closing her eyes, she tilted her face back, standing still, savoring the bliss, as the last vestiges of her makeup washed away.

She reveled in the ordinary pleasure of being under her own roof again, alone, unobserved, free to be Melody rather than some public version of herself.

Her hair proved to be a problem—she had to shiver outside the shower long enough to remove the last few pins and brush out the snarls teased in that morning by a local hairdresser—but Melody managed the task and stepped back under the steamy, pelting flow. After a thorough shampoo and a lot of soaping and rinsing, she sighed, shut off the water and got out, wrapping herself in a large bath towel, sari-style.

When the mirror had defogged, she combed out her wet tresses—she didn't have the energy to use the blow dryer, which meant she'd have to soak her head again in the morning to tame the beast, but that was fine with her. Tomorrow seemed years away.

On automatic pilot now, Melody brushed her teeth and wiped a few lingering smudges of mascara from beneath her eyes. Finally, she pulled on the nightshirt.

She left the bathroom to make her nightly rounds—all windows shut, every door locked, stove burners turned off—and congratulated herself silently for not thinking about Spence Hogan even once. It was a winning streak, a personal best; for almost half an hour, Melody reflected, her busy brain had remained Spence-free.

She gave a small sigh, deflated. He'd slipped right back into her thoughts, though.

So much for the winning streak.

When she reached the kitchen again, Melody noticed that the cat brigade had finished eating and wandered off to some other part of the house, probably her studio. They liked to sit unblinking on the fireplace mantel, so completely motionless that visitors sometimes mistook them for oversize knickknacks.

She smiled as she scooped up the empty plates, rinsed each one thoroughly and stashed them in the dishwasher. Then she dried her hands, crossed to the back door and peered at the dead bolt. She knew she'd locked it that morning, before leaving the house, but she'd been known to forget things, like everybody else.

Dutifully, Melody moved on to the next item on her mental agenda—making sure the front door was secured. She'd been pretty flustered after the encounter with Spence.

Then she examined each and every window.

Since she worked at home, and she'd never gotten around to having an air-conditioning system installed, she often kept three or four of them open during the day, hoping to catch any stray breeze that might have swept down from the snow-crowned peaks of the Grand Tetons.

The tour ended in Melody's studio, her favorite part of the house.

The space, originally the living room, wasn't huge, but it was a great place to work, with its strategically placed skylights, built-in bookshelves and the custom-made cabinets where she stored art supplies.

The tension seeped from her shoulders as she looked around. Some nights, unwilling to be parted from whatever project happened to be consuming her at the time, she actually slept in here, curled up on the long sofa, burrowed under the soft weight of a faded cotton coverlet, spinning straw into gold as she dreamed.

The cats, as she'd predicted, sat side by side on the wide mantel above the fireplace, impersonating statues. Thanks to the permanent claim they'd staked to the entire surface, Melody couldn't keep framed photographs or a nice clock or any other decorative items there, as a normal person might. She shook her head, smiling, and turned to look at the design board that took up most of the opposite wall. Every inch bristled with sketches, appointment cards, snapshots, sticky notes scribbled with reminders and ideas for new pieces of jewelry, and glossy images of watches and pendants, rings and bracelets, torn from various magazines.

Melody would never have copied another artist's work, but she liked to admire the really good stuff. Now and then, some aspect of a design sparked her own imagination and hurled her into a creative—okay, manic—frenzy that might last for hours or even days. She invariably emerged from these episodes with some new and totally original creation.

When she worked, she focused almost entirely on process rather than objectives. For Melody, the magic lay in the *what-ifs*, the little experiments, the sheer alchemy of transforming raw materials into something beautiful, timeless and utterly unique, a piece she hoped would be treasured and eventually passed down, generation after generation.

Tired though she felt, Melody was tempted to perch on the cushioned stool in front of her drafting table, open her sketchbook to a fresh page, pick up a pencil and see what emerged.

Get some sleep first, counseled her practical side.

Melody decided to take her own advice. Although she'd pulled many an all-nighter over the course of her artistic career, she did her best work after a good night's rest.

It was time to hit the sheets.

Ralph, Waldo and Emerson, still sitting on the mantel, watched inscrutably as she passed, unmoving except for their eyeballs.

Pausing to flip the light switch before leaving the room, Melody smiled again. "Hadleigh and Bex are right," she told them. "You're not ordinary earth cats, you're aliens."

SPENCE'S INNER ALARM clock woke him promptly—and completely—at four the next morning, like it always did in the summertime. In the dead of winter, he usually made it to five before his eyes flew open and stayed that way, whether he'd gotten any real rest or not.

"Damn," he muttered, sitting up, running the palms of both hands along his face. Another few hours of sleep, and he might have felt halfway human, but since staying in bed would be the classic losing battle, he tossed back the lightweight covers and set his feet on the floor.

Harley was stationed in the bedroom doorway, watching him with hopeful interest. The dog's head was cocked to one side, and his ears were perked.

"What?" Spence asked. No way was he going to let that critter make him feel guilty; he'd set out an extra bowl of kibble the night before, along with a backup supply of water. He'd also remembered to unlatch the pet door, in case Harley needed a yard break during the night.

Harley responded with a cheery little yip and thumped the hardwood floor with his tail, barely able to contain his eagerness to follow up on whatever opportunities presented themselves.

Spence sighed, drawing a hand through his rumpled hair. Even if he *hadn't* been hardwired to get up at the crack—hell, before that—the damn dog would probably have *stared* him awake.

He stood, shaking his head in pretended frustration, but the fact was, he couldn't help grinning. Clearly, Harley knew that this wasn't going to be a stay-at-home-and-wait kind of day, but a tag-along one instead, bursting with canine delights like riding shotgun in Spence's truck, sticking to his boot heels like a burr, streaking through tall grass to keep up with Reb out on the range.

Didn't matter to ol' Harley where Spence went or what he did, whether he was on foot or in the saddle, as long as he got to play sidekick.

A man had to admire that sort of loyalty.

After a shave and a shower, Spence returned to the bedroom and opened a few bureau drawers in the hope that at least one set of clean clothes might have manifested itself when he wasn't looking. No such luck.

With a towel around his waist, he made for the small laundry room off the kitchen, opened the dryer and pulled out a shirt. Yesterday's jeans would have to do, but what the hell. He'd only worn them for a couple of hours the night before, and it wasn't as if he'd been digging post holes or wrestling a roped calf to the ground at the time.

No, he thought. *He'd just been wrestling a testy woman into his truck, that was all.*

Maybe, Spence mused, he ought to apologize to Melody—again—for the *hefty* comment. He should have used *muscular*, but that probably wouldn't have gone over well, either. *Solid?* Um, no. Considering her feminine grace, he was just surprised she wasn't lighter, that was all. She must work out.

Nope. None of those possibilities would be deemed acceptable. Better to keep his distance, rather than risk stepping in it again.

Only that didn't seem exactly right, either.

Weighing the decision in his mind, Spence opened the door and left it ajar, so Harley could go outside without having to shinny through the much smaller pet door. With freedom beckoning, the animal shot through the gap at bullet speed, as if he had a date with destiny. Spence, still wearing the towel, slung the shirt over his shoulder and put the coffee on before going back to his room. He scouted around for the jeans he'd discarded the night before, found them partway under the bed and yanked them on. Then he shrugged into the shirt, noting that it could have used a few licks with a hot iron.

Oh, well. In the bigger scheme of things, a few wrinkles wouldn't matter. After all, he had the day off, and he wasn't going anywhere fancy—just to the feed store on the outskirts of town, followed by a brief stop at the supermarket. Soon as he and Harley got back, he'd be saddling Reb and riding out to see how the fences were holding up.

He planned to put the incident with the prickly Ms. Nolan right out of his mind.

CHAPTER THREE

MELODY STUBBED HER toe on the doorjamb trying to carry a filled cup and two art magazines into her studio. For some reason, one of the cats—she couldn't be sure which—had decided to weave between her legs. The balancing act was an experiment in agility and she managed to stay upright, but just barely.

Gritting her teeth, she sacrificed one of her glossy periodicals to protect the guilty feline from a splash of hot coffee. Those pages would probably never come apart again. *Thanks a lot.*

"One day," she warned all of them out loud, "I won't be so graceful."

The other two resident fuzz balls gazed blandly back at her from their perch on the mantel, and Melody got the distinct impression they wouldn't have credited her with grace to begin with, and they were probably right. Cats had a way of saying things without actual articulation or even body language. Besides, they'd seen her doing yoga—they mimicked her movements—so they could have a point. All three of them were better at it.

Damn it, her feet *still* hurt. She should write a song, something like "The Broken Toe Blues." Or "I Left My Arch in Mustang Creek." Maybe it would top the charts, since almost every woman in the world could relate.

With a little grin and a sigh, Melody shook off the whimsical idea. She was a designer, not a songwriter, and besides, she didn't have a smidge of musical talent.

Cozy in loose sweatpants and a shapeless T-shirt, she pulled out the chair at her worktable and got busy.

Or tried to, anyway.

After nearly three hours of dedicated—and largely fruitless—effort, she reluctantly faced reality. Her muse was on hiatus.

Damn. This was a big commission, a bib necklace set with precious stones for a picky client who'd collected the gems herself on various trips, and the design was hidden in a compartment in Melody's brain, but it hadn't emerged yet. Mrs. Arbuckle was infamously outspoken, so she really wanted to get it right or she'd hear about it, and not necessarily in a tactful way.

Melody was good and stuck—and that wasn't her only problem.

Resting her forehead on one fist, she contemplated the unsavory options on her list. For starters, she probably owed Spence an apology.

Probably? Try definitely.

She'd been pretty rude to him, all things considered. Oh yeah, she'd been mad at his assumption that he could pick her up and cart her off to his truck like some Neanderthal in boots and a cowboy hat, but in the light of day, she couldn't deny that he'd done her a favor. And because she'd been hungry and tired, and her feet were hurting like crazy, she'd been just plain ungracious.

Her grandmother, who had helped raise her, would not have approved of Melody's behavior—or *his*, for that matter, although that was beside the point. And even though Grandma Jean wasn't around to voice her opinion anymore, Melody swore she could *feel* it.

So yes, an apology was in order. Melody put down her drawing pen with a sigh. She knew from experience that the missing muse wouldn't put in an appearance until she'd cleared her conscience.

"This is easy to fix," she told the cats as she got to her feet, which were not back to normal but were at least safeguarded by a pair of soft, comfy shoes that would qualify as slippers if anyone wanted to get technical about it. "I'll go there, talk to the man, tell him I appreciated that he wanted to help—even if he was crass about it."

One of the fur faces—Melody was fairly sure it was Waldo, still gracing the mantel—yawned with obvious disinterest. She'd seen that expression before, and at the moment, she found it irritating. "Fine, she muttered. "I won't bore you with the details. And I won't say anything to him about being rude. Does that approach suit your royal highnesses?"

Waiting for an answer was pointless, of course. She just grabbed her purse—at least she was back to one that could hold more than a matchbox—intending to hoof it over to the Moose Jaw to pick up her car.

Halfway out the door, she stopped dead. The vehicle was sitting in her driveway. She blinked to make sure it wasn't an optical illusion. Nope, definitely there.

She had the key—the only key—in her hand.

So how...?

Spence.

Was the chief of police supposed to hotwire a car? Melody stood there for a few minutes, tapping a sore foot, and came to the conclusion that if anyone could get away with it, he could. Okay, great, now she double-owed him.

As she pulled out of the driveway, it occurred to her that she was wearing not only her slipper shoes, but also a worn T-shirt that said *Wyoming Will Rock Your Tetons* on the front, and baggy sweatpants were loosely held up by a drawstring. Glamour wasn't on the agenda today.

Fine. She planned to state her business and go. *Who cares what I look like?*

After all, this was an errand, not a hot date. Still, Melody *did* loosen her hair and let it fall around her shoulders. No use being at a total disadvantage. Spence threw her for a wide, slow loop as it was. She didn't know why, but she found herself recalling the time they'd gone swimming in the Yellowstone River on a camping trip early in that magical summer. He'd looked downright delicious with wet hair and absolutely nothing else on… Oh, yeah, that had been one unforgettable afternoon.

Let's put that memory in cold storage.

Melody drove slowly toward Spencer's property, mapping out her apology as she went. She'd say she was sorry for being grumpy, foisting the blame on her diabolical shoes. He'd act distant but nice about it all, and that would be it. Done deal. Then maybe she could actually work. Creativity was a delicate thing. When she was upset, she couldn't concentrate. So she wasn't doing this for Spence. She was doing it for herself.

When she finally cruised through the open gateway onto the Hogan ranch and started up the long drive, a plume of dust roiling in her wake, she scanned her surroundings, immediately registering that although

Spence's truck was parked near the barn, his horse wasn't in the pasture, and there was no sign of his dog, either.

Perfect. She'd worked up her courage and come all this way for nothing.

Clearly, the chief of police was not at home.

Torn between mild annoyance and stark relief, Melody parked, got out of the car and stood, hands on her hips, breathing in the grass-scented country air and taking in the scenery while she weighed her options.

The Grand Tetons loomed in the near distance, jagged and snow-capped.

She shifted her focus to the house. Nothing fancy, but Spence wasn't ever going to be fancy, and no one would expect that. The low-slung structure was functional and comfortably spacious, and it suited a cowboy lawman's lifestyle. There was a wide front porch, shaded by a sloping roof, outfitted with several wooden rocking chairs and a small table. The barn was weathered but looked like it had a new roof, and the corral was clear of any weeds, with a solid rail fence and a trough at one end.

The house and yard could have used a woman's touch, she thought—a few flower beds, maybe a window box or two, some cheery curtains at the windows.

But Spence was a bachelor, sharing the ranch with the horse and the dog, and Melody supposed the set-up was pretty much perfect for a simple man. Only Spence wasn't simple at all; he was darned complicated, vexing as hell, and that mistake she'd made years ago of thinking she understood him—it had really bitten her in the posterior.

Um, better put that memory on ice, too, sweetheart.

Melody began to feel fidgety. She really needed to *work*. It wasn't just therapeutic on a bazillion levels, it was also her livelihood, and, therefore, the only reason she was here at all. She wanted to get that apology out of the way so she could concentrate again...

Maybe she ought to cut her losses and run, get out while the getting was good. She could always send Spence an email, dash off a breezy "sorry about that" and move on with her life.

Furthermore, she could do without the drama, she told herself. Things had been running pretty smoothly but now, all of a sudden, Spence was an issue. Again.

All he did was give you a ride home, she reminded herself silently. *Lighten up.*

Inspiration struck. She'd leave him a note. That would soothe her conscience, put paid to the whole matter, once and for all.

Problem solved. Resolutely, Melody climbed the steps and just in case she'd missed her guess and Spence *was* at home, after all, she knocked on the door. No dog and no horse almost certainly meant no Spence, but with the way her luck had been going lately, she might catch him with his pants off or something.

An intriguing thought.

She rapped firmly at the door. Waited.

No answer.

Still, she hesitated to barge into another person's house. She considered scribbling a few words on a page from the sketchbook she always carried in her purse, but it was a breezy day; the message might blow away, roll across the range like a tumbleweed or wind up lodged in the branches of some pine tree.

Hell.

Melody pounded on the door.

NOTHING. SHE WAS out of choices.

After drawing a long, deep breath, she tried the knob. Surprisingly, the chief of police had left his house unlocked, but then again, she supposed Spence knew it would take some nerve to rob *his* house.

She stopped in the act of opening the door, noticing with amusement a garden gnome parked next to something bushy by the front porch. No kidding? She guessed the plant was a weed, but she had to admit it was kind of pretty with yellow flowers that she assumed would send anyone with allergies into a tailspin. Still, it *looked* as if he intended it to be there. A garden decoration like that on a ranch—what was the story? If that wasn't out of character, she would eat her pointy shoes from hell.

He was such a…*man*.

A tall, infuriating man with skillful hands and a compelling smile, who made love as if he really meant it…

But didn't. All these years she'd expected to hear that he'd gotten engaged. It hadn't happened. There'd been some talk about Trudy Reinholt, an attractive elementary-school teacher who seemed to hold on to him the longest—longer than Melody had, that was for sure—but it had fizzled out about a year ago.

Melody let herself in and stood in the living room, since there was no real entry other than some tiles in a square so cowboys could wipe their feet before they stepped onto the hardwood floors. There was a tan couch to her left in front of a river-stone fireplace, a plain pine coffee table with a dog-eared novel on it and an iron lamp that had the image of a bronco rider. His coffee cup was still sitting on the surface of the table, but to his credit, he'd used a coaster.

Would he mind her just barging in? His actions last night meant he'd given up that choice, she decided. If he hadn't been so impetuous, so…pushy, she wouldn't be standing here, uninvited, in his living room.

Yep, all his fault.

Still, she *was* an interloper. Spence craved his personal space, she knew that about him, and it was something they had in common. Solitude was a friend for both of them. *She* needed it in order to create her eclectic designs. *He* dealt with a much grimmer reality, although—granted—no one would call Mustang Creek a hotbed of criminal activity. But solitude for him was an escape from the problems he had to unravel, a chance to recover his equilibrium.

While he was in the real world solving crimes, she was in her own little realm spinning treasures.

They were opposites. She got him, and yet she didn't.

Was that the chemistry? She was light, and he was darkness?

No, Spence was pure light, just of a different kind.

She should ditch the philosophical meditation and find a pen, since there didn't seem to be one in her purse. No sketchbook either. Melody might have walked right into the man's house, but she drew the line at rummaging through cabinets and drawers. She finally fished out a bank receipt from her bag and thankfully spotted a pen on a small side table by the picture window. She'd snatched it up and started to scribble her apology, noting that the pen said Findley's Feed Store on the side, when the door opened.

"Hey."

The sound of Spence's low voice made her whirl around in time to have Harley launch himself at her in pure adoration, singing the song of his people.

So the master of the house was back.

Boy, he sure was, leaning in the doorway, that faint, devastating smile on his mouth. "Ma'am, pardon me for saying so, but I believe you're trespassing."

"I WAS LEAVING you a note."

Melody looked cute when she felt guilty, especially while trying to fend off a dog with one hand, a pen clutched in the other.

Spence's problem was that she looked cute—no, beautiful—to him *all* the time. Even in the daffodil dress, wobbling on her ridiculous shoes, she'd turned him on. Maybe it was that glimpse of one long, sleek leg because her skirt had a slit in the side of it.

The real Melody, the quirky artist with mismatched clothing and long honey hair in a shining fall over her shoulders, was eye-catching in his humble opinion. It didn't matter what she wore.

"About?" He raised his brows in question.

"About what?" She'd figured out that if she climbed onto one of the stools by the counter, Harley's exuberance was easier to handle. At a word, the dog would calm down, but Spence didn't say anything. Perched there, Melody peered at him.

"You mentioned a note?"

"Oh, right." She seemed flustered. Gloriously so. "I was going to thank you for last night."

"For what, specifically?" Spence savored Melody's discomfort, reflecting on the fact that she hadn't seemed all that grateful at the time.

"The ride home." She was blushing. "And I assume you're the one who got my car back to me. Thanks for that, too."

"No problem."

"It had to be something of a problem, since you didn't have my keys."

"As someone who's worked in law enforcement for a while, I can tell you it's not an insurmountable one."

In the course of his career, he'd met a few people who'd done a two-step, twirl and turn when it came to the law, but they weren't always bad folks, just a little misguided. He didn't look the other way when they broke hard and fast rules, but most of them, especially the young ones, only needed a nudge in the right direction. Spence was a big believer in second chances.

He wouldn't mind a second chance himself. A second chance with Melody Nolan.

He could hardly believe it, but they were actually alone. Yesterday had been different, full of activity and ceremony and guests, but in his quiet house they were together—and on their own—for the first time since he and Melody had gone their separate ways nine years ago.

"Just answer my question. How did you manage the car anyway, without my keys?"

"Called in a favor from someone I know." He moved into the kitchen, but his casual stride didn't reflect his mood. He was anything but nonchalant. Coming home to see her car outside his house—and her inside it— had done something interesting to his stomach that had nothing to do with the fact that he'd ridden back because he was getting hungry.

She looked skeptical but also flustered at being caught in his kitchen, although at least Harley had calmed down enough that she could get off the stool. "How do they turn off the car without keys?"

She'd always had an inquiring mind.

He shrugged. "The same way they started it, I imagine. And no, I didn't let a convicted felon drive your car. No arrests, just an...unusual background."

Frank was a wizard with all things mechanical, but outside of one juvenile joyride, he'd stayed out of trouble. After that initial brush with the law, they'd come to a mutual understanding—Spence didn't want to send him to jail, and he didn't want to go. He'd found it hilarious that Spence had called him.

She chose to not pursue it. Facing him, her aquamarine eyes vivid in the late-morning light, she began, "This is better done in person, anyway. I know we're no longer—"

"Lovers," he supplied helpfully, crossing his arms and propping himself against the counter.

More's the pity.

"Not in practically a decade!" His gorgeous trespasser glared at him. "I was going to say friends. That we're no longer friends, I mean. The point is, I always pay my debts, so if you ever need a favor, I guess I owe you one."

Spence couldn't help it; he laughed at her grudging tone. His drawl was deliberately exaggerated. "Why, ma'am, I'm afeard that ain't the most gracious apology I've ever gotten."

Her eyes *really* were the most beautiful color, a

shade of aqua he'd never seen on anyone else, and they flashed with a familiar fire he'd sorely missed. It had been too long since he'd really looked into them, with her looking back. Melody usually did her best to stay away from him—and if they both happened to be in the same place, she'd pretend he wasn't there. Or that she wasn't…

She slung the bag she'd brought over her shoulder, and he was surprised she didn't topple over because it was obviously heavy. That was confirmed when she listed a little to one side. "Don't pull that country bumpkin act with me, Spence. After that *hefty* crack last night and the way you manhandled me, you're fortunate to get an apology at all."

Harley sat there with his head cocked in that way he had, apparently fascinated by their exchange. The dog was so darned smart he probably understood every word, too. If Spence even mentioned the word *walk*, the dog was at the door, and heaven forbid he should carelessly drop the word *treat* because then there'd be a streak of black and white making a dash for the pantry, straight to the correct cupboard.

Melody was getting ready to leave. Apology over, duty done.

While he still wondered why she'd bothered, he didn't want her to go. That glutton-for-punishment mentality of his clearly meant he should get his head examined by a professional.

Oh, yeah. And he was about to prove it.

"Hold on." Spence lifted his brows. "I already know the favor. The one you promised me."

"You do? Okay." She eyed him suspiciously. "Shoot."

She sure as hell *should* be suspicious. His intentions were distinctly based on a certain portion of his anatomy that was clamoring to be in charge. Her mouth was soft and tempting in the light coming through the kitchen window, the view outside framing her in a vista of mountain peaks and blue sky. The sun lit her hair with a glorious shimmer of gold.

If he asked her for what he wanted, she might refuse, so he improvised. "Don't move."

"That's the favor?" There was confusion in her voice. And a slight tremor.

"Yep."

"What are you up to, Hogan?" Her eyes widened as he took two steps, closing the distance between them.

He relieved her of the purse or bag or whatever it was. He muttered, "What's in this thing? Have you been diving shipwrecks to pick up cannonballs?" It thumped as he put it on the counter. Then, quick as heat lightning, he caught her around the waist.

"None of your business, and what the hell are you doing?"

"Kissing you."

"I don't think—"

"Perfect," he interrupted as he lowered his head. "Thinking should not be involved."

It had been a long time since that passionate summer when they couldn't get enough of each other, but his senses hadn't forgotten a damned thing. Her taste, the curves of the body pressed against him and a fierce surge of desire he'd certainly never felt with any other woman.

Maybe if he hadn't been in constant contact with her for the past few days he wouldn't have done it. While it was awkward to run into each other in town and at various Bliss County events, they both used avoidance like a personal shield.

They'd done this for nine years. But he still thought about her every day. That was too telling to ignore.

What if they put as much effort into resuming a relationship as they did avoiding it? Perhaps it could work.

It must be Tripp's happiness rubbing off on him, giving him some sort of romantic bug that was as infectious as the flu.

Melody made a noise of protest and slapped his shoulder.

Not exactly romantic enthusiasm.

In return, he deepened the kiss, half expecting a knee to the groin.

Then her hand relaxed on his arm.

That was something he might not have noticed if he wasn't so attuned to her body language, but he felt every atom shift, the cosmos adjust, and Melody softened against him.

Physically, they'd always been good together…

If she made that sexy little sound of enjoyment that he remembered like a song stuck in his mind, he'd be dead in the water.

She made it. Big splash as he went in and started to drown.

Instant erection. He knew she could feel it, too, because she stirred slightly, in an erotic movement that was instinctively female, and if he hadn't been busy giving her the kiss of her life—he was sure trying— he would have groaned out loud.

What happened next was up to her.

Neither one of them was breathing evenly when they

finally broke the kiss, and he nuzzled her neck, waiting for her to say something, anything, to indicate how she felt about what they'd just done. Knowing Melody, she might come to her senses—smack his face and storm off, peeling rubber as she drove away.

He really hoped she wouldn't come to her senses.

He certainly wasn't being practical.

Luck was with him; she wasn't, either. She looked him in the eyes. "I have no idea what that was about."

"Yes, you do." He brushed his fingers across her cheek. "I'm going to recant what I said last night. You're lovely in yellow. I'm very partial to you in yellow. See how well I can apologize? Besides, it was a joke."

"Too late to smooth that one over. Maybe you should kiss me again."

"I'd like to do a hell of a lot more than that."

"That isn't exactly a state secret at the moment." Her reply was typically sassy, but she didn't pull away.

A treacherous flicker of triumph shot through him. *Whoa, there, cowboy, don't get too full of yourself yet. Give her something more.*

"Mel, did you ever consider that it's never too late?" He whispered the words against her mouth, and the sun was warm on his shoulders as he pulled her closer. "For us, I mean."

He didn't wait for her answer. This kiss was even better than the last one. That could be strictly his opinion, but as one of the two participants, surely his vote counted.

Melody took a long breath when it was over. "I know I'm being stupid, but I don't care. Bedroom?"

"You aren't…" He started to argue, but trailed off.

Leery as she was of trusting him again, he was equally afraid of making promises until he understood exactly what she wanted. Until he knew that they both wanted the same thing.

He swept her into his arms but was wise enough to not say a word as he carried her down the hall to the desired destination. It was time he learned to keep his mouth shut.

CHAPTER FOUR

MAYBE IT WAS Hadleigh and Tripp's romantic wedding
wedding that had sent her personal universe into la-la
land, and maybe it wasn't.

Melody wondered if with just two fire-hot kisses,
the man holding her had changed his mind about ticking off the avoid-at-all-cost box.

"It'll take me two minutes to get out of these
clothes," he said. "Let me undress you first." It was
so endearing that she burst out laughing. It felt good.

"Oh, out of my sexy sweatpants and T-shirt?"

"I don't need fancy duds to know what you'll look
like." He peeled off her shirt, raising her arms. "The
shirt is see-through to a discerning man like me with
a good memory. I remember what's underneath, so I
don't notice the frills." He added in a low voice, "Come
on, Melody, you know I think you're beautiful. *That*
was never our problem."

No, he was right. With him, in his arms, she'd always felt every inch a woman. In fact, she'd become a
woman. At twenty, even in this day and age and halfway through college, she'd been a virgin. Not a conscious choice, really, but she'd had the nagging thought
that it might have been. She was the naive fool who'd
saved herself for him, as she'd realized later, when she
faced the bitter truth.

FOR A VERY long time she'd had a crush on Spencer Hogan. When it turned into a love affair, she'd gone in feet first, like jumping off a cliff. It had been awkward when he'd grasped that she had zero experience, but all in all, they'd managed pretty well, probably because he sure hadn't saved himself for her. She was well aware that even in high school he'd had a reputation as a player.

Over the next few months, practice had improved the situation. They'd practiced on every horizontal surface available until it came time for her to enroll for fall college classes. They'd continued their relationship—or that part of it, anyway—even after that disastrous proposal of hers, followed by his humiliating rejection, in early July. All summer long, they'd been lovers. She'd still thought they had a future.

Then he'd cut her loose.

He'd wanted a summer fling, so why couldn't she just do the same thing now?

That annoying inner voice, the one she wished would shut up, whispered, *Because that's not you, dummy. Especially when it comes to this man.*

He was beautiful, too, with all that dark hair and those oh-so-blue eyes. At least she'd put on a new bra with matching panties when she'd gotten dressed, since that was all she had. She hadn't done laundry in a while, thanks to the wedding festivities.

He ran his finger along the scalloped lace edge over the curve of her right breast. "My X-ray vision missed this. Nice."

She retorted, "It's a laundry issue, so don't think I wore it for you."

"I hope you won't mind if I admire it more off you

than on." He deftly undid the clasp in front and slipped it off her shoulders. At some later time, she'd probably resent that level of expertise.

Don't think about that.

In his usual audacious way, he just picked her up and deposited her on the bed. His room was masculine, but then again, he was Spencer Hogan, male through and through. A rough-hewn bed with a headboard made of pine logs took center stage. It was covered with a bedspread in browns and greens patterned with pine trees, and there was a single dresser, a nightstand with a reading lamp and a door to what she assumed was a closet. A window with a view of the mountains drew the eye. No other decorations.

The view alone was probably the reason there wasn't a single picture on the wall. What was the point? No framed picture could match it, spring, summer, fall or winter, but her attention was currently riveted elsewhere.

When he shed his clothes, she could see that his body certainly hadn't changed, still honed and muscular, his broad chest tapering to a taut waist and narrow hips. She knew he worked out because she'd seen his truck at the local gym; Bex owned it and she went there, too. She also knew that he rode Reb every day, rain or shine.

His aroused state reminded her that sexual attraction was never their problem, either. Any more than mutual appreciation of each other's looks had been. On the physical level, they'd had no complaints.

"You won't need these." Her panties went next as he hooked his fingers in the thin bits of lace and drew them down her legs.

When he stretched out on top of her, her heart was beating at a pace that would send the average race car driver slamming into a wall at curve three. He stroked her breast and said the most romantic thing possible, which certainly didn't help matters.

"I've missed you."

Three simple words if you discounted the contraction. But he looked and sounded as if he meant them.

He also looked hot. And sexy. And just…Spence.

"Are you talking to me, or my breast?" Melody ran her fingers through his thick hair and let him have his way. "I—"

He interrupted whatever she was going to say— she wasn't sure what that was, actually—with another scorching kiss. *Enough talking.* That was also Spence. Pillow talk wasn't his style. He was a man of action in *every* way, so that hadn't changed.

Neither had the way he could so quickly ready her with a touch, with his kiss; even a meaningful look could do the trick.

Not that she really needed foreplay, but he was considerate enough to make sure by gliding his hand over the curve of her hip then sliding a finger deep inside her. "Wet and hot. You've missed me, too."

If only she could deny it.

She ran her hands down his bare back. "Hurry."

The rasp of the drawer of the nightstand being pulled open momentarily distracted her from the haze of her lust-induced delirium, and he extracted a foil pouch, tore it open and covered himself. That was something else she'd address later. He had condoms on hand.

He entered her in a slow movement that managed to convey that he wanted to go faster but wouldn't rush it. He was the lover she remembered, finesse balanced by a hot-blooded approach to making love. He could accurately gauge her level of arousal and handle the situation accordingly.

Then it all took off.

He moved and she moved, lifting her hips in instinctive response, her body knowing what she wanted.

Spence knew it, too. He increased his pace right on cue, the erotic rhythm perfect. She felt her climax building, did her best to put it off because it was embarrassingly quick, but couldn't. She lost it.

The most gratifying part, besides the orgasm of a lifetime, was that Spence lost it, too, and she was sure her reaction pushed him over the edge faster than he'd intended.

Both of them breathless and perspiring, he pulled her with him as he rolled to the side. His tousled dark hair was in stark contrast to the white pillowcase. After a moment, he said in a voice that was much huskier than his usual cool tone, "And here I thought I wasn't seventeen anymore. That was damn fast."

Clearly they'd both needed what had just happened, but if she analyzed it, she'd probably jump up, jerk on her clothes and run. So nix to the psychological aspect of what might have been a very big mistake.

"No apologies necessary." She drew her hand along the contours of his chest. He felt solid and very real, even in a surreal moment like the aftermath of wild sex with a man she'd vowed to avoid for the rest of her life.

Bex and Hadleigh were going to strangle her for getting involved with Spence again—if she ever told them about this. Not to mention that it was Sunday morning. She was normally a regular churchgoer, but she'd just renewed her sinner's card, instead, by making love with Mustang Creek's most notorious bachelor.

Not to mention her *stupidity* card.

His breath was warm against her mouth, and his lashes lowered. "I'd like to make it up to you if you have the time. My unseemly speed, I mean."

There was *nothing* to make up.

"I have to feed my cats. I haven't done it yet this morning."

He laughed, his eyes a crystalline blue as he gazed at her. "Can I get a better excuse than that, please?"

The second time they made love it was slower, more measured but just as intense, and she held herself together a little longer, but by the third time she hit that sweet spot, Melody wasn't even sure she could remember her own name.

In bed he deserved a Hollywood star on a sidewalk somewhere.

Out of it, she wasn't positive they understood each other. At all. Emotionally speaking.

The buildup to the wedding had been trying, although she supported Hadleigh and Tripp with all her cheerleader might, even in those torturous shoes, pompoms waving. They'd all been cheerleaders in high school, way back when...

Spence said something, and she registered the cadence of his deep voice, but she was tired, physically and mentally. The sheets were soft and smelled faintly like him, and all the bustle of the past few days came crashing down. She and Bex had been running around like headless chickens, handling all the details to keep Hadleigh sane. Melody nestled into the pillow like a bear finding a cave as the weather turned cold.

"Hey, Sleeping Beauty, I just asked you a question."
A gentle hand caressed her shoulder.

"Hmm. What?"

"You want to talk about this?"

"About what?"

He chuckled softly. "I'm going to run into town. Do you want me to feed your cats while you take a nap since I'll be in the vicinity?"

What did he say? Nap. Yeah. What a glorious word. She mumbled, "Sure."

Then drifted off to sleep.

SPENCE WASN'T POSITIVE what to do.

Okay, he needed to get this straight. For the first time since the dawn of human beings, since creatures crawled out of seas or grabbed an apple in a garden somewhere, depending on what school of thought you followed, a man wanted to talk to a woman about their relationship, and she just went to sleep.

It was supposed to be the other way around.

So…he watched her sleep. Melody had half turned toward him before she'd conked out, one hand under her cheek, her lashes casting shadows on her cheek-bones.

It wasn't even noon.

Harley whined at the bedroom door. Spence had shut him out—he didn't want a canine audience while he and Melody were making love—and it was getting close to lunchtime. Spence got out of bed, pulled on his jeans again and headed toward the kitchen. Melody didn't stir.

After he fed his dog, he figured he ought to rustle

up some human-grade food. Trouble was, he didn't have much in the house.

He dumped the high-end kibble—the stuff he traveled twenty miles one way to buy—into the dish and Harley went at it, gobbling it up with a gusto that made that trip worthwhile. Then he said, "Want to go into town?"

Harley did an imitation of a champion high jumper by the door out to the back porch.

Big yes.

Spence got his keys and hers, since they were on the counter, grabbed a piece of paper from the drawer and wrote a note for Melody, which was an ironic twist to an already unusual morning. Then he hit a number on his phone. The owner of the Ride 'em Café answered on the fourth ring and he said, "Good morning, Carly."

"Back at you, Chief. You sound chipper."

He *was* feeling chipper, although he was fairly sure that was a word he'd never use to describe himself. But yes, he was in a very good mood. There was a beautiful naked woman in his bed—naked except for that bracelet. He was going to have to ask Melody if she ever took that off. And it was a bright sunny day.

Carly Riggs was from the South, which could account for her killer fried chicken, and he ordered two dinners to go, the usual sides. He remembered his first date with Melody and added two slices of cheesecake. If they were meandering down memory lane, they might as well go all the way. She didn't do much in the dessert arena unless she'd changed a lot, but she'd always loved cheesecake.

Be back with lunch was what he'd written.

He hesitated but that seemed clear enough, so he left

it at that. Harley jumped into his truck once they'd hot-footed it outside, and he drove to town.

Beautiful day, birds singing, cartoon cupids darting around with their arrows…

What had he just done? Spence's hands curled around the steering wheel as he took the turn off the property. He'd seduced Melody.

She might have joined in with a flattering amount of enthusiasm, but he knew she hadn't come to the ranch expecting a roll in the hay, so he had to take responsibility. It was all on him.

He really wasn't some kind of Lothario, but that was his reputation. It had come about mostly because once he started dating women who weren't Melody, he was quick to lose interest.

He wondered how she'd feel if she found out how old those condoms were. Surely they held up pretty well in those foil packs. He didn't sleep around, no matter what everyone gabbed about. At one time, especially after their breakup, he'd dated lots of women, but his heart hadn't been in it, and that was a problem, as he'd discovered.

"Her cats are weird according to what I've heard from Tripp," he said to Harley as he drove into Mustang Creek proper. "You'll have to stay outside."

His dog gave him a look that spelled out clearly he thought *all* cats were weird.

That was a valid point in Spence's view. He took a breath and expelled it. "I wasn't looking to get involved again," he confided. "At least I didn't think so. Not until this weekend…"

Sprawled in the passenger seat, Harley whined in commiseration, his white paws crossed.

Some jerk was speeding, going the other way on Main, and as they passed he took a moment to radio that in. He was never truly off duty, but that was fine.

He pulled up at Melody's house, took Harley as far as the front porch and told him to stay then let himself in, pausing to look around.

Melody had turned her living room into her studio. There were sketches scattered across a worktable, and Spence resisted the urge to examine them because that would be an invasion of her privacy, even though she'd given him permission to go inside. The place was cozy, with a comfortable sofa and a patterned rug, and the artist in her was evident in an unusual mobile by the window. Squares of brilliant stained glass hung from strands of twisted copper. It didn't take much intuition to know she'd made it, and Spence stood there for a moment, admiring her handiwork. He knew she was gifted, but fine arts hadn't been her major the summer they were together. Back then, she'd planned on going to law school.

Changing her mind had been wise; she'd certainly nailed *that* piece, and he knew her jewelry sold well. During tourist season the local shops did a land office business in the stuff and clamored for more.

But that aside, there was one small problem. There were no cats to feed as far as he could tell.

No meows, no brushing against his legs, just utter silence. It was summer, and he sincerely hoped she hadn't left a window open and they'd all escaped. It was possible that they were hiding because he wasn't familiar to them—cats were very canny critters with a knack for self-preservation.

Or maybe they were hiding in plain sight.

He suddenly realized that there were three cats sitting on the fireplace mantel—looking almost like works of art themselves. He stared at them. Their tails were curled in perfectly matched question marks, and they seemed identical, but then again he was far more used to horses and dogs. Occasionally cats took up residence in his barn, but they fed themselves on the inevitable mice. It was an eerie sensation to see that these felines were studying him as if assessing his status as an interloper. Friend or foe?

Tripp had been right. They *were* weird.

"I have her permission," he told the trio defensively. "Besides, I'm here for your convenience. She wants me to feed you." He thought about his relationship with Harley, the understanding they had. "Anyone care to show me where the food is?"

That ploy actually worked. Go figure.

One of them jumped gracefully to the floor and with his tail twitching, led him to the kitchen, where he stared at a cabinet.

There did turn out to be cans of cat food in that cabinet, so he opened one—how much did a cat eat? He divvied the contents into three servings, refilled their water bowl and left. On the porch, Harley thumped his tail in support, and Spence could swear there was a sympathetic look in his eyes that said *cats*.

"I might get points for being helpful." He opened the truck door to let the dog jump in.

When they reached the café, the joint was hopping, but that was typical for a Sunday morning. Spence nodded at just about everyone as he went to the counter to pick up the food. Maybe he'd been in Mustang Creek too long, but he knew every person in the dining area.

Carly was the one who waited on him, and as she rang him up she asked with raised brows, "Two meals?"

"I'm really hungry," he said evasively, handing over the money. This town was small, and gossip spread like the proverbial wildfire.

"You must be." Carly's tone was as wry as the expression on her face.

"Ravenous," Spence confirmed. With Melody still in his bed, there was a double meaning to that answer—a private one, anyway—so technically it wasn't a lie. He took the bag out to the car, throwing Harley a stern look as the dog sniffed the fragrant air. "You've already eaten, remember?" he drawled.

The chicken *did* smell great, though. The aroma tormented him all the way back to the ranch.

Things turned awkward the moment he stepped into the house. Melody was dressed, pacing the kitchen, her eyes accusing. "You took my keys so I couldn't leave?"

Spence suppressed a sigh. Sure enough, the idyllic morning was headed south. He set the keys on the counter with a musical jangle. "I asked if you wanted me to feed your cats. You said yes, so I did."

"Oh." She seemed chastened. "I haven't gotten much sleep lately. Sorry."

"That's okay." She seemed flustered, so he held up the bag of food. "Lunch? Carly's chicken, mashed potatoes and coleslaw."

"I should go." Melody scooped up her keys, hoisted the three-ton handbag and then turned. "You fed the cats?" she asked, a beat behind. "How did that go?"

He'd gained ground and then lost it. Spence knew at least enough not to push. He replied, "I asked where the food was, one of them showed me and they came and ate. End of story."

"You're joking." She sounded genuinely startled.

It was a good thing he really was hungry since apparently he had two lunches to eat. The north fence needed repair, and digging post holes burned a lot of calories, so nothing would go to waste. "No, I'm not kidding. Why?"

"They *liked* you?"

"I have no idea one way or the other. I put food on plates and they ate it."

"They did?"

This conversation was getting away from him. "Because of the food? Is there some reason they wouldn't? Hungry cats. Someone giving them food. Seems simple enough."

"It's not that simple. But never mind," she murmured as she walked out the door.

But hopefully not out of his life again, Spence thought as he heard her car start. He absently reached into the bag and pulled out a container.

They'd separated once before, which had been his choice. He'd changed his mind on that score.

Spence explained it all to Harley while he ate a double portion of fried chicken.

CHAPTER FIVE

MELODY WAS THINKING of starting a club for the romantically challenged. She'd be the president, treasurer and secretary, all rolled into one. As the founding and probably only member, she might even award herself a fancy plaque or a trophy, just for the hell of it.

Thoroughly unamused by the prospect, she pulled her car into the driveway and parked, briefly resting her forehead on the steering wheel.

The question of the hour was whether phenomenal sex was a fair substitute for common sense.

The jury was going to be out on that one for a while. All men, and the verdict might be yes, but then again, she was proof that a few other women might vote that way, too.

Melody walked through the door to see all three cats on the couch in their classic sphinx pose, paws forward, heads lifted as they watched her come in. She dropped her purse on the floor—she really needed to clean it out. She hated to admit Spence was right, but it had accumulated more than one human being should lug around. "So I'm an idiot," she told the cats. "Don't rub it in."

The consensus was that Ralph, Waldo and Emerson agreed with this assessment. She hurried to the bathroom, throwing off her clothes on the way. Maybe a shower would clear her head. She'd just spent an extremely energetic morning having sex. Really unforgettable, steamy sex that she should put out of her mind.

And her heart.

Especially her heart, she thought as she stepped into the stream of hot water. Spence had casual affairs, but she didn't. He had condoms at his bedside, which proved it.

She needed to talk this through with someone she trusted.

Hadleigh was on her honeymoon and therefore out of reach, but she could unburden herself to Bex. *After* she'd worked on the commissioned piece, of course. She wasn't positive she'd fess up completely, but she could admit that being together with Spence for the whole wedding gala had thrown her off—which was not a lie.

At all.

At the very least she needed to mull it over, and as she'd found when a problem presented itself, talking about it out loud, with a friend, worked best. Besides, Bex was nothing if not forthright, and a good sounding board, and what were friends for, anyway?

Her cell rang.

She'd turned off the spray and was reaching for her towel when it happened. The illuminated screen showed Spence's number, and she said a word no lady should ever utter. But after a moment, she picked up.

"You lit out of here pretty fast," he said without a greeting. "You okay?"

That was a difficult question to answer, Melody thought, and he had quite a bit of nerve asking it. With admirable calm, she said, "Spence, I've lived without you for nine years. Why would I not be okay now?"

In retrospect, that had been kind of a low blow.

He was silent for so long that Melody wondered if they'd lost the connection. Finally, though, he spoke again. "I was wondering, since you skipped out on lunch, if you'd like to have dinner with me."

Dinner?

Tonight? No. Too soon, too much, too fast.

She'd end up in his bed again. A trust had been breached—and it was with herself. She had to, once again, question her own judgment.

"I don't know." The truth, but that sounded a little harsh, so she modified it. "I mean tonight is impossible."

"Heavy schedule, I get it." The hint of sarcasm might even have been well-deserved.

According to most people, honesty was the best policy. Melody inhaled deeply. "I appreciate the offer, but I need time to sort out what happened this morning."

"I tried to talk to you about it, but you started to snore."

"I don't snore!"

"Everyone snores now and then, and it was just another lame joke. I meant we need to talk, and over dinner would be nice."

"I'm not sure what I want. What should happen next." That, also, was the truth.

"If the next thing you say is 'It's not you, it's me,' I'm going to arrest you."

One thing she'd say for him, he could always make her laugh. "On what charge?"

"Overuse of a platitude."

"I didn't realize there was a law against that."

"By the time your expensive lawyer figures out that there isn't, I'll have made my point, so do us both a favor and don't say it. Do you *want* me to call you again?"

That was blunt. She chewed her lip, and one part of her screamed *yes*, and the other part said, *unless you want to take a runaway train to a collapsed bridge, tell him no.* "Can I get back to you on that one?"

His tone was careful and quiet. "That puts the ball in your court, Mel. You aren't twenty this time."

When he ended the call, she stared at the blank screen on her phone. What did that mean? She looked over at the sphinxes on the couch. They hadn't moved a muscle. "There's no way this man is good for me unless he's serious. Other than that he relieved some sexual tension I didn't even know I had."

The cats had no comment, of course. Apparently, the sexual tension part was TMI. One of them licked his paw.

THE GOAL OF her day was to work, so she set out to do more sketches, something to wow her wealthy and eccentric patron, the one who'd pay her a small fortune. It would be nice to make some progress.

As usual, when inspiration flowed, it…flowed. She became engrossed, focused, and her pen took on a life of its own.

She drew a portrait of Spence.

She'd always been an easy study, quick with a brush or a pencil, and since his face was so fresh in her mind, she had no problem picturing the unique curve of his lips as he smiled, or the way his raven hair curled against his neck, or the clean line of his jaw…

"Howdy, sister girl."

She glanced up to see Bex breeze through the door without so much as a knock, a personal-size container of ice cream in each hand. The screen banged lightly back into place. Her friend said, "I think after yesterday we both deserve a little of this. Part one of the pact fulfilled. Let's celebrate with a few calories. Do you want the praline or the chocolate fudge?"

It was good to see her, but that was Bex, spontaneous and with a mind-reading sensitivity that could be unsettling, especially now. Melody hastily closed her sketchbook, hoping Bex wouldn't notice. If she was caught drawing a picture of Spencer Hogan, there'd be some 'splainin' to do. She didn't even know how she felt about the whole thing yet, so *that* would be impossible to pull off.

"Praline," she said, jumping up. "I'll get the spoons."

"I see the triumvirate is in an Egyptian mood today." Bex followed her into the kitchen and settled comfortably at the old table, an heirloom Melody had inherited, its distressed patina the result of years of scrubbing. Melody had never entertained the thought of getting it refinished. It was beautiful to her, reminiscent of her grandmother in her apron, cleaning up after Sunday dinner, or her grandfather reading the paper with a cup of coffee in front of him.

She was out of regular napkins but she did manage to scrounge up a few cocktail napkins that said *All My Girlfriends have One Thing in Common. They Wine Well With Others!* Hadleigh had given them to her once upon a time before she and Tripp had made up with a vengeance, when they'd commiserated with each other over some vino. They seemed appropriate now.

"You sure bolted out of the Moose Jaw early," Bex said, whipping the lid off her carton and scooping out a generous spoonful. "Or else you went and hid in the bathroom or something. I looked there, actually. No you."

"My feet insisted. They plotted a prison break." She dipped in, too. The ice cream was heavenly. Ice cream for lunch… As Bex had said, she deserved it. There was no way she could've sat and munched down on fried chicken with Spence, making polite conversation, after what had happened between them. "Besides, I told you I was getting out of there."

"Your car was still in the parking lot." Direct as always, Bex looked at her pointedly, licking her spoon. "How'd you get home?"

That question was actually a relief. It meant that all of Mustang Creek didn't know Spence had carted her off. If anyone had seen them, Bex would know about it. Melody stammered, "I, er, I caught a ride with someone whose car wasn't hemmed in like cattle in a feed lot. How was the rest of the party?"

"Cowboy wild. It was fun."

"Do I sense a pensive note?"

"I'm happy for Hadleigh and Tripp. Goes without saying." Bex looked resigned. "We all are. It really was beautiful to see them pledge their lives to each other. He's so in love with her. I have to admit to a certain envy I just can't help. I've been to a lot of weddings but none like theirs. They have something special. I want *that*. Yesterday reinforced it."

Since Melody knew exactly what she was talking

about, she nodded. "I'm in the same boat. The ship of fools."

The mind-reading must have kicked in because Bex said, "Spence looked like a million bucks. What is it about a tux, especially on a hot guy? Then he strolled into the bar in those jeans and looked even better. I think I was standing right there when you noticed the same thing."

He looked better yet wearing nothing at all. "I noticed," Melody admitted, weighing her words carefully. Her friend could sense a lie the way a shark scents a single drop of blood in a million gallons of sea water. "But my first experience with Spencer Hogan didn't turn out all that great. I'm gun-shy."

And he asked me out to dinner tonight. I declined. Probably because of those ready condoms. He does have a really cute dog, though…

"I know you are." Bex regarded her from across the table, spoon in hand. "But what about the pact? Would you ever give him a second chance? I don't know if I should mention this, but I saw him watching you the entire time these past few days. During the rehearsal, the dinner afterward and even during the ceremony when he was supposed to be playing best man."

"We sat next to each other at the rehearsal dinner. He had no choice but to talk to me. He's not perfect, but he's polite."

Bex asked through a spoonful of ice cream, "You sure it's over?"

She wasn't sure of anything, particularly at the moment. "That was nine years ago."

"So? Chemistry is chemistry. Tripp and Hadleigh had their differences and look how that turned out. I'm going to venture a guess at what they're doing right now." Bex glanced pointedly at the black cat clock on the wall, its tail moving in a steady rhythm. "Never mind that it's just afternoon."

An echo of her own thoughts. Damn. And she herself hadn't held out until noon. One kiss, the feel of Spence's teasing mouth at the juncture of her shoulder and neck, and she'd caved.

Twice. *No, let's be honest.* Three times.

"Spence Hogan has a lot of baggage. His past, not to mention *our* past. I'm not positive I'm interested, even if he is."

Now she'd ventured into the realm of Sort-of-Lies. She *was* interested, but she was skittish. A person could survive one broken heart, she was proof of that, but could she get through it twice?

Doubtful.

Hadleigh could easily be the exception in their secret pact. Relationships didn't come with an instruction manual. If Melody wrote a book on the subject, and she was the last person on this green earth who'd qualify, she suspected it would be panned by the critics.

Bex finished her ice cream and pushed the container to the side. "Don't be hasty."

She was far too insightful for comfort.

"What?"

"He's never slept with Junie. I think most of his reputation is based on the fact that he *looks* like someone who could have any woman he wants. Spence and Junie are childhood friends. They work together. End of story."

Her bizarre day had just gotten more off-kilter. Melody stared at one of her two best friends and tried to dredge up a reasonable response. She settled on, "Can you explain how you came to that conclusion?"

"No." Bex got up to dump her empty container in the trash. When she turned around, she looked determined in a familiar way as she leaned back against the counter. "Mel, one of the reasons we're such good friends is that you know I keep secrets right next to my heart. I don't reveal sources, but the rumor about Spence and Junie isn't true. I'd say most of the rumors about him are just plain fabrication. He's easy on the eyes, but that isn't his fault."

To a certain extent it might be, because a man didn't get to be thirty-six and have those flat abs without exercising, and he had to lift weights—and Bex was the one who owned the local gym.

He's definitely *easy on the eyes. You should see him naked.*

Okay, she really shouldn't say that or her intuitive friend might assume she'd seen him sans apparel lately. Like a few hours ago.

Lamely she muttered, "He seems to keep in shape."

"You noticed. Yeah, he was staring at you, and you looked his way more than once, too."

She got up. "Is there a particular point to this conversation?"

"H-E-double toothpicks, there sure is, as your grandmother used to say." Bex watched her move to the sink. "I so loved that woman. She could genteel-swear like no one. For instance, today is hotter than Blixen. I remember her saying that as she served us those cookies with the sprinkles on them. Blixen? What does that mean? Can't be the reindeer when we're talking about high summer in Wyoming. She was such a character."

"I loved her, too, but you're drifting off topic, Bex."

Bex sobered. "I can't speak for him, since he's his own man, but if I had to call it, Spence is still interested."

The question was, in what?

THE GROUND WAS hard as hell.

Spence drove down the post-hole digger and winced as the reverberations rocketed up his arms. They could use some rain, no doubt about it.

That was the only thing in this life he was certain about at the moment.

Shirtless and panting, he wiped a bandanna across his forehead and grabbed a drink of water. Harley sat in the blowing grass, head down on his paws, and watched him work while Reb grazed.

He'd be more than content to work away at a chore that wasn't the most pleasant in the world, since he was out of doors, it was a nice day and all of that was good, but...

His interesting morning was now like a burr under his saddle.

Melody had turned him down. No date for dinner, nothing.

Really?

She hadn't turned him down for sex, though. She'd been on board for that, and he couldn't deny that her response to every touch, every whisper, had been even better than he remembered, but he also couldn't deny that when he'd called her, there'd been a distance between them.

It was possible that he deserved it, but he was damned if he could figure out why.

He slammed the post-hole digger into the ground. "She's going to run like a spooked mule deer, isn't she?"

Neither Harley nor Reb made a sound, but they did look up in unison. There was sympathy in their eyes, and that made him feel somewhat better but solved none of his problems. Reb came closer and snorted softly as he nudged his shoulder. He stroked the horse's nose. Huskily, he reassured him, "It's going to be okay. I need to find a balance and so does she. Once upon a time, I disappointed her, but I still stand by that decision."

The single best thing about talking to a horse and dog—as long as no one else overheard and slapped an insane sticker on your medical record—was that they just listened.

"She was too young." He swept his hair back with a gloved hand, probably leaving a streak of dirt behind. He needed a shower anyway after a job like this, so that point was moot. "Give me a break."

They did. That might be why they got along so well.

His phone rang. It was a miracle that he had reception at all, and he pulled it from his pocket and tugged off a glove so he could answer it. Junie said, "Howdy, boss."

"You're calling me on a Sunday. What's going on?"

"The good news or the bad news?"

"Junie, give it to me straight."

"Thought you might like to know Estes ticketed the speeder you called in. Reckless driving. Thirty over the limit when he hit the outskirts of town. The kicker is that the driver was Judge Randolph's kid, so Estes didn't arrest him, although he could have. He's all nervous now, Estes is, second-guessing himself. Not the kid's first ticket."

A new headache he didn't really need. "Thanks for the heads-up," he said with a sigh. "I expect I'll get a call, though Randolph would be the first one to hit the driver with what he calls 'the full weight of the law.' Tell Estes I'll handle it."

"I expect you're right about the call. You recovered from the wedding yet?"

"I'm fine." He wasn't exactly thrilled at the question. Had he been so obviously rattled by the whole best man routine? He liked to think he was pretty even-keeled and that he kept his feelings to himself. But then again, they'd known each other a long time.

"I'm glad," she said cheerfully. "By the way, after this weekend shift, I'm off tomorrow. See you Tuesday."

"See you then." He pushed a button and shoved the phone back into his pocket, wishing it was the Old West, when a man could find some space from his problems, not walk around with cell phones that could reach him anywhere. However, he was sensible enough to know that was an illusion. Problems were non-negotiable and they existed no matter what.

Problem one on *his* horizon: a very sexy blonde. The judge limped in a distant second.

Three more fence posts to go. Good. He wanted to go back to the house so tired he'd just sit on the porch and watch the sunset before he fell into bed.

His only consolation was that he had two pieces of cheesecake to eat.

CHAPTER SIX

WAS IT EMBARRASSING to duck behind a display of turnips in the produce aisle?

Melody was going to guess the answer to that one was a hands-down yes.

But there she was, lurking in turnip land just because she caught a glimpse of a tall, dark-haired man whose profile was so achingly familiar she would swear it was indelibly etched in her brain. Had she been thinking about anything but him since the morning after the wedding?

Um, no. The commissioned piece was going nowhere fast.

Spence looked over the tomatoes, haphazardly picked absolutely the wrong one in her opinion and moved on down to the lettuce. He didn't show much judgment there, either, tossing a bag of prewashed greens into his basket.

It had been nearly a week now, and she was still trying to sort things out.

Just her luck, when she straightened and tried to slink away, he turned at exactly the right moment and spotted her.

Brazen it out, you big yellow-bellied coward.

She said, "Oh, hi. Grocery shopping?"

That was brilliant.

His mouth twitched. "Nope. Looking for a used car. You?"

"I needed some…" She refused to say turnips, even though they were handy. Instead, in her sheer genius mode, she chose, "…stuff."

That was when she decided that if there was an award for world's lamest person, she'd have a statue to set on the mantel next to the cats. Good job.

His blue eyes held such a look of amusement that she felt a flush move up her neck and into her cheeks. He said conversationally, "Luckily for you, they do have *stuff* here."

It was time to regain at least some of her composure. Melody squared her shoulders. "I didn't expect to see you here."

"We live in the same town."

"I'm aware of that," she muttered. He sounded so infuriatingly reasonable. She grabbed a produce bag and tossed in a few turnips, just for show. Her grandmother used to mash them with butter and some lemon pepper, and they were quite tasty. She could probably use the fiber, right?

"You look good." There was a subtle sensual edge to the compliment.

So did he in his usual worn jeans and denim shirt. He always seemed in need of a haircut, but he managed to pull it off. She felt grateful that she'd taken the time to put on a sundress and some strappy sandals—no heels—before she ventured out in public.

"See you around." He turned abruptly and walked away.

Left with her plebeian veggies, she watched him move. He had the long-legged gait of a true cowboy, and his wide shoulders drew the eye. He tipped his hat at an elderly lady as he passed, and Melody could only describe the woman's reaction as simpering, although she'd never quite understood the definition of that word before.

Enough.

She needed cat food—no forgiveness there if she ran short—and she picked up some chicken breasts and spinach for a salad, and then on a whim, chose two nice steaks. For what special occasion, she wasn't sure.

Keeping her options open?

She couldn't deny that she'd been thinking about Spence a lot and was considering asking him over for dinner instead of going out, but her mind wasn't made up. There was that fork in the road, and she was trying to figure out which path was the best choice. Where was Robert Frost when you needed him?

The road less traveled.

Second Chance Lane. Almost no traffic. Plenty of parking.

She went through the check-out and then straight home. It felt downright unbelievable when she passed Spence's truck on the main thoroughfare. As if nature, fate, the powers that be, whoever or whatever was in control of the universe, were all conspiring against her.

Gritting her teeth, she walked through the front door, unloaded her groceries under the unwinking scrutiny of the triumvirate, as Bex called them, and then sat down at her worktable.

That was a good sketch of Spence, if she did say so herself. A wasted effort, but it had settled her mind at the time, and that was worth it right there. Determined, she worked on the design for the commissioned piece, complete with the amethysts, fire opals and freshwater pearls and turquoise, ending up with a fair idea of where she was going, although she was still dissatisfied with the details.

The knock on the door that interrupted her proved to be a teenage boy from the local flower shop with a charming bouquet and no card. She rushed off to get him a tip then surveyed the selection of blooms as he drove off in a rattletrap car.

Daffodils, interspersed with ferny greens.

Spence.

That demolished her concentration, sent it into oblivion with no hope of return.

They were exquisitely beautiful, and she clipped the stems and put them in a vase her aunt had given her as a graduation present, a lovely piece she admired for its symmetry of form, with graceful curves and a frosted etching of a garden on one side. She carefully placed it on her desk.

If she had a better handle on what he wanted, exactly, she wouldn't have sat there and stared at them abstractedly for more than an hour.

Was he…courting her, to put it in old-fashioned terms?

No. Two kisses, and she'd melted into his arms. His bed. Spence Hogan didn't *court* women; they came to him. Even married women flirted with him; she'd seen it firsthand, though she tried to stay indifferent to his personal life. For all she knew, he took them up on it, but to be fair, she hadn't ever heard *that* about him.

The flowers seemed to stare back, though, petals furled gracefully, green stems upright.

"What's he got in mind?" she asked them, thinking out loud. "All theories are welcome."

They didn't answer. Neither did the cats.

To complete her glamorous evening, she ate some leftover pizza and watched the evening news—nothing good there—then toddled off to fall into bed.

Alone.

But she dreamed...deeply.

Of Spence, and it wasn't all sunshine and roses. Her general unrest was evident in the landscape of her dreams, and when she got up in the morning, she was unreasonably annoyed with him. They'd been walking through a meadow, and he was always two steps ahead of her. And he had an umbrella while she was walking in the rain. The dream-Spence wasn't at all gallant, but she had to admit lack of courtesy was not one of his many failings, so she wasn't sure where that came from. Her psychology diploma must have gotten lost in the mail somewhere.

What did that mean?

She sleepily drank her coffee and pondered the convoluted workings of the human brain when it was set loose without a bit and bridle in the guise of rest.

Maybe, based on the elusive symbolism of her dream, he was just hard to understand.

He'd sent her flowers. Why had he done that? And how did she feel about it? And the biggest question of all—could she ever trust him again?

IT WAS AS though he couldn't please anyone the entire week.

Spence punched up his computer screen, irritated by just about everything. The situation with Judge Randolph had turned out better than he'd feared—that had ended up being the highlight of the past few days. Although he was still surprised by it, the man hadn't asked for a single favor when it came to the charges, thanking him gruffly for not hauling his son in, but not contesting the ticket.

In typical Randolph fashion, he'd stated plainly that his son was a pain in the ass right now, and he was going to take away his expensive car.

Spence couldn't agree more. Save the hardworking taxpayers money by freeing up jail space and teach the kid a lesson without involving the courts. Perfect.

But otherwise, he couldn't jump up and down with joy.

Melody hadn't called. There was nothing from the Nolan camp but silence, and he had a bad feeling that wasn't going to change. Junie was out sick with some sort of virus, so he was scrambling to find someone to cover for her, and of all things, his mother had sent him a letter. Or a card. Addressed to General Delivery, Mustang Creek, Wyoming.

His mother. The same woman who'd dumped him on his aunt's doorstep?

He hadn't even opened the envelope. It had been delivered to the police station, so she must have looked him up on the internet and found out where he worked and what he did.

His decision was to not make a decision at the moment. He had enough on his mind.

WHEN TRIPP'S CALL came, he was knee-deep in neglected paperwork and could have passed for the grouchy creature on that TV show for children, the

Muppet who lived in a trash can. He answered the phone with one exasperated word. "What?"

Tripp said with relaxed amusement, "I expected a warmer response. Like remotely friendly. I'd ask how it's going, but I'm not sure I want the answer."

"It's going." Spence shut down the screen. He'd been at it for twelve hours, anyway. "Where are you?"

"On a white sand beach."

"I hate your guts."

Tripp laughed. "You should. We're having a great week. But we're both looking forward to getting back to Mustang Creek. Hadleigh says hi, by the way."

"Glad you're having a good time." It was asinine to do it, but he asked, anyway. Tripp had called him, so maybe... "Has she talked to Melody by any chance?"

"That's an interesting question. Just about an hour or so ago, in fact. Uh, why?"

"I was kinda wondering if my name was mentioned." His phone might be ringing off the hook, but it certainly wasn't Melody on the other end. His mood wouldn't be so black if she'd just call him, dammit. Even if it was merely to say thank you for the flowers. Despite the absence of a card, she had to know they were from him.

Tripp took a moment to respond. "Here's the thing, Spence. You have to tell your wife everything. That's the pact you make. If you want to tell me why you're asking about Melody, Hadleigh's going to find out, too. Because if I ask her if Mel mentioned your name, *she's* going to ask *me* why I want to know. Fair warning."

He was gentleman enough not to blurt out that they'd slept together, so he settled for a sin of omission. He told the truth, but only part of it. "Long story short,

I asked her out to dinner but she was busy that night and was supposed to get back to me. I haven't heard from her."

A low whistle came from the other end of the line. "You and Mel again, huh? You might want to keep in mind that if you break her heart a second time, Hadleigh and Bex will take out a hit on you."

Spence muttered, "Can everyone give me enough credit to realize I didn't mean to break it the first time? She needed to finish college. I still stick by that decision. And it was *her* decision not to forgive me."

"I know. I remember we discussed this over a case of beer right after you broke it off. If it's any consolation, *I* give you that much credit. Tell you what, I'll ask my wife. *My wife.* I can't believe I love saying that, but I do. I'll ask her if Melody mentioned you, but like I said, that means Mel will probably realize you asked."

His pride had taken a beating all week as it was, so he didn't really care. Maybe it was better if she *did* know. "Warning duly noted."

"The real reason I'm calling is that we're having a party at the ranch when we get home. A week from Saturday. You on?"

"You even have to ask?"

"Kind of, since a favor is involved. I was hoping you'd be in charge of the bonfire and order refreshments of the liquid persuasion."

"Sure thing."

When they hung up, he sat there, staring a map of Wyoming he had framed and hanging on the wall of his office. Melody would be at the party, no doubt about it.

She couldn't avoid him forever.

Oh, at the grocery store, she'd tried. Unfortunately

for him, she'd been wearing a simple pink dress with thin straps that showed off her shapely shoulders. It was the familiar shimmer of her hair that had first caught his eye, though. Or maybe he was so aware of her that his radar signaled whenever she was in his vicinity.

It had taken some willpower not to ask her out again, but he liked to think he was a man of his word and tried to live his life that way. He'd promised her the next move was hers.

That had been a damn foolish play, but it was done, so he was stuck with it.

Tripp's admonishment rankled, too, but his friend might have a valid point. How serious was he about Melody, about wanting a second chance with her?

The wedding had tilted his world sideways. And making love to Melody had been a revelation of sorts. He *wanted* her, he knew that.

Just when, in a relationship, did desire turn into love?

That was one hell of a question, and he didn't have the insight to answer. Not yet.

Because if they were talking about love, he wasn't sure he'd ever fallen out of it.

CHAPTER SEVEN

"NEUTERED MALES," Melody mused out loud to Ralph, Waldo and Emerson as she went into the Warrior Two position, "are much easier to get along with."

They did their version of the same yoga stance, straightening their tails and lifting a front paw. She usually found it hilarious, but she wasn't feeling all that jocular this morning.

Last night she'd run smack-dab into Spence again. This time it was at the liquor store where she'd stopped off to pick up a nice chardonnay as a special treat, since she'd finally finished the design for the bib necklace and wanted to celebrate.

He was there, he explained in that sexy drawl of his, to do Tripp a favor and order a couple of kegs for the upcoming party, since they were still out of town.

"He looked good, as usual," she explained gloomily to the feline contingent as she switched, appropriately enough, to the cat pose, making sure her back was hollowed and then arched. "It would be helpful if he'd grow a big wart on the end of his nose or something."

Now she'd wished that on him, it would probably happen to her, instead.

Needless to say, her cats managed the stretch perfectly.

What a bunch of show-offs.

She went on. "If I didn't know he's too busy for it, I'd swear he was doing it on purpose, following me around."

He hadn't so much as mentioned a dinner date, not last night, not at the grocery store two days ago, either. He also hadn't called again, but he'd been unfailingly polite when they crossed paths.

She'd be unreasonably irked by that, but he was simply doing what he told her he'd do.

Okay, she *was* irked.

She'd thanked him for the flowers yesterday, at the liquor store. He'd said he was glad she liked them. Nothing more.

If only she wasn't so confused.

The solution for that, she'd discovered, was work. After she finished her yoga session, she changed into comfortable jeans and a T-shirt, whipped her hair into a tidy ponytail and prepared a cup of tea. Then she made a beeline for her worktable and started to tweak her new design, an inevitable part of the process. There were still decisions to make, like where to put the freshwater pearls, fire opals, turquoise and amethysts her client had bought on her travels. Engrossed, she didn't look up for hours, not until she had to flip through her drawing pad to go back to some of her original ideas and found the picture she'd drawn of Spence.

Even at home she was running into him, she thought darkly, staring at his image.

Perhaps she should take a well-earned break. This shindig that Hadleigh and Tripp were throwing was supposedly casual, but she knew her friend, and Hadleigh was going to do it up right. So Melody wanted a new outfit for the occasion. Working from home, she tended to put on her "uniform," as she called it, and wear the same thing every day with just a slight variation on that theme. All her jeans were faded, and some of her T-shirts were collecting stains and starting to look a little disreputable. New shoes, too—cute comfortable flats; heels were out of the question—might not be a bad idea.

A shopping trip might be in order. Maybe Bex was free.

She was, as it turned out, at least for a long lunch. "My eyes are crossing since I'm buying new equipment for the clubs and doing research. The best elliptical machine? Talk about a million choices. Yeah, I could use a break."

Mustang Creek didn't have a mall, but there were a few designer shops and the usual retail stores, so they could wing it, and she'd be in better shape than she was now.

They went to O'Henry's on Main first. The restaurant was nestled between two buildings with wooden fronts and had a big glass window; the owner was also the chef and a native Wyoming son who'd gone off to New York. Then he'd felt the pull back to a simpler lifestyle and come home. His food was exceptional, so good it made you want to lick your plate. Since the inside room was packed, they chose a table on the patio, one with a brightly striped umbrella, and decided to split a decadent sandwich that included brie, ham and apples. They ordered sparkling water to accompany it.

"I hope the weather's like this for the party," Bex said, gazing upward. "Not a cloud in the sky."

"Me, too." As casually as possible, Melody brought up her current unshakable problem. "I ran into Spence yesterday. He was helping make some of the arrangements—the liquid kind. Sounds like it's going to be quite the event."

Bex smiled mischievously. "I volunteered us both to help, too."

Melody had to laugh. "So did I. With the decorating." She and Hadleigh had quickly discussed it at one of their prewedding get-togethers. "I'm doing the lanterns. Remember the night I drove her home because you had to leave early? That's when she told me she wants paper lanterns. You're far more organized at supervising staff than either of us. You've been nominated as the official kitchen queen."

"I can do that."

Bex nodded. "So...Spence asked you out to dinner, huh."

The arrival of the waiter precluded the need to answer immediately. The sandwich looked fabulous in all its gooey glory and she was hungry, but she didn't pick up her half right away. Instead, she stared at her friend. "How do you know that?"

"He told Tripp."

"Who blabbed it to Hadleigh, who then shared it with you." Melody took a sip of her water and sighed in resignation. "Are there no secrets in this town?"

"You know the answer to that already, Mel." Bex managed to take a fairly ladylike bite, with only a small dribble landing on her plate. She rolled her eyes in enjoyment. "I could eat this every day. Breakfast, lunch and dinner. Now, by the way, is the point in our conversation when I say I told you so."

Melody opted for the knife and fork method to tackle her lunch. From experience she knew she couldn't pull

LINDA LAEL MILLER   103

off the other option with any dignity left. "I said I was busy that night."

And she'd needed privacy, time alone, after spending all morning in his bed having gymnastic sex that had brought her an entirely new perception of the big O, even after their previous relationship. She was older now and more comfortable with her sexuality, no longer that twenty-year-old with so many stars in her eyes they blurred her vision. She could enjoy the fact that he was a considerate lover, but not expect much more. She'd had a couple of short-term relationships that just hadn't worked out, but if nothing else, those experiences had taught her a lot about herself and what she wanted. Part of the point of the marriage pact was *not* to settle.

"Were you?" Bex looked skeptical. "Busy, that is."

The sandwich *was* absolutely delicious, the conversation not so much. "I have that new commissioned piece. So the answer is yes, I *am* really busy right now."

Bex pointed at her plate. "But you still need to eat, don't you? I assume you didn't skip dinner."

Was she being censured for turning Spence down? Here she'd thought both Hadleigh and Bex would warn her against a second involvement. "If you make a comment about how *hefty* I am, I'm going to make you pay for lunch."

"Huh?" Bex sounded puzzled. "Hefty? You? You have the kind of body the rest of the world works out to achieve. If everyone looked like you, I wouldn't have a business. What are you talking about?"

"Never mind." Melody waved her fork for emphasis. "I am extremely leery of getting involved with Spencer Hogan again, even if it's only dinner. Your faith that his reputation isn't deserved might just spring from the fact that you've always liked him."

"Not always." Bex sobered, and her voice was quiet. She dabbed at her mouth with her napkin then carefully laid it back in her lap. "Not that summer nine years ago. I wanted to strangle him for hurting you. But… Have you ever read a historical romance novel?" She made a theatrical pretense of introspection, tapping her finger on her cheek. "Wait, yes, you have, since you and I traded copies for years. There's a well-worn saying in those books that reformed rakes make the best husbands. Maybe you remember it."

"I'm familiar with it, and very funny." Melody used her fork to sweep up an errant chunk of brie that had escaped her sandwich. "Can I delicately point out that's fiction?"

"There's usually truth in those classic plots." She suddenly changed the subject. "Do you really think Spence is shallow?"

What a question. Spence? There was probably an incredulous expression on her face.

"Oh, please. I think he's the total opposite of shallow. He's…he's an extraordinarily complicated man." Time for another change of subject. "Okay, can we discuss our shopping trip now? I need head to toe. Except for a few dressy dresses, most of my current wardrobe looks like I borrowed it from some local hobo. The other night I went to the grocery store in a dress—because I was too embarrassed to wear my casual clothes. It's the definite downside of working at home. I don't think I own a pair of jeans without a ragged hem or a hole somewhere."

Either the distraction worked, or more likely, Bex

knew when to back off. They finished lunch in a companionable mood and then hit the shops. Two new pairs of jeans, plus two silk blouses later—one red and another in a blue-green shade Bex swore matched her eyes—they parted ways. Oh, and she was also the proud possessor of a cute pair of navy open-toed flats. That was a particularly happy purchase, since they were a name brand *and* they happened to be on sale.

As Melody walked back to her car, she thought about Spence. Of course. He was like the refrain of a popular song playing on her personal radio. She'd bumped into him so often lately she was almost surprised she hadn't seen him in the women's shoe section of the downtown store. What he'd be doing there, she had no idea. Maybe he'd be apprehending a stilettos thief. Or chasing a shoplifter...

She chewed her lower lip. Why had he mentioned the dinner invitation to Tripp? Men didn't usually share that sort of information, did they? Especially if they'd been turned down.

Though, technically, she hadn't said no; she just hadn't said yes.

As she loaded her purchases into the trunk, she contemplated her choices.

Call him.

Bad idea.

Right?

Right.

She slammed the trunk lid with more force than necessary.

SPENCE PICKED UP his pen and made a note then figured he'd call it quits for the day, since his various personnel issues finally seemed resolved. He'd worked several days of back-to-back shifts. It was time to close his files and turn off the computer. Leave the office, head home.

A nice ride beckoned. He'd neglected both his horse and his dog for too long.

Besides, he needed to clear his head.

An hour later, on horseback, he took a deep breath and stopped at the edge of a meadow full of Indian paintbrush. Reb shook his head, restive at the rein, obviously wanting to run. A horse had a special way of communicating that left no doubt what he was thinking. Next to them Harley yipped in agreement.

Fine. It suited his mood, too.

He loosened the reins, touched his heels to Reb's sides, and they were suddenly gone. Nothing like it when the power of the horse was beneath you, the sky was a very wide blue and the air smelled of pine-scented mountains. The ridges were thick and dark this time of year, layered like sedimentary rock, the different trees defining the elevation at which they grew.

He slowed for Harley to keep up, but even that short gallop helped him.

There were some irrefutable facts swimming out there like a runaway raft in a flooding river full of rapids, the first of which was that he'd never fallen in love except for Melody. Lust was different. His passing interest in the women he'd dated didn't count.

Not even close. Everyone around them thought he'd broken her heart, but his had shattered, too, when he'd turned down her proposal—for her own good—and she'd stubbornly walked away. He was tired of taking all the blame.

He'd dated. He'd tried. He'd failed at every attempt for a reason.

The minute he'd kissed her again, a small voice had whispered that *she* was what he was missing in his life.

She was bright, and she was beautiful, and he wanted to see her over the breakfast table each and every morning as she drank one of those awful cups of tea she liked.

Unfortunately, she'd give a mule a run for its money. Nobody was better at planting her feet and refusing to move an inch, and he had the feeling that they were each pulling in the opposite direction.

Was there a manual? *How to Win the Lady: Advice for the Lovelorn Male in His Hour of Need.*

If so, he should purchase a copy right away, read it and take notes.

The idea was ridiculous enough that he wanted to laugh, but he could actually use some guidance, he reflected with a grimace as the sun began to set behind the Tetons.

His phone beeped. The message said Junie was returning to work. He could use the break.

The sunset was breathtaking. Streaks of crimson and violet and sapphire as the light faded behind the mountains. He sat there in his favorite spot on earth and mulled everything over until he came to a decision, one he'd probably made a long time ago but hadn't wanted to acknowledge.

His mind drifted to the card from his mother, which still sat unopened on his desk. Postmarked Bozeman, Montana. In about three minutes at his computer, especially with the databases he had available, he could find out anything about her he needed to know.

Was that particular part of his life better left alone? Unopened and unexplored? He wasn't sure.

His thoughts inevitably made their way back to Melody. He wanted to marry her. He wanted to marry Melody Nolan, sleep next to her every single night, and the image of her large with his child was there, too, like a shimmering desert mirage. Out of reach at the moment, but possible.

He loved her.

She loved him, too, if she'd just admit it. Otherwise she would never, ever have spent Sunday morning in his bed. He *knew* her. She'd never give herself lightly. One kiss had been taking a chance. Two kisses had lit the world on fire. What had happened afterward was proof that they hadn't moved on, either of them.

It had only taken about a decade for him to realize it.

At that point he came up with a plan that had a devious slant to it. At least it felt like that to him. He was more a shoot-from-the-hip sort of man, but he needed to think it through carefully.

It could be the most ludicrous idea ever—or a stroke of brilliance.

He didn't do more than shift in the saddle before Reb understood that he needed to turn back to the ranch, so the horse swung fluidly around. Harley jumped up and followed at a full run.

They all seemed to understand. They were on a mission.

CHAPTER EIGHT

MELODY ABSENTLY ANSWERED the phone without glancing at her call display. A crisp voice said, "Melody. How are you this morning?"

Eccentric Important Client alert.

She gave the conventional reply. "I'm fine, Mrs. Arbuckle. You?"

"Good, good. How's the necklace coming along?"

The phone call wasn't a surprise. She hadn't promised it by a certain date, but because of the wedding and one very distracting police chief, it was taking a lot longer than she'd expected. *So focus on the positive.* "I have the design done, except for a tweak here and there. I love it, and I hope you will, too. It just needs to go to the next stage."

"Excellent, but I'm actually calling about something else."

"Oh?" Melody asked with some caution.

She'd known Mrs. A. forever, it seemed, because she was a Mustang Creek—and for that matter, Wyoming—celebrity. The woman was slightly intimidating with her forthright approach to life, and if she didn't like someone or something it was no secret. So when she'd commissioned the necklace—the truth was Mrs. Arbuckle had basically announced to her that she was going to do it—Melody had accepted the task with mixed feelings. Joy because of the challenge and the beauty of the gems deposited on her worktable, coupled with a twinge of apprehension that her client might not like the end result.

"I need a second piece made and want you to be snappy about it. The necklace can wait."

Melody blinked. *Snappy* wasn't always easy in design or production, but she wasn't about to point that out.

Lettie Arbuckle was not only the head of the Bliss County Historical Society, she was also a patron of almost everything that even hinted at the arts in this state. She'd inherited a fortune from her family's widespread mining interests and knew a lot of influential people. Influential people with scads of money. Careerwise, she was a gold mine.

Besides, under her domineering exterior, she was undeniably generous and had recently donated the money for a new wing to the regional hospital, and she supported countless charities. The new library at the high school was named in her honor.

Melody, pen in hand, was ready to take down instructions. "I'd love to. What did you have in mind?"

"I want the perfect engagement ring."

"You're getting married?" She was taken off guard or she wouldn't have blurted out such a personal question, but Mrs. A. was seventy if she was a day. Not that older people didn't find romance and permanence—look at Jim and Pauline Galloway, for instance—but she had a hard time picturing the man who could take on Mrs. Arbuckle's formidable personality. The woman had been married once, she knew that much, to a Mr. Arbuckle; gossip had it that he'd simply faded away and that she saw more of him when she visited his grave than she ever had while he was alive.

"Not me. Bite your tongue, young woman. If I could find a man who understood and loved me unconditionally like my dear Roscoe, I might consider it, but otherwise, I don't think so."

No mention of the late and apparently unlamented Mr. A. Roscoe was the little terrier she took everywhere, even into restaurants—whose staff looked the other way, because she was, after all, who she was.

"It's for my nephew. He's a cowboy, and you know how romantic they are, so he wanted me to arrange for the ring."

Cowboys, in Melody's experience, were not at all romantic or sentimental. Sure, they could be rugged and sexy as hell, but romantic was a stretch for her, and she'd lived in Mustang Creek almost her entire life, so she should know. Actually, it was possible she knew *him*. "Okay. Tell me what he wants."

"No."

"Excuse me?"

"My dear, I want you to design the ring *you'd* like to receive if your true love was on bended knee, promising you his undying devotion. This is your area of expertise, not mine and certainly not his."

"But I have no idea of his tastes. Diamonds? Emeralds? Rubies? What?"

"You choose. No stipulations. I told him I trust you. Besides, his tastes probably run to a new saddle or custom boots. How would he know what she wants? That's why I'm calling *you*."

Desperately, she tried to get at least a glimmer of information. "How much does he want to spend?"

"I get the impression he doesn't care as long as it's perfect. Besides, just send me the bill. It's my wedding gift to both of them."

No pressure. It only had to be perfect. Not a high standard.

"When does he want it? Do we have a timeline?"

"Didn't I say snappy?"

The call ended because Mrs. Arbuckle had a habit of doing that; when she'd said what she wanted to say, she just hung up. Melody looked at the blank screen on her phone and then said to the cats, "I like her, but that woman is a little wacky at times."

Emerson yawned from the mantel. Old news, apparently.

Still, a new commission was always a good thing, and she could use the money *and* the break from thinking about Spence all the time.

Hadleigh and Tripp should be touching down in Cheyenne right about now in his private plane. Blushing bride, handsome, adoring bridegroom. If that wasn't inspiration, what was?

So she had carte blanche to create the perfect ring? That was exciting—and kind of scary. She licked one corner of her mouth and turned to a new page in her sketchbook. Any artist would be intrigued, and if Mrs. A. was paying… Fine, she could design a ring, that went without saying, but she usually had precise directions. Often *too* precise.

This bride didn't want a marquis diamond, but preferred a square cut. That one disliked sapphires and wanted white gold. Another thought bigger was always better. The list of demands went on and on.

Personal taste was…personal. Lettie Arbuckle had

hired her for an almost impossible task. Second-guessing someone else's taste.

Pensively she sat there, pen poised. It seemed as if everyone was getting married except her. And Bex was in the same canoe, paddling upstream to nowhere. Not that the act of getting married was the appeal of the marriage pact they'd all made; it was marrying the right person. Melody consoled herself that she had a fulfilling life, the feline triumvirate, a nice little house, her work, lots of friends.

Yet no husband, no childish laughter in the yard, and most of those friends were married.

Oh, God, she *was* going to be the weird cat lady, wasn't she? She should have skipped the silk blouse and just bought a faded housedress at a secondhand store.

No, skip the pity party, for heaven's sake. Melody assured herself that she was happy for the girl with the romantic cowboy lover.

And she was. Truly. She just wanted it for herself, too.

Oddly enough, all of a sudden she missed her mother. Melody was normally satisfied with their occasional visits and frequent phone calls. Yet, every once in a while, she could, quite frankly, use a maternal hug.

This was one of them.

So she picked up her phone and called. "It's me."

"I see that." Her mother laughed in her gentle way. She'd be drinking tea. She usually was. "I'm so glad you called. We always talk on Sunday, but you skipped it this week, for perfectly understandable reasons. How are Hadleigh and Tripp? They back from their honeymoon yet?"

"Almost." She wondered whether she should mention why she'd suddenly needed to hear a friendly voice. "They're throwing a party for their return. I offered to make those special lanterns Hadleigh likes."

"You *would* offer because you're you, and I predict they'll be fabulous."

She wasn't sure what to say next. Telling her mother she was even *thinking* of getting involved with Spencer Hogan again would not be met with warm approval. She'd cried a small ocean of tears on her mother's shoulder the last time she was that foolish, and she doubted her only parent had forgiven him.

Her mother certainly wouldn't approve of her falling into bed with him.

She shouldn't so much as drop his name.

So she substituted her recent news. "Mrs. Arbuckle gave me another commission. I just got off the phone with her."

"Rubbing elbows with the elite, I see. Congratulations. I expect Lettie hung up on you as usual?"

Melody laughed. "You'd be correct. So what's going on with you?"

After an update and evading the usual request that she visit soon, Melody ended the call. She squared her shoulders, turning her focus to the ring, idly using her pencil, letting the ideas flow.

After all, *snappy* was the word of the day.

Mrs. A. had said to think of this ring as the one *she'd* want. What would that be?

She was an old-fashioned girl at heart, so a diamond, probably. She wasn't into flashy, and she had slender fingers, which to her meant a modest-sized stone, but in an unusual setting. A couple of gems on the side, maybe? Not rubies and not emeralds. Aquamarines to set off her eyes?

She toyed with that concept for a while, doing several sketches, and wished she'd requested a contact number for the young man. Knowing Mrs. A., she wouldn't have given it. The woman was about as moveable as a boulder dumped midstream by a glacier eons ago. She did exactly as she pleased.

Nice gig if you could get it.

Melody went back to work. The ring of her dreams was at least a ticket out of Spenceland, and she needed the express lane.

BAD BILLY'S WAS pretty packed, but then again, there was some sort of biker caravan going toward Yellowstone, and they'd apparently all decided they wanted a cheeseburger at the same time. The parking lot was crammed with bikes of all makes and sizes.

Just Spence's luck that a couple of guys had jostled each other, taken offense, and then it erupted into a fistfight.

Peacekeeper time, but when he walked in, the place seemed as usual.

He liked bikers; they were generally good down-to-earth folk, but they could also be on the volatile side now and then. Get in their grille, they got in yours.

Spence leaned on the counter that was scarred from a thousand meals being pushed across it and asked the owner, "Trouble over?"

"They're eating at the same table now and talking like old friends, if you can believe that," Billy said in a harried voice. "Turns out they're both from Indiana. That made them blood brothers or something, although

I'm confounded as to how they exchanged that information while trying to pound the shit out of each other. Sorry for the call."

"No problem. I always prefer an amicable resolution." Spence grinned, looking around at the packed tables. The air smelled like charred meat and French fries with a hint of ketchup. "I'd order but you seem plenty busy."

"I can scrounge you up the meatloaf special to go in about two minutes."

Bad Billy's made a mean meatloaf, that was for sure. "Make it two orders, and I'll take one back to Junie. She's been pretty sick, and she's still kind of pale."

"Heard that." Billy moved efficiently behind the counter, picking up an order slip, clipping it to the rotating metal ring for the kitchen, and spinning it with the skill of someone who'd done it a time or two. "Poor darlin'."

It wasn't as if everyone in Mustang Creek didn't know Billy had a crush on Junie. "She's fine," Spence assured him.

"Good to hear." Billy gave him a swift, shrewd glance and wiped his hands on his apron. "How's Melody Nolan, Spence?"

That stopped him dead in the act of asking for an iced tea to go with the meatloaf. "What?"

"I was at the Moose Jaw the night of the wedding."

"Oh." Well, heckfire, he'd hoped there were no witnesses. Before this, no one had said anything. He probably looked like a steer that had been hit with a ball-peen hammer.

"Saw you pick her up like she was yours and carry her off to your truck." Billy chuckled.

Like she was yours. That phrase had such a nice ring to it.

"Her feet hurt." That was an undeniable fact. Melody would even back him up on that one.

Billy's eyes twinkled as he swiped a rag across the counter. "Spence, don't try to fool an old fool. I could swear you just went a little red. She's a beautiful girl, and once upon a time you two were an item. If you carted her off for purposes other than to, uh, help her tender feet, I'm not gonna say anything, but you know I always call it like I see it. You had a real determined set to your shoulders, son. I've seen it once before. Seems to me that was at Hadleigh Stevens's first wedding—the wedding that wasn't—when Tripp Galloway hauled her out of there in the nick o' time. Never did like that Smythe boy, anyway. Tripp stopping that ceremony was the best thing he could've done."

It was true that Hadleigh had been about to make a major mistake, and Tripp had wisely intervened. Spence said evenly, "Not exactly the same situation. Can I have corn with the meatloaf? I'm betting Junie will want green beans."

"Sure thing." Billy bustled off, and Spence dug out a twenty, put it on the counter and accepted the bag a few minutes later. He left the change behind to cover the tip and skedaddled.

When he got back to the station, Junie, who'd been nearly wiped out by the stomach flu, looked pathetically grateful for the food. She said, "I haven't felt like cooking. I haven't felt like anything. Did Billy send this?"

"With his love," he responded drily on his way into his office. "He'd marry you tomorrow, you know.

Charged me for mine, but yours was on the house. He knew I'd tell you, too. It must be his way of courting you, hoping he can win your heart with his meatloaf. I didn't realize at first that he hadn't charged me, so he got quite the tip."

"He's so sweet."

"What can I say? He's a sucker for a shit-kicking woman who can get away with a short denim skirt on a Saturday night."

"You sooo know how to make a girl feel good about herself, Chief," she said, not sparing the sarcasm.

"I try." He shut the door to his office, dropped into his chair and devoured his lunch as he punched up his computer. Tripp had sent him an email.

Back in Mustang Creek. Great to be home.

He sent back:

Great to have you here.

It was.

Mind dropping by to discuss the party?

You just got back. Are you up for it?

Melody is coming over, too.

That was just plain bribery. An officer of the law should be above being tempted by something so blatant.

He wasn't.

Well, when it came to crime, he was above it, but when it came to Melody, he wasn't. He typed in:

I don't have any plans. Sounds good.

Hadleigh's so tired of eating out she just wants me to grill a few steaks—prove to her that she's back in Wyoming. Bring Harley.

Muggles, Harley and Tripp's dog, Ridley. Those three were as much fun to watch together as a fireworks show.

What else can I bring?

Yourself, and maybe a bottle of that wine the girls like.

He drew a blank.
As if Tripp could read his mind, he typed in:

Ask Mel or Bex. I don't know, either.

They'd obviously been friends too long.

Will do.

It was pigheaded of him, but he wasn't about to call Melody, since he'd made the grand declaration that it was her turn to call him, so he shot Bex a text, instead. While waiting for the information, he answered several messages from the Bliss County courthouse and went through his mail.

Bex came through with the name of the wine about an hour later, and added a sly:

We'll pour Mel an extra big glass and mellow her out.

Nice to have friends in your corner. With a grin she couldn't, of course, see, he shot back:

I'll buy two bottles.

CHAPTER NINE

THE RANCH LOOKED prosperous, but then again it would. After Tripp had returned to Wyoming, he'd sunk a considerable amount of cash into reviving his stepfather's property, and being Tripp, he'd done it right.

Melody drove her yellow BMW by a pasture of grazing cattle and winced at the dust that was no doubt coating her beloved car.

A glance in the rearview mirror told her that, on the bright side, her light, barely there lipstick, a subtle pink, was fine, but also, that was unmistakably Spence's truck coming up the drive behind her.

It wasn't as though she was surprised, because she knew he was helping Tripp and Hadleigh out with the upcoming party. Still, she silently berated herself for the way her pulse accelerated.

He pulled in beside her and slid out of the truck in one lithe movement. Harley bounded out and dashed over with his usual enthusiasm. She slammed the car door on her skirt and would have dropped the potato casserole she'd brought if Spence hadn't been quick on the draw. He caught it and said one word to the dog, who obediently sat down.

"He's in love. What can I say, except please forgive his sad lack of manners. He's taken a shine to you."

Her face on fire, she muttered something akin to a

thank you, managed to get the door open and free herself. Harley assisted by licking her ankles. She finally met Spence's amused eyes. "I've always been cursed with coordination issues."

"Well, it would be unfair to every other female on this planet if you were beautiful, smart *and* coordinated," he said gallantly, but his mouth was twitching with laughter. "I'll just carry this in for you and keep my dog under control."

He could hold the dish in one palm and balance it perfectly. And she'd made such an awkward move. She wanted to strangle him.

"Thanks."

"No problem."

He was as devastating as ever in the usual denim shirt, jeans and boots, and she'd give him credit for the way his shirt exactly matched his eyes, but doubted it was planned. Spence could get up in the morning, put on any old thing and look terrific.

Damn him.

Was it that she was searching for any reason to be mad at him?

Well, that one seemed as good as any. He was just too handsome, and she resented him for it.

"I hope this is that potato thing you used to make." He waited for her to go up the steps first. "The one with all the cheese. I have to admit to a mighty weakness for that."

It was, and she'd remembered. She crossed the wide porch. "Could be."

"I think that dish is what made me fall in love with you in the first place."

She sent him a sharp look as she put her hand on

the screen-door knob. His expression was completely bland, but it was feigned innocence. It had to be.

She wasn't in the mood for games, and he needed to know it. "Spence, let's get something straight. The morning after the wedding happened. I accept that, and I take my share of the responsibility. But you need to do that, too. I'm going to be as clear as possible. I am not interested in one of those casual relationships you're so famous for. As *you* so kindly pointed out, I'm not twenty anymore."

He stood there, still expertly balancing the dish, unfazed. "Nope. You aren't the girl who thought it would be a wonderful idea to elope years ago. You're a woman, Mel. Can we sit down and talk about this rationally?"

"And discuss what?"

"Us."

At that key moment, Hadleigh appeared in the doorway, whipping open the screen door, offering Melody a big hug. She had a fine tan, and her topaz eyes sparkled. "I missed you."

Melody hugged her right back. "I missed you, too. You look fantastic."

"Hey, what am I, chopped liver?" Spence said it mildly and also received a hug, still irritatingly able to hold on to the casserole dish with no visible effort.

Never, even under the pain of impending death, would Melody admit she'd made it just because she knew he'd be there. The man was hopeless when it came to potatoes. It was a weakness she had shamelessly exploited; she'd even piled on extra cheese.

But…*us*?

Was he serious? *How* serious?

"Let me put this in the kitchen and make a quick trip back to the truck." He deposited the dish on the stove and went out again.

Melody looked around. It was a true ranch kitchen, but Tripp had remodeled it when he'd returned to Wyoming, and the spruce cabinets, butcher-block island and white marble countertops with a farmhouse sink, suited the place. All the appliances had custom cabinet covers, too, so the rustic feel wasn't compromised. Hadleigh had hung one of her gorgeous quilts on the wall by the eat-in area of the kitchen, and it was all, in a word, stunning.

"Looks great." Melody meant it.

Hadleigh's smile was wry. "The man paid more attention to the run-down barn than the most important part of the house, so he gave me this kitchen reno as a wedding present."

"Great choice."

"I think he just wants me to cook for him."

Melody grinned. "Really? I remember you made great frozen pizza when we were in college."

"I liked your boxed mac and cheese, too." Hadleigh was never shy about shooting back a response. "Bex is on her way. She just called."

The door opened as Spence returned, and chaos ensued. It was with no small satisfaction that Melody noticed that he was almost knocked off his feet since the doorway was only so big and three decent-sized dogs decided to come in with him at the same time.

He was carrying a sack and nearly dropped it before managing to get through the melee and deposit it on the counter.

Whatever happened with the rest of the evening,

this was a high point, Melody thought. It was endearing to see Muggles, Ridley and Harley greet each other, but they were bouncing off the walls. Canine love abounded to the extent that Tripp, who came in the back door at that moment, his dark blond hair rumpled by the Wyoming wind, hauled the three of them outside before they could break something. He smelled like grill smoke and fresh air, and gave Melody a kiss on the cheek. "Bex just pulled up." Then he pointed at the dogs. "Out, you three hooligans. This isn't a circus, it's a house. Let's go. You can play outside."

The voice of stern male authority worked wonders, and they obediently went out the back, trotting single file.

Both Melody and Hadleigh were laughing when Bex came in, Spence holding the door for her. "What's so funny?"

Hadleigh shook her head, leaning against the counter. "Just the dogs. Ooh, please tell me that's your fruit salad."

Bex plopped the bowl on the table. "Of course. I look forward to the challenge when someone asks me to bring something else. I swear I can cook."

Melody and Hadleigh looked at each other and said, "Won't happen."

At that point, Spence set two bottles of their favorite wine on the counter. "Enjoy, ladies. This is for you. I'm going to go out and help Tripp."

"Help him do what?" Melody asked. "Drink beer?"

"Grill. Control the dogs. I don't know." The charm in his apologetic smile was palpable and affected each one of them before he walked out the door.

He wielded that darned smile like a loaded gun.

Melody said to her two friends, "Crack open that wine, please. I think I need some."

They laughed out loud, but at least Hadleigh hurried to comply, taking several antique glasses from the cupboard and handling the corkscrew with impressive skill.

Melody knew the glasses had belonged to Tripp's mother, inherited from her grandmother. She begged, "Can I have something plastic, please? Those glasses terrify me. I'm so afraid I'll break one."

"Special occasion." Hadleigh shook her head. "Special glasses required. My husband always tells me that she insisted all her fancy dishes be used. I'm *married* to her son. Time for a toast for the three of us, and let's pretend she's here."

They even poured a fourth glass and solemnly faced each other. Bex said, "Here's to Tripp's mom—and the marriage pact."

Glasses clinked. "Hear, hear."

There was silence as each took a solid gulp.

"As for the wedding, we were there for the festive event." Bex's smile was half-mocking. "Remember us? In those dresses? We're going to get you back for those, by the way."

"It's summer. They looked…summery." Hadleigh might be protesting, but her expression was full of mirth. "And feel free to retaliate. I thought they were pretty, but I'll admit the color could have been better."

"You did that on purpose!" Both Melody and Bex said, perched on stools in the remodeled kitchen, their mouths open.

"I suppose it could be seen that way. I swear I thought you'd both say no to the yellow, and I guess that's why I picked them. When you manned up and accepted that color without a single complaint, it was just too funny. I couldn't resist going ahead and letting you wear them."

All three burst out laughing.

Tripp and Spence chose that moment to walk back in the door, crowded by the romping dogs, so there was another traffic jam in the doorway, and the wary look on their faces caused another fit of merriment.

"What's so funny?" Tripp was the one to ask, his tone cautious. "Please tell me it has nothing to do with me." He glanced over at Spence. "Us."

Melody was too busy wiping tears of laughter from her eyes to answer. It was Bex who said on a hiccup, "Not you, us. So relax. Private joke. How soon should we put the potatoes in the oven?"

"The coals will be ready pretty soon. Whenever you want."

Melody got up to take care of it, sliding the dish onto the rack. "It just needs to heat through."

Tripp turned to Spence. "Tell me that's the potato thing with the cheese."

Spence took the plate of steaks out of the refrigerator with the ease of someone who'd been in the house many times before. "That's what I hear."

"Score." Tripp seemed genuinely delighted.

Spence turned around. "Hope to."

Melody flushed at that laconic reply; she couldn't help it since he was looking at her. The warmth spread upward from her neck and cheeks, even though she tried to fight it. Both Bex and Hadleigh were also staring at her now. She'd bet even the dogs were gazing in her direction.

"The three of us are going to bring our wine out to the deck while you all cook," Hadleigh finally said. "It's such a nice night."

"Good idea if we can get these goofs out of here again." Spence pointed at Harley with a stern finger. "You sit until the ladies go outside. Spill one drop of their wine, and you'll be in disgrace for the rest of the evening."

All three dogs sat swishing their tails. There was power behind that tone and at least Mel, Bex and Hadleigh were able to safely exit the kitchen. There was a pretty copper-topped table with several comfortable chairs near the grill, and the view, of course, was the star of the show. Rugged peaks and vistas of pasture with horses and grazing cattle, the grass waving gently in the continuous wind that was as much a part of the landscape as the mountains and the winding rivers.

No sooner had they settled down than another car pulled up, tires crunching on the gravel. Hadleigh took a sip of wine and rested her elbows on the table. "That would be Tate Calder. His boys heard the dogs would all be here, and we had a few extra steaks, so we invited them, too. They've just moved here from Kirkland, Washington, and the kids love the animals. Hope you don't mind. Tate's wife died a few years back and… well…he's really nice."

And, Melody thought, taking a sip from her glass, he was really a hottie. Wavy chestnut hair, dark eyes and a memorable flyboy kind of smile. He was maybe early thirties, young for a single dad, good-looking and successful by all accounts. Ex-pilot like Tripp, who had—from what Hadleigh had briefly explained—decided he had to chuck it all because he couldn't be gone for days at a time with a six- and an eight-year-old to raise alone. He was thinking of starting up a business, or so Hadleigh had mentioned, and had already bought some land; for the moment he was renting in town as he figured out exactly what he wanted to do. Tripp had sold him on Mustang Creek as the quintessential small town, a great place for kids, so he'd left the Seattle area for a place that was affordable and where he knew at least one friendly face.

Maybe that would expand to two. There was some matchmaking going on.

Not for her, thank goodness. Spence was hard enough to handle without male competition. Since the whole world seemed to know about his dinner invitation, no way would Hadleigh try to set her up with someone else.

Bex had better watch out.

She was in the crosshairs of a conspiracy.

Two NOISY BOYS, three rambunctious dogs, a gorgeous sunset, and Spence was sure that the three beautiful women on the back porch were plotting against the men.

Call it a hunch. An educated guess.

Tate Calder was still an innocent when it came to the women of Mustang Creek, but hey, it was every man for himself.

Dinner had been delicious. Tripp knew how to grill a steak, not to mention skewers of onions, mushrooms and zucchini. Melody had outdone herself with the potatoes, and Bex's fruit salad was legendary. Spence had been told she wouldn't part with the dressing recipe for anything, but he suspected Melody and Hadleigh would coax it out of her one day.

Now they were just sitting around the back porch, enjoying the encroaching twilight, doing what men and women always seemed to do—divide up into separate gender gatherings. None of the guys had much of a clue about quilting, exercise studios or jewelry design, which seemed to be the ongoing conversation at the other table, but ranching, *that* they knew about.

"How's the new foal doing?" Spence asked Tripp, picking up his iced tea. The other two men were drinking beer, but no way was the chief of police going to drive even a short distance with any alcohol in his system. When he had the occasional drink, and that wasn't often, it was strictly at home.

"He's a beauty." Tripp ran his fingers through his hair. "I was up half the night with Starburst when she dropped him, but it was worth it. He's in the north barn. You should take a look."

"Love to," Spence responded, meaning it. "Maybe I can persuade Melody to walk out there with me. It's a nice evening."

Tripp raised his brows.

Tate said, "I'm sure the boys would love it, too, if I can round them up. Did we ever have that much energy? Jeez."

Spence laughed, but it was with a tinge of pain when he thought about Will. "Hadleigh's grandmother used to call us—her brother and me—The Whirlwinds. So I think the answer is yes. They should sleep well tonight. So will Harley. Just watch him. He's getting tuckered. I predict that within the next few throws of that ball, he's going pull his usual stunt and hide it so he can take a siesta."

On cue, his beloved mutt followed his usual protocol and caught the ball midair and then, instead of galloping back to continue the game, disappeared around the corner of the house.

Muggles had long since given up the game and was snoozing at Hadleigh's feet, but Ridley and the boys looked disappointed. Not for long, though, since Ridley improvised by finding a handy stick in the grass.

Problem solved.

Spence, Tate and Tripp all burst out laughing.

"Let me guess, dirty joke?" Melody walked past with an empty wineglass. "Does anyone need anything? I'm headed inside to put this away."

Spence saw an opening and went for it, jumping to his feet. "I'll help you."

She frowned. "I think I can put a glass in the dishwasher all by myself."

"I was wondering if you'd like to walk over to the barn to see the colt that was born last night."

She gave him the same suspicious look she'd given him before he'd kissed her the morning after the wedding.

Before he'd taken her straight to bed.

If the sound he'd just heard was Tripp Galloway stifling a laugh at the pause before her answer, he'd punch his best friend in the nose at a later date. He smiled at Melody with what he hoped she'd interpret as an innocent invitation and casually slid his hands into the pockets of his jeans.

Innocent, he was not.

Maybe it was the wine, maybe it was the beautiful

night, but she acquiesced in the end. "A walk might be nice. Those potatoes alone probably contained my daily ration of calories."

If they didn't have a riveted audience, he would've pointed out that he wouldn't change a thing about her body—it was the truth—but everyone except the dogs and the boys seemed tuned in.

Bex swept by and plucked the glass out of Melody's hand. "I'll take this. I need to visit the little girl's room, anyway. Go for your walk."

Thank you, Bex!

Spence motioned toward the barn. "Shall we?"

He didn't make the mistake of offering his arm because her cool demeanor told him she'd snub the gesture, but he'd been tempted. He watched a lot of old Westerns. Maybe he needed to curb that habit.

As they walked down the porch steps, he remarked, "I love this time of night when the sky goes indigo and the stars are just coming out. There really is nothing like it."

Melody gazed up. "I know."

The air smelled sweet, like summer. Her hair moved in the breeze, and he knew it would feel like silk under his fingers, so he had to fight off the urge to reach out and catch a strand.

The barn was a weathered structure but well-maintained. That familiar smell, which included the earthy scent of manure, was clean and poignant, and it reminded him of everything he loved about living in Nowhere, Wyoming.

Reminded him that he wanted to raise a family right here, in Bliss County—with the lovely woman at his side.

His boots crunched gravel. At least she was wearing sensible shoes this evening.

Sensible. That had been part of the problem. When she'd proposed to him nine years ago, Melody hadn't been all that sensible. Sweet and smart and sexy as hell, but so unworldly he'd had to step in, and while he wasn't an oracle or anything, he'd known rushing into a marriage was a bad idea. It hadn't worked out for Tripp, either, who was divorced from his first wife.

The new arrival, awkward and long-legged, was in the second stall with Tripp's prize mare, a coal-black beauty named Starburst for the striking shape of the white patch between her ears. She nickered softly as they approached. Spence stroked her nose and admired the little guy, a tiny replica of his sire, a stallion owned by a friend of theirs who'd won a number of ribbons at the state fair and then showed well all across the country.

Spence's voice was soft as he talked to the horse. "You did good, mama."

Melody peered into the stall. "Yes, she did. He's darling."

Privately Spence doubted any male of any species wanted to be described as *darling*, but kept that to himself. They weren't arguing at the moment, so that was something.

The truce didn't last long.

He managed to put his foot in it by joking, "How were the turnips, by the way?"

Her eyes narrowed a fraction as she turned to face him. "I happen to like turnips. They were delicious."

Thus started what he would ruefully label The Great Turnip Fight.

"Oh, come on, you were trying to duck out of sight. Afraid you can't resist my infamous charm?"

He said it in a teasing tone, but she sure didn't take it that way. In truth, he'd found the incident amusing, but it had stung a little, too, that she wanted to avoid him so much she'd lurked behind a bin of root vegetables.

Melody's hands went to her hips, and she raised her chin. "You know, you are so full of yourself, Spencer Hogan. That must be why you keep condoms in your nightstand. Just in case."

Whoa, *that* was the problem?

Very reasonably, at least he thought so, he countered, "I had them there. I don't necessarily *keep* them there. But they came in handy, didn't they?"

At that moment, judging by the look of fury that swept across her features, he decided he should give a seminar called *How Not to Court a Woman: The Wrong Thing to Say at the Wrong Time.*

"How often do they come in handy?"

That question was about as dangerous as a rattler with its tail shaking. "I don't keep a log or anything."

Okay, he was sinking into a black hole of bad judgment, but she'd put him on the defensive. It only got worse as he tried to climb out of it. "I meant it isn't like I could just come up with a number."

Idiot. Imbecile. Dolt.

"Probably because you can't count that high." The anger in her voice came through loud and clear.

"Thirty-six."

CHAPTER TEN

HAD HE REALLY just said that?

Melody whirled around, figured the pitchfork propped against the barn wall was a little too drastic, and scooped up a fistful of straw and flung it at Spence. It was a satisfying moment. He'd taken off his hat for dinner, and flying bits caught in his dark hair and sprayed his red shirt.

"Okay, that was badly phrased," he admitted, brushing at his clothes and shaking his head. "I swear to God I'm not *trying* to make you mad."

A small rational voice told her that *she* was the one who'd fallen willingly into his arms once he'd asked for that kiss, but it was drowned out by the much louder voice reminding her that Mustang Creek's sexiest bachelor hadn't even had to sweet-talk her into his bedroom. She was a damn fool to believe he was sniffing around for anything more than sex.

Great sex, but still…

She bent over and grabbed another round of ammunition and said through gritted teeth, "Yet you make it seem so effortless. You've slept with thirty-six women?"

He ducked, but again her aim was pretty accurate. The fact that he was laughing now didn't help. "Mel, look at me. I didn't mean to imply that I find it handy to keep condoms by my bed. I meant I'm responsible enough—because I'm thirty-six years old!—that I wouldn't have unprotected sex with you or any other woman unless we'd discussed it beforehand."

Or any other woman? Nope, that *really* didn't help the situation. He deserved another faceful of straw. Like a truckload. She couldn't scoop up that much and heave it, but threw as much as two hands and some real determination could manage.

What she needed to do was acknowledge that she was jealous of all the women who'd breezed through his life, jealous of Junie no matter what Bex thought about that rumor—and she was scared stiff she'd get seriously involved with him again.

Or that she already was.

"Dammit," he finally snapped, warding off another straw attack. "I get that you're mad at me. I just don't get why." He moved then, so quickly she couldn't dodge out of the way, catching her by the arms and tumbling her backward until she lost her balance and they were suddenly lying in the pile of sweet-smelling straw. He was on top, his mouth mere inches from hers. "Now we're talkin'," he said huskily. "This is *much* better."

"Get off me." She shoved at his shoulders, but he might as well have been one of the mountains she admired every day. Immovable. Worse, he had a smile on his all-too-handsome face.

Then he kissed her.

Oh, she saw it coming; he made sure of that, slowly lowering his head, letting her feel his breath against her lips before he delivered the real deal. Persuasive and warm, his lips molded to hers, took possession, and her bones seemed to melt as his tongue began a leisurely exploration of her mouth.

Her hands, which had been pressed against his wide shoulders in a futile protest, loosened, and her arms slid around his neck in a repeat performance of what had happened at his ranch.

He wasn't irresistible, she reminded herself, more like a virus she couldn't seem to shake.

The bracelet she wore around her wrist, the one with the charms she'd created for the pact, gleamed against his dark hair when she opened her eyes. The weight of his lean body was pleasantly balanced, and there were several horses stretching their heads over their stalls, watching the strange antics of their human counter-parts with equine amusement—or so Melody assumed.

His gaze held hers before he kissed her again, this time with less tenderness, the heat level so combustible she was surprised the straw didn't start to smoke.

"Where is it, Daddy? Where is it?"

The sound of an excited childish voice came through, but Melody barely registered it. The next second, Spence had broken off the kiss, muttering something she didn't quite catch. Suddenly three rowdy dogs and two boys came spilling into the barn, tumbling all over themselves, followed by Tate Calder. Melody could see his expression change as he noticed them in the straw. At least they were still fully clothed and not *doing* anything. He said hastily, "Oops, sorry, just riding herd on the crowd. We're out of here. Didn't mean to, er, interrupt anything. They can look at the colt some other time."

Spence recovered with disquieting ease, lifting her to her feet in one swift movement and shaking his head to dislodge the straw still clinging to his hair, all the while acting as if nothing happened. "No problem. Come on, boys, want to see the foal? Right over here."

That left Melody plucking the straw out of her own hair, with the dogs milling at her feet. She coughed in embarrassment, her face hot, and saw the amused look in Tate's eyes. She didn't even try to make up an excuse. "Um. Spence and I go back a ways."

"If you think I didn't cotton on to that before we all barged in here, you're selling me short." He had a nice easy manner. "My lips are sealed."

At that point she didn't know whether to question Hadleigh's efforts to set her up with this man or condemn them. Bex was a peacekeeper, an even-keeled influence on everyone around her. He seemed the same diplomatic type, and maybe he'd be a good match for her friend. Or maybe they were too much alike.

Once Bex had been in love with Will, and he'd died on deployment overseas, which had sent her life into a downward spiral. She'd turned her grief into a devotion to building her business.

As for Spence and her, they were *definitely* too alike. Pigheaded, her grandmother would have labeled it.

She listened to Spence with the boys, watching him out of the corner of her eye as he picked them up one at a time so they could look at the colt. He was good with them. The mare trusted him, too. You could see it; she didn't balk at letting the boys pat her head and even tug at her mane.

The best indication of character, Melody had always thought, was how an animal reacted to a person. Spence inspired that kind of trust in the people of Mustang Creek, too.

The feline triumvirate had tolerated him, and they were a demanding bunch, no doubt about it—excellent judges of character.

"Tripp said he's a good guy, and now I see why they're best friends." Tate shrugged casually. "Obviously, I trust his judgment or Hogan wouldn't be holding my children."

"Well, there's that chief-of-police thing he's got going," she said, her throat a little constricted. "He's trustworthy. Your children are in good hands. Literally," she added, smiling as she glanced at the younger boy. Tate held him by the waist, and the child leaned into the stall, intently studying the foal.

Tate turned back toward the house. "Ya'll mind walking the hooligans back? I'll go thank Hadleigh and Tripp and pack up the truck. The boys love to help me. It only takes twice as long when they do."

"No problem."

Bex was doomed, Melody thought as she watched him walk away. That was a fine cowboy ass, and he was unquestionably her friend's type. He wore his hat well, too, she observed, tilted forward at exactly the right angle.

Melody knew that *she* was doomed, too.

There was something about Spence and those boys together that went straight through her. Straight to her heart.

Would he hold their children that way?

She was hopeless.

Or, worse, hopeful.

They walked back to the house, the boys between them, each of them holding the hand of one child. The dogs gamboled at their heels, and the night air held the sweetness of summer.

Hadleigh, Bex and Tripp were still on the porch, probably finalizing the party details. Tripp asked the boys as they climbed the steps, "So what do you think of the ranch's newest colt?"

"Really cool," the older one answered. Then he announced, "They were kissing."

For the second time that evening, Melody blushed as if she was sixteen. Talk about wanting to sink through the floorboards. The worst part was that none of the adults present seemed to need any clarification, despite the leap from *cool* foal to whoever was kissing whom. Hadleigh was the one who patiently explained, "Well, Spence and Melody like each other."

Bex looked at Melody pointedly and added, "Sometimes they forget that, but yeah, they do like each other."

Tripp got diplomatically to his feet. "Spence, want to walk out to where we're going to have the bonfire and we can set it up?"

Leaving her to the tender mercies of Bex and Hadleigh? Melody didn't think so. She said in a rush, "I have to finish the lanterns, and I have a new commission, so time is tight. Tate will be right back for the boys. Dinner was wonderful. See you tomorrow night."

As she beat a hasty retreat, she heard her hostess call out, "Coward. We're *going* to talk about this."

SPENCE SWUNG THE wood splitter with a heave that might just have been the result of unresolved sexual frustration. What might have happened if the kids and the dogs hadn't arrived when they did was anyone's guess, but *his* guess was a roll in the hay. The log cracked with a satisfying sound.

Tripp picked up the wood and gave him an appraising look. "So, you have some kind of plan?"

It was a warm night; Spence unbuttoned his shirt to his waist and pulled it off. He was sweating, and it wasn't entirely due to the exertion or the temperature. "Plans for what?"

"How to convince Mel you're the one."

"What's makes you think…" he started to say then shook his head. "Strike that, I already know what you think, and you aren't off track. I hurt her once. She doesn't trust me. All the gossip in this town doesn't help my case, either. I'm considered a player, but most of it's undeserved." He briefly rested the ax on the stump and studied his best friend. "You know me, Tripp. I'm not a saint or anything. I've slept with a few lovely ladies, but none of it counted for much. Melody's always been different. Special. We had an argument, if you can believe this, over how many women I've slept with, because I couldn't remember off the top of my head. So I said something stupid—thirty-six—then told her I was talking about my age. I was. I meant, in a sort of convoluted way, that I'm old enough, mature enough, to act responsibly toward any woman I date. Any woman I've ever dated. It isn't that there's a long list, and I don't put notches in my bedpost or anything like that."

Tripp heaved up another log and set it in place. "I do know you. That's what this conversation is about. Let's get back to my original question. How's this gonna go down? I'll be blunt here and tell you exactly how my wife sees it all. Nine years ago you had a fling with

Mel for a few months, then you dumped her, and now you want another shot at it. Why should she give you a second chance?"

Spence picked up the ax and defended his position, saying flatly, "It wasn't a fling," before the ax came down with a solid chunk, and wood chips flew.

"I realize that." Splitting and stacking wood on a summer night was hard work, and Tripp evidently decided Spence had the right idea, because he took off his shirt and tossed it aside. "But it's taken almost a decade for you to admit it."

"That's not true." He swung at the next log his friend put in place. "I've never denied it. Look, we've already had this discussion. More than once."

"Are you going to ask her to marry you?"

That was blunt, even for Tripp. Spence paused to catch his breath. "I'd answer that, but can you swear you won't tell Hadleigh?"

"No."

He said, "Then this conversation is over."

Tripp looked irritated, but they'd been friends long enough that he backed off. "Fine," he said gruffly. "But a man can't kiss a girl in a barn one day and walk away the next."

"You want me to bring over those extra camp chairs I have in my barn?" Spence pointedly changed the subject.

Tripp went along with it, stacking more split wood. "That's a good idea."

"Moe Radner might pitch in, too. He spends every day off hiking and camping out and has a lot of equipment." The deputy would be more than willing to lend them outdoor furniture for the party. "By the way, he wants us to organize a trail ride for some of the local boys, courtesy of the police department and the ranger service. He has a lot of buddies who work for various parks. He once told me up front that he was headed down the wrong path as a kid until he discovered he loved riding and camping. He wants to do that for kids who might be in the same kind of situation he was. I agree."

"I'll contribute money for a good cause any day. Even lend you a horse or two." Tripp wiped his brow.

"Well, this must be my lucky day." Hadleigh's voice, tinged with amusement, stopped their conversation as she strolled up, her long brunette hair shining. "There's nothing like two bare-chested cowboys to make a girl's heart flutter."

"*My* bare chest better be the only one that makes your heart flutter," Tripp said to her with a pretend glower. "I take it everyone's gone?"

Her gold eyes showed a glimmer of laughter. "Yep. Melody swears she has more to do than humanly possible, Tate had a couple of sleepy kids to get into bed and Bex has some sort of corporate meeting first thing in the morning."

Spence figured that the way the two of them were looking at each other was his cue to exit, stage left. He cleared his throat and put down the log splitter. "I should collect Harley and go, too. I'll see you both tomorrow night, and thanks for dinner. I'll bring those chairs."

He shrugged back into his shirt, whistled for his dog, and a few minutes later was in his truck, heading down the driveway.

For the briefest of moments, he considered calling

Melody, but decided against it, knowing he'd be shot down if he pushed too hard. So he just drove home, Harley curled up in the passenger seat. That dog was really worn out.

He suspected Harley would sleep well.

Somehow he doubted the same would be true for him...

CHAPTER ELEVEN

OCCASIONALLY THINGS JUST fell into place.

Melody thought the price for this diamond was a little high, but then again...

It was perfect. And, after all, Mrs. A. had requested perfection.

She said to Ronald Keith, "Tell me what you know about this stone."

Old and spare, he was the canniest antiques dealer in Bliss County, and he knew everyone, so she was able to get the stone's provenance. Wearing his usual patterned flannel shirt even in mid-summer, he leaned forward with a conspiratorial air, resting his bony elbows on the glass case. There was no one else in the shop, but he kept his voice low. Melody would have found it funny, but she was too entranced with the diamond. Its cut and brilliance were too striking to pass up.

"Well, word has it that it's the diamond Rochester Pierce gave his wife the day he asked her to marry him."

She managed to wrench her gaze away from the jewel for a moment. It was really gorgeous, the setting old-fashioned enough to support Ronald's claim. "The senator?"

"That's the one." Ronald straightened. "It's got good karma, too, since they were happily married for over half a century. The estate sale was pretty brutal. Not all their children are still alive, and the grandchildren bickered so much that all of it went up for auction."

She was really entranced. The diamond was of rare quality, at least a carat and a half. A little showier than she'd planned, but the setting could be redone, or even kept for a different piece.

She could only hope that Mrs. Arbuckle meant it when she'd said price was no object.

On the other hand, Melody would have bought this, anyway. She could set it and resell it for a small fortune.

She dealt with Ronald quite a lot and knew he was an honest man. She doubted he was asking enough for this ring. He'd certainly recognized its quality. "I'll take it."

"Good." He smiled. "That's why I called you. I didn't think anyone else would appreciate it and make it shine again, like you will."

"Flatterer."

They always flirted a little; it was part of the negotiation.

He didn't hide his grin. "What can I say? I like pretty girls."

She flashed him a smile in return. He was charming in his own way, although old enough to be her father. "I'm light-years away from being a girl, but I thank you for thinking of me. Our usual deal?"

He nodded. She often paid him a percentage of her commission when he brought her special finds.

They frequently did business when he picked up interesting finds like this one—which was perhaps the most interesting yet. She carefully set the ring by the cash register. "Okay, any other hidden treasures I need?"

A bit of dickering later—she hated that part but Ronald loved it, so she couldn't disappoint him—she had a necklace she could easily disassemble and turn into several pieces. She also bought a couple of silver bracelets missing their settings, but they were solid and worth redoing.

Ronald's assistant was someone she remembered from high school. Cassandra Downing had hung out with the popular crowd and married, as they said, "well," but had divorced her husband, who happened to be the town lawyer, a few years ago.

As she carefully wrapped up the purchases, Cassandra said pleasantly, "Good choice."

Melody agreed. "If I worked here I'd spend my money as fast as I made it."

Cassandra handed over the bag with a smile. "Oh, it is tempting."

Satisfied, Melody left, stepping out onto the sidewalk, and immediately called Mrs. Arbuckle to leave a voice mail. "I have a one-of-a-kind center stone for the ring. It's just…stunning. It has historical significance, too, so I'm sure you'll be pleased."

She certainly was, but she'd promised those lanterns for the party tonight, and they weren't quite done, though after last evening, she had mixed feelings about the whole thing.

RALPH, WALDO AND EMERSON were all snoozing on the couch, and they ignored her *and* her nice haul as she pulled it out to admire, their poses like synchronized swimmers, all limbs arranged in exactly the same positions.

"Look, guys." She held up one of the bracelets triumphantly. "Good shopping day."

Not an eyelid moved. What a girl had to do to impress them, she wasn't sure.

Whether the cats liked the diamond or not, she loved it. Holding it up to the light, she admired the flashes of brilliance, and the cowboy's engagement ring began to take shape in her mind. The old setting would be salvageable, too, with a different gem.

A win-win.

She sat down and went to work on the necklace first, trying to figure out how to assemble the gems so it would wear comfortably, as well as be decorative. Jewelry design wasn't just about the aesthetic impact. She was completely absorbed in her design concepts, and not until her stomach rumbled did she remember that she'd missed lunch. It was 1:45, according to the clock on her wall, and her feline roommates were staring fixedly at her, as if she'd neglected them, ignoring their dietary requirements. Then a car pulled into her driveway, and she was finally shaken from her trance-like engagement with the drawing board.

It was Bex with a paper bag and a friendly but speculative smile. Since they had lunch together several times a week, her appearance wasn't a big surprise. "I'm guessing," she said as she came in, "that we're going to be too busy helping tonight to actually eat. How are the lanterns coming along?"

"Just about done." She'd finished them last evening, working well past midnight. They were scattered all over the studio, ready to be transported to Hadleigh's gala.

"Glad I'm not the artistic one," Bex observed, surveying the Melody's creations everywhere, taking up most of the space. "This looks like a lot of work. No wonder you ducked out last night."

Melody eyed her warily, waiting for some comment about Spence, but thankfully it didn't come. Her stomach made another embarrassing sound. "Hey, it's almost two. Let's go into the kitchen. I have to feed the cats, anyway."

There was nothing wrong with feline hearing in her house. Ralph, Waldo and Emerson jumped up with alacrity. She got out their food while Bex unloaded grilled chicken sandwiches with lettuce, tomato and the heavenly sauce created by the owner of the local bakery. She refused to divulge the recipe for it in her lifetime, or so she declared. Melody had tried more than once to duplicate it at home, but had eventually resigned herself to the fact that there was some mysterious ingredient she'd never be able to figure out. So she fulfilled the craving by simply buying sandwiches from Myra's Hometown Bakery.

The delicious aroma alone made her mouth water. She poured some lemonade into two tall glasses, and they sat down to unwrap their sandwiches. "How was the meeting?"

"Extremely corporate." Bex grimaced. "Nuff said. I know doing the graphs and pie charts is a necessary evil, but I'd rather just have Accounting tell me it's all going well and leave it at that." She sighed dramatically and stretched her arms over her head. "Franchising the business sure changes things."

"Do you miss being the person entirely in charge?" Melody was curious. She'd thought once or twice about opening a shop, but that would mean she'd have the headaches of hiring and supervising employees and renting a suitable space. So far, doing commissioned pieces was lucrative enough to give her a great deal of freedom. Local merchants carried her pieces, and Mustang Creek was tourist-busy in the spring, summer and winter, due to its scenic location. Fall tended to be quiet, but it was nice to get a break now and then. Plus, she loved it when the aspens turned golden and the air had that crisp bite to it.

Bex had taken a huge bite of her sandwich, so she thought over her answer while she chewed and swallowed. "I'm still adjusting. Since the company's going to be publicly traded, I don't have total say, of course, but I own fifty-one percent of the shares, so I still have a lot of clout. On another subject…are we going to take bets that Hadleigh's already pregnant? She didn't have more than one sip of her wine, even though it's definitely her favorite."

Come to think of it, that was true. Melody wiped her mouth with a paper napkin—she'd remembered to buy some—and put her sandwich down. Slowly she said, "Now that you mention it, I did notice that. I just thought she was too busy playing hostess… Holy cow, Batman! That was fast. Must've been quite the honeymoon."

Drily, Bex commented, "You *have* seen her and Tripp together, haven't you? Besides, we both know they decided to try right away."

Inspiration took off. "I need to make her another

charm. What do you think? Stork? No, that's too cli-
chéd. How about a mare with a foal? Side by side."

"That sounds perfect, but don't get ahead of yourself." Bex was visibly amused. "We don't *know* anything."

True. And she still needed to finish the necklace, as
well as that engagement ring. Melody swallowed the
last bite of her sandwich and licked her fingers. "Mind
helping me carry the lanterns out to my car and we'll
go hang them up?"

Serenely, Bex said, "What are friends for?"

THE RASH OF break-ins continued.

It was starting to become a real problem, especially
in a place like Mustang Creek. Spence frowned at the
most recent report that had landed on his desk and
wondered if he should call in state detectives to help.

Six reports in six weeks now. In his jurisdiction that
was a lot. No place was crime-free, but in Bliss County,
they usually didn't see much of this kind of thing.

The thieves seemed to operate in a consistent way,
too, so he was sure it was all carefully planned. So far
no one had been hurt, but as an officer with a lot of
years under his belt, he knew that could change soon
enough. They stole mostly small portable things, particularly electronics, always from private residences,
never shops, although they weren't above taking personal items like leather jackets.

Ross Hayden had just had the trolling motor for his
fishing boat stolen from his garage, along with a cache
of antique woodworking tools.

Considering the details of these thefts, he'd say the

burglars knew the people they robbed, but that was based on his gut and no facts whatsoever.

It infuriated him to think that someone he might smile at on the street was doing this. Not just because it was happening right under his nose, but because that person was betraying a trust of place and safety. The *Mustang Banner,* published on Wednesdays, had picked up on it by now, and every single week there was a new piece about one theft or another. He was tired of being front-page news.

With that in mind, he probably wasn't as congenial as he should have been when Moe Radner came into his office. "What?" he asked sharply.

The young man looked at him and shifted uneasily. "Something wrong, boss?"

"No. Well, yes," he replied. "These robberies are bothering the heck out of me. What do you need?"

"I wanted to tell you the trail ride's full."

"Already? That was fast." The announcement had gone out the day before. That news improved his day. If they were going to do this, at least the idea was being met with enthusiasm.

"Well, yeah, I thought so, too. But we have one, uh, small problem."

"How small?" He asked it wryly, leaning back in his chair. When someone said that, describing a problem as insignificant, it was rarely true.

His deputy rubbed his cropped hair sheepishly. "I didn't think of this before, but we have some miffed parents, because we're only offering this for boys. I even saw that a couple of girls had signed up and I had to call their parents and tell them no way. I did my best to explain that grown men aren't going to take young

girls on a camping trip, not without female chaperones—much less with a bunch of boys to ride herd on.
That's asking for all kinds of trouble," he said indig-
nantly. "Anyway, we don't have enough horses. But
I wanted to let you know that a few people out there
aren't happy."

Spence hadn't actually seen that one coming, although in this day and age, anything that even smacked
of gender discrimination was a problem. He twirled
his pencil in his fingers, thinking it over. "I suppose
we could do a second one just for girls. We'd have to
find some women to manage it, since I wouldn't even
know where to begin. One or two of us would have to
go along to make sure everyone stays safe." He shook
his head. "I didn't understand teenage girls when I
was a teenage boy, and I sure as hell wouldn't understand them now."

"The only female ranger I know who'd really be on
board with this is out on maternity leave, so obviously
I can't ask her," Moe said. "The other two might be interested but they're filling in for her while she's off."

It occurred to Spence that Hadleigh might help them
out. She had her own horse, too, a pretty little mare
Tripp had bought her last fall. Maybe she could rope
in Bex and Melody, too. He had no idea where their
riding skills fell on a scale of one to ten, but this was
a trail ride, not the Kentucky Derby.

He could always pitch the idea at the party tonight
with a heads-up to Tripp first so he'd have back-up.
That would only work if a newly married man was
willing to give up his blushing bride for a few days.
But Hadleigh was an adventurous woman, so she just
might go for it.

"I might be able to make some arrangements," he said. "Now, did you run those files through the state database?" He was looking for any similarities to the crimes they were experiencing in Bliss County. "I was hoping you'd get some sort of match."

Moe shook his head. "If you want my slant on it, they must be local, Chief. Living in Mustang Creek, and stealing in Mustang Creek. They don't seem to be hitting any other towns."

Well, shit, he'd thought that all along. "It's too slick for it to be a bunch of kids. I think we need to look more closely at the victims. Do they have anything in common? Are they connected in any way? Do they go to the same church? Where do they work? Who are their neighbors? Anything that could tie them together so we can understand why they're targets."

"On it." Moe seemed relieved about Spence's solution to the trail ride problem, but also serious about this shadow clouding their horizon. He'd told Junie, and Junie had told Spence, that he'd always thought he'd try for a spot in the FBI; then he'd found out field agents didn't get to choose where they were assigned, and he loved Wyoming way too much to leave the mountains.

Spence understood that.

Yeah, there was a lot he loved about this place, and it included one stubborn blonde he was fairly sure he just couldn't live without.

He glanced at his computer screen and registered the time. "I'm out of here," he told Moe.

CHAPTER TWELVE

THE LANTERNS LOOKED fabulous, Melody thought with justifiable pride. She surveyed the effect and felt a sense of satisfaction because the *wow* factor seemed to impress all the arriving guests. The gold and crimson glow reflected the burst of color over the mountain peaks as the sun went down.

As predicted, Hadleigh had done this up right, and Mother Nature was cooperating.

There was a live band tuning up, a dance floor behind the house set up by a local company and a large tent that held tables and chairs. The buffet consisted of good old-fashioned beef barbecue, baked beans, coleslaw and a variety of desserts, including a Key lime cheesecake and Bad Billy's signature brownies. It was the only dessert he offered, and people drove upward of an hour just to get them. How Hadleigh had wheedled him into making some for the party was a mystery. He refused to do catering but he was fond of Hadleigh and Tripp. He was in his mid-fifties now, and they'd all known him since he was the JV basketball coach.

Except, remembering the pact, Melody reminded herself that they weren't those girls anymore, the girls who'd grown up together, and life wasn't slumber parties and gossip and giggles. They were women, all of them almost thirty, and it wasn't so much the biological clock ticking, as the happiness clock chiming in the background.

She didn't *need* a man to make her happy, but she sure *wanted* what Hadleigh had with Tripp.

As the real wedding reception—the one that actually involved the bride and groom—it was quite an occasion. Melody was delighted to help with more than just the lanterns, but everything seemed to be under control, so she just sipped a glass of beer, grateful for the mountain breeze.

"May I have the first dance?"

The smooth tone made her look up, although it wasn't as if she hadn't seen Spence arrive earlier. He was his usual unforgettable self in worn jeans and a white shirt, with a loosely knitted navy tie and polished boots. She regarded him with what she hoped was indifferent composure.

In truth, her pulse had sped up. And that annoyed her.

"The band hasn't started playing yet."

"I thought I'd jump the gun in case you get all booked up. I expect your dance card will be full. You're the most beautiful woman here."

His relaxed smile was probably deliberate, and she could all too clearly remember that searing kiss from the night before. The spectacular evening backdrop didn't hurt, either, and she had to tell herself that he might or might not be truly interested.

Well, interested, yes, but in what?

"I appreciate the flirtation, but we both know you don't have much of a need to sweet-talk me." The beer must have had a mellowing effect, because she let out an exasperated breath.

At least he was smart enough to not push the issue. "I'm just telling the truth." His gaze dropped blatantly to examine the curve of her breasts under the clinging material of her pink blouse for a moment before he politely raised it, but there was a definite gleam of mischief in his eyes. "I like you in that color. Nice."

"Hmmph."

They just looked at each other until he finally reminded her of his initial question. "So, first dance?"

Maybe he'd bribed someone, but the band started up right then. When she peered around the corner of the house, she saw that Hadleigh and Tripp were already on the makeshift dance floor, in each other's arms. She nodded, since as maid of honor and best man, they were supposed to make an immediate appearance.

"Let's do it."

"Hey, that's music to my ears." Spence took her cup, set it on a convenient table and clasped her elbow, urging her over to where the crowd had gathered. "I'd love to do it."

"I hardly meant *that*."

"Too bad." He pulled her toward him as they stepped onto the floor. "For this moment, though, just dance with me."

It would've been preferable if he hadn't drawn her just a little too close, especially with an audience looking on.

She would also have preferred it if he hadn't smelled so good. She hoped she didn't react visibly, but couldn't count on it. His muscled shoulder was hard under the palm of one hand, and his fingers threaded through the fingers of her other hand as he held her.

It was a love song, of course, and Melody couldn't

risk looking into his eyes. Instead, they just danced, without conversation, and he seemed content with that, too. His body brushed hers, reminiscent of another sensual dance they'd done, and if they hadn't practically burned down the barn the night before, it might've happened again, right then and there. Just as well the boys had burst in on them the night before, she told herself firmly.

She sensed that everyone around them was drawing all the right—or was that all the *wrong*?—conclusions about her and Spencer Hogan.

She wished she knew what was going to happen next.

If she had to make book on it, she guessed he was going to sweep her off her feet and then infuriate her in some way. History had that habit of repeating itself. At least *their* history did. Why he had to be so hard to handle was something she didn't understand.

Maybe that was part of the chemistry. He was completely predictable in some ways—intelligent with a strong sense of right and wrong, tough as nails when he needed to be, possessing an easygoing sense of humor. But he was also immovable in his beliefs and ethics, and that didn't bode well for anyone on the other side of the law.

That uncompromising quality was a valuable trait in a police officer, but in a husband? Perhaps, if he decided to settle down, but so far Spence hadn't suggested he was ready to head in *that* direction, although he'd be happy to head for the nearest bedroom. The nearest altar? Not so much. He'd sure never shown her any sign of that.

Therein lay their biggest problem.

"I love the way your hair smells," he murmured. "Like flowers."

"It's called shampoo, and please don't smell my hair in front of all these people."

He laughed, and she had to admit that was a ridiculous thing to say, so she laughed, too, albeit somewhat reluctantly. She amended her comment to say, "Everyone is watching us."

"So they are. Anyone ever tell you that you can be as prickly as a cactus?"

"*You* have once or twice. I just think we're dancing a bit close for such a public event."

His smile was wicked. "And here we go again, disagreeing. Because I don't think we're dancing close enough."

His arm tightened around her waist, and his lips grazed her temple in a subtle caress.

The man might as well have taken out a billboard sign that said: *I Am Hopeful I'll Have Sex With Melody Nolan Later Tonight.*

The first song ended, and grateful for the reprieve, she stepped away. "I need to go see if Bex needs help. She's working with the catering staff in the kitchen."

He let her go without argument.

She was illogically disappointed as she hurried toward the brightly lit house. One of her favorite vendors, an older woman who ran a shop that stocked her jewelry, stopped her briefly, airily waving her hand, a knowing glint in her eyes. "Whew, seems kind of warm out here, doesn't it, darling? You're a little flushed. Wonder why."

Melody felt an urge to strangle a certain chief of police. She knew Mustang Creek. Gossip was like a match to dry sagebrush. "Uh, yes, a little warm, but it's such a lovely night, Mrs. Perkins. All those stars," she responded pleasantly then dashed inside.

Bex was filling a chafing dish with barbecued chicken. Melody grabbed her arm and dragged her into a corner. "Can you please do me a favor?"

Her friend looked at her inquiringly, strands of hair curling because of the heat in the kitchen. "My usual answer would be 'of course,' but maybe you'd be kind enough to tell me what I'm promising."

"I need you to run interference between Spence and me tonight."

"Run interference? You make it sound like you're playing a football game or—"

Melody caught her apron and gave it a tug, interrupting. "I'm not kidding, Bex. I need some space."

Bex nodded. "I heard about the dance."

"Already?" That surprised even her. "It just ended. I came right inside."

"*Have Gossip, Will Travel* mean anything to you? Two people popped in to steal some of Billy's brownies—the word's out about those, too—and they said something about you and Spence."

Melody didn't even ask what. She didn't want to know. "So, will you help me?"

"Like I said—of course."

HE WAS CLEARLY being railroaded.

Spence wasn't sure whether to be amused or irritated. Melody chose a chair as far from him as possible during the eating portion of the evening, and both Bex and Hadleigh had chatted his ear off for the past hour.

The party was in full swing, people were having a ball, but the band was winding down and it was time to start the bonfire, so he finally managed to track down Tripp.

He said mildly, "I could swear both Bex and your wife actually like me, or have I just been fooling myself for years?"

Tripp looked like he was having a good time, his mood expansive. "You're a fool occasionally, Hogan, no question about that, but what specifically are we discussing?"

He straddled a chair and rested his arms on the back. "They won't let me get within ten feet of Melody."

"I kinda noticed that they were acting like trained cattle dogs cutting a calf from the herd. I think you might have overdone that first dance."

It was impossible to not chuckle at the comparison. "Uh, take a note, Mr. Galloway. Do not refer to your wife or her best friend as dogs, got it?"

Tripp looked properly mortified, a plastic cup of beer halfway to his mouth. "I guess that wasn't my best call. Tell on me and I'll kick your ass. What I meant was they seem to be like wolves chasing a deer—to use another animal image. Hmm. Not positive that one's any better. Well, okay, so they're keeping an eye on you but running in a pack. Melody is dancing with everyone else, and if I was a betting man, I'd guess she's asked her posse to step in."

"To protect her from me?"

Tripp rubbed his jaw. "I'm going to give that question a miss. Enough of *this* topic. Hadleigh mentioned the trail ride and campout for the girls. I can't be gone from this place for three days, but maybe I can get Jim on board so you aren't completely outnumbered."

It was a good suggestion. Jim Galloway, Tripp's stepfather, had recently remarried and moved into town, but he'd always been a rancher and a rider and knew his way around the outdoors. Not only that, he had boundless patience and the appropriate grandfatherly demeanor.

"Ask him." Spence might have said more, but right then his phone vibrated, and when he dug it out of his pocket, he saw it was dispatch. It wasn't as if Junie didn't know where he was, so he frowned. If she was calling him, it meant something.

He flicked a finger across his phone. "Hey."

"You aren't going to believe this, but we have another break-in. Thought you might want to know about this one, even though you aren't on duty."

He looked at the bright lanterns and listened to the laughter and swore inwardly. "Okay, give it to me."

There was a brief hesitation before she said, "A guy out walking his dog heard the sound of breaking glass and realized it came from a house two doors down. He has a German shepherd, you know Curtis, and he walked over to look. Apparently, the dog was having fits, jerking him halfway across the yard, and he saw the window had been knocked out of the kitchen. He didn't have his phone so he had to go home to call it in. By the time he did that and walked back, they were gone." There was a pause. "You'll recognize the address."

It felt as if a leaden ball had settled in his stomach. He just *knew*. "Let me guess. Melody's house?"

"You've got that right, boss."

Her place was, after all, the perfect target. Small,

valuable items. He took in a deep breath. "I'll tell her, and we'll be on our way."

"From what the boys said, they didn't do the interior any favors. Nothing actually destroyed, but they trashed it."

"Are the cats okay?" That was going to be her first thought. If anyone broke into his house, he'd panic about Harley right off the bat. The dog would more likely be clamped to the thief's backside with his full set of sharp teeth, but if the thief was armed, a dog didn't stand a chance.

"No mention of any cats."

"Tell whoever responded there should be three cats and to immediately block that window. Put some cardboard or something over it. Make sure they secure it. Also tell them not to touch a thing. We want fingerprints."

"Got the message, boss." Junie was a good dispatcher; she took everything in stride, always stayed calm.

There was no way he wanted to ruin the party. He ended the call and thought about it for a moment as he tried to regroup.

If he told Melody, she'd flip—because he couldn't promise her that the cats were safe. She'd want to be there, searching for them. And he needed her there to assess the damage, identify everything that had been stolen. What he had to do, he decided, was figure out how to get her out of the party without letting anyone know the real reason for their abrupt departure.

Sometimes tried and true worked best.

He walked over to the dance floor, where she was doing a pretty impressive line dance, and stopped dead in front of her, caught her startled gaze and leaned over to scoop her up over his shoulder, bottom up, his arm clamped around her knees. "We're leaving, everyone," he announced, waving grandly. "This was some party."

Laughter erupted.

Maybe the earlier dance *wasn't* a mistake.

Melody made an inarticulate sound because his shoulder was no doubt pressing into her diaphragm and tried to kick him, but fortunately didn't succeed.

Nothing like having the upper hand in a sneak attack, so to speak. He walked off the dance floor, resting his free hand on her bottom, whistled for Harley and marched to his truck.

"Are you insane?" she finally managed to get out, smacking him none too kindly in the middle of his back as he trudged across the area designated for guest vehicles. "Spence, what's wrong with you?"

Laconically, he said, "It worked for Tripp." He also remembered the night of the wedding, hauling her to his truck to spare her blistered feet. *That* maneuver had worked out well, he thought, as he remembered her in his bed the next morning…

"I'm less likely to marry you than ever!" she yelled.

"Nice to know you were even thinking about it. Take it easy, will you? I have my reasons, and I'll tell you on our way back to town. I didn't want to disrupt the festivities with bad news."

She was seething, he could feel it, but that quieted her down a notch. "Like what?"

"Give me a minute." He let the dog in the vehicle first, since Harley was the more tractable, and then deposited Melody in the front passenger seat. He took the liberty of buckling her seat belt, although he was risking a fist to his jaw, sternly told the dog to stay in the back and went around to the driver's side.

The Wyoming stars were bright but his mood, needless to say, wasn't. It seemed cruel not to be honest about a problem like this one, so he said without preamble, "I just got a call. Your house was broken into and probably robbed. They took out the kitchen window. I need you to stay calm and focus on any details that stand out. I have a deputy there, but I told him to not touch anything. I'm sorry about our exit from the party. I thought people might think it was funny if I just took you out of there in a sort of…dramatic fashion, and all that effort put into the party wouldn't go to waste. There's nothing anyone else can do. They might as well enjoy themselves."

Melody was speechless, and that wasn't something he'd seen before. Not very often, anyway. In profile her face was very still as she stared out the windshield. Finally she said, "Someone broke into my house?"

"Afraid so."

The expected panic ensued. "The cats! They hate strangers. Drive faster."

"I'm not going to break the law by speeding. We'll stay within the limit and get there safely. I expect those cats have the burglar tied up in a closet somewhere, anyway."

"Maybe." Her voice cracked as she tried to laugh. And failed.

"Please, Spence, I'm so worried about them." Her whisper was almost inaudible.

That did it. He did speed up, just a little, when he saw the shine of tears in her eyes. He reassured himself that he was still within the allowable limit—and he *was,* after all, responding to a call. They hit the county highway and made it into town in reasonable time.

He saw the law-enforcement vehicle in front of her house, lights still flashing, which was showy but not necessary. Except that after a seventh break-in, maybe it was a nod to the public, signaling that they were on it.

He grabbed Melody's arm as she went to jump from the truck. "Do me a favor and try not to touch anything. There's always a sense of violation with a burglary, but if you'll just let us do our jobs, I'd appreciate it. Collect the cats, and we'll take you wherever you want to go, okay? If you notice something missing, speak up, but otherwise, we don't need you to do anything."

"I'm not an idiot," she snapped as she got out of the truck. Then, being Melody, she had to turn and shoot back at him, "Except when it comes to you!"

She ran up the walk.

The next hour wasn't pretty.

To her credit, Melody wasn't hysterical over the pulled-out drawers, scattered pillows or even the ransacked state of her studio, but she cried silently over the absence of her cats, tears trailing down her cheeks.

He had to admit he couldn't take it.

While the responding deputies took photographs and fingerprinted the obvious surfaces, Spence helped her search under every bed, the couch, the nooks and crannies of the entire house, and finally had to acknowledge the cats weren't inside. He told the deputies, one being Moe and the other a county veteran, "Stay inside with her, take a statement like you would with anyone, while I look around outside. Keep Harley inside. He means well, but he's just going to get in my way."

Moe nodded. "Will do."

Now, he was really used to dogs, but cats were unknown territory. Spence tried to think like a cat, gave up after a split second, and scoured the yard with a flashlight for the best place to hide if he was a small critter.

At the farthest end of the yard, under a giant lilac bush that had taken over that corner, he suddenly spotted three pairs of unblinking, glowing eyes.

All lined up.

Oh, it was them, all right. Relief washed over him in a wave. He figured he could save Melody from a raging fire or a deadly avalanche, but she'd appreciate this more.

The kicker was, of course, trying to get them all three of them on board with the idea of going back inside with him. How did one man carry three hefty cats—if he could even begin to coax them out? Crouching there, he thought it over.

So he did what any heroic officer would do and texted for backup. Found them. Need you.

Melody burst out the door. He was slightly surprised the cats didn't scatter, but they must have been used to her impetuous nature because they didn't move when she dashed up and dropped to her knees next to him.

"Thank goodness." She kissed him then, just a peck of gratitude on the cheek. Still, a kiss was a kiss in his book. Then she began the process of trying to convince her precious roommates that they should leave their safe haven.

They were having none of it.

Spence was ordered back into the house to get a bag of cat treats from the same cupboard where he'd been shown the food, and it was just possible that he saw a smirk on the face of the county deputy as he walked past carrying the brightly colored little bag.

Moe, standing there with Harley at his feet, grinned. "Anything for a pretty lady, right, boss?"

Spence shot him a lethal look, and he shut up.

He had to admit she knew cats. The treats worked like a charm.

All he needed to do was rattle the bag, and three forms cautiously emerged from under the bush. Then they followed him into the house as if he was the Pied Piper, their curved tails twitching.

Melody dispensed the treats, and after they'd daintily devoured them, they jumped on the mantel to inspect the mess in her studio. But not until they'd flicked a glance of disdain at Harley. With the cats safe and sound, Melody informed him that all the jewelry pieces she was working on were missing, and some of her tools, as well.

She looked...well, shattered.

He was going to damn well fix that.

"I have a safe, actually, but I don't use it much," she confessed, a few tears resurfacing. "This is Mustang Creek, after all. Luckily, I did put some of the gems Mrs. Arbuckle wanted in the necklace she commissioned in there, but I just bought a gorgeous diamond for an engagement ring she ordered, and it was here on my worktable, so I could study it while I did the design. I have insurance, of course, but that stone simply isn't replaceable."

"We'll need a full written inventory, with photographs. The state has a special unit to investigate fenced goods on the internet. Luckily, your pieces are one of a kind. With enough information, they can flag each of them."

"My computer is missing, too," she said bitterly, "but I take pictures of the pieces with my phone before I store the digital files. At least that was with me this evening."

"That's welcome news." He meant it. "You know, and mind you I'm not saying I'm glad this happened, but it might be the break we need. If a trolling motor gets stolen, no one thinks twice, but a Melody Nolan piece is a different story."

Although the quality of the stolen items had escalated with this particular theft, the MO was similar—entry through a broken window, the mess left behind—so Spence was convinced that they were connected.

"Happy to help," she said gloomily.

He turned to the deputies. "I've got this from here. You boys can go."

Damned if he didn't notice another smirk. Apparently, it was no secret that he was more than a little interested in Ms. Nolan. Once word about the way he'd carted her off from the Galloway party got around town, he was going to catch some ribbing.

Worth it.

Spence eyed the trio of cats. "I'd suggest we go out to my place, but I'm guessing that idea would not be met with universal household approval, so Harley and I will just bunk down here. In the morning I'll call Gary at the hardware store, and he'll come fix your window."

"Oh, that's subtle," she said, the sarcasm unmistakable.

"I'll sleep on the couch. Do you really want to stay here alone?"

HE HAD HER THERE.

Alone? No, thanks. Besides, the triumvirate was okay with it. Despite the presence of a dog, in their eyes clearly a lower life form.

Melody had to agree with his earlier assertion that there was a sense of violation in the knowledge that people had broken into her house, taking whatever they wanted, frightening her beloved pets. In the process, they'd destroyed any feeling of personal security. It was generous of Spence to offer to stay. He was right, too, as little as she wanted to acknowledge it—having a man and a dog in residence might allow her to get some sleep. Besides, the cats required a lot of persuasion to get them into a car on a good day, and this was unfortunately not a good day. Or rather, night. And she couldn't possibly leave them in the house after what had happened.

At least the party had been a success. She was happy for Hadleigh on that score.

She picked up a pillow and put it back on the couch and helplessly surveyed the chaos. Books scattered, drawings everywhere, even her DVD collection was all over the place. "I don't know where to start."

Spence walked up behind her and put his hands on her shoulders, rubbing them lightly. "The bastards left the kitchen alone, aside from the broken window. A cup of tea might be nice. We can take a deep breath and clean up in the morning."

The man did have a way with those talented hands. She relaxed a fraction as he soothed her knotted muscles with his thumbs. "Not a bad plan."

"Occasionally I have good ones, believe it or not."

She turned around, her gaze softening. "I have never doubted your intelligence or integrity, just your motivation. But I'm emotionally incapable of having this discussion tonight."

He seemed to understand, his right hand coming up to touch her cheek in a brief caress. "I'm really sorry about all this."

He was hardly responsible for what had happened, but she got the impression that maybe he felt he was. "I think I'll skip the tea. I'm just going to brush my teeth and fall into bed."

Harley was completely in favor of that; he followed her into the bedroom, jumped onto the bed as if he slept there every night and settled at the foot of it. With a brief thump of his tail on the double-ring wedding quilt Hadleigh had made for her, he laid his head on his paws and closed his eyes.

"Some watchdog," Melody said with a suffocated laugh, kicking off her shoes.

His tail thumped again, but his eyes stayed closed. The signal was clear. He was in for the night.

She went into her master bathroom, grateful the thieves hadn't vandalized that, too, and got ready for bed, putting on a pair of shorts and a worn T-shirt.

Sexy stuff.

She went back out into the living room/studio in her bare feet. Spence had removed his boots and stretched out on the couch, his arms crossed behind his head.

"Just come and sleep in my bed," she told him. "I'm

not in the mood for anything but actual *sleep*, but…it would be better to have you there."

He glanced up at her. "Sure?"

He looked so tall and solid and safe. Given recent events, she was *very* sure. "Yes. Besides, your dog's already settled in, so the more, the merrier."

He got to his feet. "I'm going to walk around the house one more time, make sure everything's secure."

"Thanks."

Melody crawled into bed, aware that she was still tense, until Spence came into the bedroom and began to quietly undress, except for his boxers. When he joined her, she immediately spooned into him. She felt the warmth of his body against hers, listened to Harley still snoring softly and finally, finally she relaxed.

He draped an arm around her waist. "I'm right here."

If she hadn't been so vulnerable and shaken, she might not have whispered into her pillow, "I have no desire to fall in love with you again."

"It's okay if you do." The reassurance was accompanied by the slight tightening of his embrace. "I promise."

At any rate, she *thought* she heard that as she drifted into an exhausted sleep.

CHAPTER THIRTEEN

FIGURATIVELY SPEAKING, THE next day felt as though a tsunami had blasted the coast of Wyoming—although, of course, the state had no coast.

Moe hadn't been kidding about the irate parents and their complaints over the trail ride. Spence saw that his inbox was jammed with complaints. He needed to approach Hadleigh right away, but the night before had been complicated for them both, no doubt about it.

The latest robbery had him severely pissed off on a personal level, although he had to admit that waking up with Melody snuggled next to him, her shapely bottom pressed against his groin, had been a sweet perk, despite the whole untenable situation.

Except there was no way he could lose the erection that had kept him awake half the night, and his unsatisfied body certainly didn't improve his mood. In the light of day, the damage to her house looked even worse, but other than the window, nothing was actually broken, and he'd done his best to help her clean up before he left for work. She'd thanked him very nicely as her trio of cats watched her give him another chaste kiss on the cheek, and he'd departed, feeling like a deserter. The place was still a mess.

After dropping Harley at home, taking a lightning quick shower and throwing on some clean clothes, he'd made arrangements to have her window re-paired ASAP.

His morning went from bad to worse.

There was a traffic accident on Main Street involv-ing the mayor. Spence answered that call himself.

Somehow, a load of cattle, headed for auction, had somehow nudged open the door to their transport truck when the driver stopped for gas, and meandered through town, causing that accident. The driver, while he could drive a semi-trailer truck, knew nothing about cattle, and the mass escape had to be handled. Luck-ily, Spence could herd cows even without a good cut-ting horse, and there were plenty of cowboys around to lend a hand. With the assistance of these good-natured citizens pitching in, the cattle were all herded back into the truck, but it took a while. One stubborn cow had discovered the joys of a bed of hostas at some-one's residence, and refused to budge. Much to the amusement of the onlookers, Spence finally had to rope her and use his truck to urge her away from the buffet of plants. The owners weren't home, so he'd had to leave them a note explaining what had happened. They weren't going to be pleased when they saw their ravaged landscaping.

Then there was a fistfight between two boys during the beginning of football practice at the high school, and the elderly coach—the same one he'd had back in the day—couldn't deal with it because they were tak-ing some serious swings at each other. A concerned parent watching the practice called the police.

Fine, but in the end, that turned out to be a case of overreacting; when they got there, the incident was al-ready over, and handshakes had been exchanged. He'd even talked the principal out of suspending them since no one was hurt.

He couldn't wait for this day to be over. It wasn't murder and mayhem, thank God, but all the small stuff added up to a big headache.

When he finished work, he went straight home to his horse and his dog. He needed to unwind, and a long ride was just the way to do that.

He saddled Reb, took him out to the big clear pasture and the river, and ran him full tilt along the bank, giving him his head. The horse understood he could go as fast as he wanted, and at one point they were racing flat out, reins loose, the wind in Spence's hair. He finally had to pull up, laughing and patting his horse's damp neck. "Hold on, partner. You seemed to need that and so did I, but let's walk back. We should both cool down."

After that… He wanted another night in Melody's bed, but not one of playing the gentleman.

As for Reb, he might be feeling so frisky because Spence had been neglecting him. With the wedding, the burglaries, the party and Melody, he hadn't had much time to get in his evening rides.

They splashed through the creek, the pebbled bottom reflecting the dying light, and he pondered the robbery. Melody swore she hadn't told anyone about the diamond she'd paid a nice chunk of change for, which meant that trail led back to the antiques shop, where she did business fairly often. And yet, he knew the owner was upright and trustworthy, so maybe that wasn't such a promising lead. The theft might also have been random. It could simply be that the thieves broke in, the diamond was just sitting there and they took it. Spence had the feeling Melody wouldn't make that mistake again, but the pang of regret he experienced was heartfelt.

"This is an imperfect world," he mused out loud to Reb. "Full of imperfect people who behave badly at times. I'm supposed to be the one keeping them in line. Tell me, if you were me, what angle would you take with this case?"

In answer, Reb put down his head and drank from the stream, loudly and with horsey enthusiasm. Spence laughed. "A lot of help you are."

But as he sat there in the saddle, where he usually did his best thinking, he decided that being forced to stop for five minutes while Reb drank his fill actually *was* some help. Horses—and people—went where they knew they could get what they were after. Melody's house hadn't been a random target, and the more he thought about it, the more certain he felt.

Follow point A to point B—that was the usual blueprint in police work. But there was also the gut feeling that steered you in the right direction. Finished slurping up water, Reb shook his head, and Spence absently held the reins as his horse meandered out of the creek bed up the embankment.

The thefts were well-planned; in each case, no one was at home and although there had been considerable disruption at Melody's house, there was a common thread of no real destruction.

Yup, same folks.

The aspens whispered back, agreeing with him.

When he rode back to the house, he found Tripp sitting on his front porch with Ridley and Harley, booted feet propped up on the railing, holding a bottle of beer.

He waited until Spence slid off before he said lazily, "That was quite the exit last night, my friend, and now I know why. I heard about the robbery. After I thank you for not making everyone go AWOL on me and spoil the party, wanna fill me in? How's Melody, for starters?"

"Too damn beautiful for my peace of mind." No matter what, a decent man never put up a wet horse, so he nodded. "Give me a minute to get Reb taken care of, and by the way, I hope you brought more of those. I might even have one. Mustang Creek's had enough of my time today."

"Go take care of Reb. Hadleigh's with Mel, so I'm footloose and fancy-free. The dogs can stay here with me."

Those two lazy mutts seemed way too comfortable with the idea of sleeping side by side on the porch instead of making their typical trek to the barn. Spence grinned at that as he unsaddled his horse and brushed him down. Then he gave him some oats as an apology for his recent neglect, not just the usual hay, and opened the gate to the fenced pasture. Back at the house, Tripp took a bottle from the cooler he'd brought, handed it over and said, "I thought I had the best view in our grand state, but yours is mighty fine. Not that I haven't sat in this exact same chair before, but this is one pretty night. So, what happened?"

He twisted off the cap, took a long swallow of light lager before he dropped into a chair. "Someone broke in and tossed the place, stole from her, scared her cats—and that's quite an accomplishment since they even scare me—and got away without anyone seeing anything."

"What's your hunch?"

It wasn't as if he hadn't been thinking about it all day—and night, since he hadn't slept much.

"I was just asking Reb that." He laughed and felt a fraction lighter. "He didn't have a lot of insight, but I figure we have someone working the community. These aren't random burglars. I'm sure of it. They're going into these houses with a mission because they know what's there. Any ideas?"

"Glad my opinion's second to Reb's."

"He was handy, that's all. Sometimes it helps to think out loud. Think this through with me now over a cold one."

"Don't have to ask me twice. When I heard about it, I was furious for Mel's sake. Let's not even discuss how Hadleigh feels. Anything happens to her friends, and she's on it, both barrels blazing. If I was whoever broke in, I'd watch for a *High Noon* moment when she finds out who did it."

Spence surveyed the Tetons and had to admit it was a privileged view. He tipped the beer to his mouth again, took another swallow and said in measured tones, "I agree with Moe. This is a local problem. The thieves are obviously aware of the comings and goings of anyone they target. If you think for a minute that the idea of someone keeping track of what Melody's doing doesn't freak me out, you'd be wrong."

"Ask her to move in with you."

He turned slowly and gave his friend a direct look. "I was waiting for the answer to another question first. But," he said with a deep sigh, "I still have to find the right time, the right *way* to ask it."

Tripp threw back his head. "Ha, thought so. I'm

going to win that bet with my wife. But I'm serious. Melody's house was broken into. Is she safe?"

It was a worry, no doubt about it.

He muttered, "When people bet on my personal life, it annoys me. I also do my best to keep the peace in this town. Mustang Creek is generally a nice place to live. I'm angry on a number of levels."

"I'm not denying that this is a peaceful town. It's safe except when people break in and steal your valuables. What if she'd walked in on the crime? She's a woman living alone. Anything could've happened."

He wished his friend hadn't brought that up. In fact, he wished Tripp didn't have a point. He stared over at their boots, perched on the railing. Tripp had much nicer footwear since he had them custom-made, but then again, he didn't live on the taxpayer's dime, and Spence was a down-to-basics type, anyway. He exhaled audibly. "I'll ask you again, since you think you're so blasted smart. We don't have a single witness, and the perpetrators of these crimes seem to know the victims and their habits well. So where would you look?"

Brow furrowed, Tripp thought it over. "I'm not a detective, but I agree it has to be local. Makes sense. Pretty much everyone around here knew about the party. Hadleigh and Mel are close friends, so our thief or thieves knew she'd be at the ranch."

"So far you're getting about a C in Lawman 101."

Tripp rolled his eyes. "Hey, if you want to fly a plane, go ahead and give it a try. I'm just thinking out loud—like you asked me to."

"No, thanks on the plane. My feet stay firmly on the ground whenever possible." Spence stared at the label on his bottle of beer but didn't really see it. "I haven't been able to tie this together yet, and it's really frustrating. I know the crimes are related, but I haven't put my finger on the connection. I'll find it, but—"

"Maybe you should talk to Jim," Tripp broke in.

"Your father? Why?"

"He's retired, he lives in town and he knows just about everyone. Maybe he'll have an idea or two. He's a man of few words, but when he speaks each word is like gold.

"He's always been shrewd about people. He sure knew when I'd crossed the line as a kid, no matter how careful I was to hide it," he said wryly. "Oh, and why don't *you* ask him about going on that trail ride with a bunch of giggling girls? I haven't had a chance yet."

Not a bad suggestion. Spence inclined his head in a nod. "Might just do that."

"Know what else you should do?"

"What? I wouldn't bother to ask, but you're going to tell me, anyway, so why put off the inevitable?"

"Buy Melody a horse. Worked for me. Hadleigh and I ride out every night in this kind of weather. Relax, talk, enjoy where we live. You can keep it here. You've got lots of space, and Reb would probably like having a companion. As a wedding gift, seems to be a good one."

Much as he hated to admit it—because Tripp would gloat—it was an excellent idea.

He drained his beer. "Okay, thanks for that. I'll start looking around."

Tripp drained his own beer, set the bottle down with a plunk and said smugly, "No need. I think I can hook you up."

Hadleigh had made her a cup of tea. As she'd explained to Melody in the past, her grandmother had taught her to serve tea the "proper" way—in a china cup with saucer—and as a result, she had a plentiful supply of both.

Melody accepted her tea with both hands and took a grateful sip. "Thanks for helping me clean up."

"Are you kidding? Of course I would!" Her friend sank down on the couch next to her. "It looks almost normal now that everything's back in place. I can only imagine how you feel."

"Mad as hell," Melody said without hesitation. "Spence warned me I'd feel violated, and oh, I do, but I'm also furious. Besides the diamond and my works in progress, they took most of my tools so I can't even work. The mess, too—that was just spiteful. They didn't steal my CDs, but they threw them around. Maybe they didn't like my taste in music."

Hadleigh touched her shoulder. "I'm so sorry. And I can't help feeling sort of responsible. If you hadn't been at the ranch—"

"Don't make me dump this tea on your head," Melody warned her. "Like *you're* responsible? Please. Besides, then I might have *been* here. That would be even worse. Walking into it afterward was bad enough."

"At least Spence was with you." Hadleigh's expression was bland—to the extent that she could pull it off, anyway. "Word has it he was here all night. People talk, you know, and his truck was still in your driveway this morning."

The cats hadn't budged from the mantel all day, except to eat and at litter box time. They obviously felt disturbed by the break-in, as well. Melody sent a silent message of apology their way, not that it was her fault any more than it was Hadleigh's, but she was their human guardian. So, in a way, it did fall on her...

They got the message. They blinked in unison. Did that signify forgiveness? Melody chose to believe that it did.

"I can tell we're going to talk about that. Spence being here, I mean." Melody said it with complete resignation. "Should I take out a notice in the paper announcing that nothing happened? I was tired and distressed and didn't have a kitchen window. He was being nice."

"He's in love with you."

Having someone, especially one of the people closest to her, state that so starkly, made her eyes suddenly burn. "He's supposedly been in love with me before."

"Hot damn, you can sure dig in your heels." Hadleigh set down her cup so hard it rattled in the saucer. "He *was* in love with you before, and he is now. If the entire world can see it, why can't you? Why are you so blind?"

"He's in love with sleeping with me." That came out sounding a little more forthright than she'd intended, but Melody stood by the words. "Everything else is up in the air."

"Including a certain part of his anatomy? Well, that's exactly my point."

She had to burst out laughing, the levity welcome. "You are so bad."

Hadleigh laughed, too. "I know. Tripp would be the first to agree with you."

They settled down again, and Melody put her feet on the coffee table. Special circumstances allowed special vices, although the cats looked surprised. No paws permitted on the coffee table. House rule. Melody clarified. "I'm trying to figure this all out."

"Yeah. I remember the process—excruciating introspection."

Melody nodded.

"Spence isn't all that easy to understand. If you take Prince Charming and combine him with Billy the Kid, maybe you'd get it."

"Can't disagree with that one." Hadleigh grinned. "At least this time it was you carted off like a sack of feed."

"Then you remember the feeling." Melody didn't point out that Spence had done that to her once before—after Hadleigh's wedding. But nobody knew about that—right?—and she wanted to keep it that way.

"How could I forget?" They both laughed again then looked at each other. Hadleigh said quietly, "When Tripp did that, it was the best thing that ever happened in my life—except the day I married him instead of Oakley. You might want to keep that in mind."

Trouble was, she hadn't noticed Spence asking her to marry him. "If he's serious, I think we should get to know each other better."

Melody's best friend gaped at her as if she'd jumped into the deep end. "You've known him since you were six years old. Check the calendar, sister. That wasn't yesterday."

"Thanks," she said drily. "I've seen the forecast, and imminent spinsterhood, if you'll pardon the old-fashioned term, seems to be the dark, rainy cloud on the horizon. I'm saying that summer nine years ago ended badly, and that's something I've been thinking about. Remember the pact? I want to get married one time and one time only. I totally misunderstood his level of commitment back then. I don't want to make that mistake a second time. As the saying goes: Fool me once, shame on you, fool me twice, shame on me."

Hadleigh seemed to consider it and then nodded. "All right, I see your point. What's your plan?"

There was no plan. And therein lay the problem. Spence was a wild card, whether you were talking poker *or* baseball.

"I've decided if he wants to take me to dinner, I'll accept," she finally said, "and that would be a good start. Help me out here. I figure that what needs to happen is the separation of sexual attraction and friendship. You know, so we have a better understanding of each other. Do you agree?" Melody ran her fingers through her hair, briefly closing her eyes. "I don't want to be *that* girl, the one who uses sex to get what she wants. It's flattering that he's so interested, but I need more. Spence has never told me how he feels about marriage. As a matter of fact, he's never told me how he *feels*. Period. End of story."

"He didn't have the easiest childhood," Hadleigh said, curling her legs up under her.

"I know. Neither did you. Neither did I. I still remember the day I found out my father was sick."

"But he didn't reject you. He fought his battle with cancer so he could stick around as long as possible for you. Besides, we're women. We tend to work through our problems by talking about them. Men, on the other hand, usually just ignore their emotional issues."

Truer words were never spoken. But Melody was still prepared to argue. "I can't handle a relationship based purely on physical attraction."

"Maybe you should tell him that."

"And force his hand one way or the other?" She got restlessly to her feet, unable to sit still. "I know he cares about me. And it's probably a foolish sentimental notion, but I have to know he *loves* me. If he asked me to marry him tomorrow, and I thought he wasn't one hundred percent in *love* with me, I'd say no."

"So go to dinner with him, for heaven's sake. Do *something*." Hadleigh brightened. "Wait. The trail ride! That's perfect."

"What trail ride?"

"Spence wants us to chaperone a trail ride for teenage girls. That'll provide quality time together and no chance of even sharing a sleeping bag. Three days. I was going to ask you and Bex to help out, anyway."

Three days in the saddle? She wasn't a complete tenderfoot, but...

"I haven't been on a horse in a while." She had to be honest.

"I doubt many of the girls have, either. When he asked me if I'd participate, Spence promised an easy pace. Just enjoying the scenery and being outdoors is the whole point. Cooking over a campfire. Spence swore to me that the guys will do the cleanup, set up the tents, saddle the horses and handle all the details. Tripp can't go, but he's going to ask Jim to come along."

She adored Jim Galloway, so that sounded good. Melody wasn't positive she and Spence would spend a lot of "quality" time together on this outing, but it was an intriguing opportunity.

"I suppose it would test his devotion, dealing with a saddle-sore woman," she said, only half joking. "Since I can't work until I replace my tools, do you mind if I come out tomorrow morning and take a ride on Sunset, just to practice?"

Hadleigh grinned. "Atta girl."

CHAPTER FOURTEEN

SPENCE TOOK THE piece of paper from his desk drawer and smoothed it out again, at odds with himself emotionally, something that was unusual for him. He'd always been action-oriented, which was why his job suited him. If a decision needed to be made, he made it and damn the torpedoes. What happened next was what happened. He'd deal with it as it came.

The portrait was interesting.

He studied it, head tilted, wondering if it was just a physical representation or a subjective and emotional one.

He didn't think he looked that remote and wondered if that was a personal perception of hers.

He was on horseback in her sketch, and she'd done a good job with Reb, too. There was a hint of mountains in the background, but it was mostly him, clad in his usual gear. He seemed to be looking into the distance, his features shaded by the brim of his hat, his mouth unsmiling.

He felt guilty for having this picture, and equally guilty for being the star of the show.

He'd, in essence, swiped it.

Yes, he, Spencer Hogan, police chief, had stolen it from the floor of Melody's studio when he'd stumbled across it after the robbery, crumpled and in the corner.

During the vandalism, the thief or thieves has ripped apart her sketch book. Once he saw that the portrait was clearly of him, he'd tucked it away in his pocket without saying a word.

He should probably return it, but that would just embarrass both of them, because she'd know *he* took it, and he knew *she'd* drawn it. When, he wondered, had she made this sketch? Recently, he'd guess; that pad was the one she was currently using.

"Knock, knock. You look a million miles away, son."

The familiar friendly voice brought him out of his contemplation. The door to his office was open, and he glanced up to see Jim Galloway there, dressed in his usual ranch attire even though he lived in town now. His battered hat had been replaced by a brand-new Stetson, no doubt at the insistence of his wife.

As he strolled in, Spence got to his feet and offered his hand. "I see you got my message. I'd have stopped by the house."

Jim's calloused grip was as firm as ever. "I was out and about, so took a chance you might be in. Save you the trouble. Us retired folk have a little more time on our hands, though I have to say the missus keeps me hoppin'. Got to admit I'm curious. What can I do for you?"

"Have a seat." He gestured at the chair by his desk. "I've got two favors to ask. Listen, Junie makes a mean pot of coffee. Want a cup?"

"Old cowboys live on coffee. Black, no sugar."

Spence went out to the small break room, poured a cup and brought it back then sat down behind his desk again. "I want to pick your brain about this recent string of burglaries. Tripp's suggestion." He smiled. "He seems to think pretty highly of you for some reason."

Jim chuckled. "The feeling is mutual." He sobered almost immediately. "I've taken to locking my doors. Gets my hackles up. I've even told Pauline to keep 'em shut up tight when she's alone. If I can help in any way, I'd be happy to."

Spence picked up a computer printout on his desk and leaned forward to hand it over. "Here's a list of the victims so far. Of course, it's possible that they were chosen at random, but I don't believe that. There are certain similarities, and my gut tells me these crimes are planned. Since you know just about everyone around here, I wondered if you could think about it. Tell me if you see a connection between these seven people."

With a small grimace, Jim fished a pair of glasses from the pocket of his shirt and slid them on. "Can't read without these damn specs anymore. It's better to get old than not to get old, if you catch my drift, but there *are* inconveniences."

Spence thought about the card still sitting unopened in his desk drawer. He'd had no idea if his mother was still alive until that card had arrived. She'd be in her late fifties now, which wasn't old, but it wasn't young, either, and life could deal a person an uncertain hand as it played out the game.

When he was younger, he'd often wondered what had happened to her, if she'd remarried, if he had half siblings out there, but as an adult, he'd put it behind him. People could change a lot of things in life, but not the past. Once he'd come to terms with that, he'd stopped thinking about it, stopped thinking about *her*. But then that card had to turn up.

Jim squinted at the list, obviously mulling it over. "I might have to ponder this a bit. What could sweet little Melody Nolan have in common with crotchety ol' Lily Rayburn? That pious pain in the ass could have a passel of people who dislike her, but not Melody."

Spence hid a grin. First of all, he doubted Melody would enjoy being called little and sweet, and certainly Mrs. Rayburn wouldn't enjoy *her* description. "Among assorted other things, like a DVD player, a television and some small appliances, they stole Mrs. Rayburn's prize teapot collection, some of which she bought in England. That seems pretty strange to me. The average thief isn't going to know what to do with that. Sure, they can fence the other stuff—that's easy—but teapots? And unless you come prepared, how do you even carry them without breaking or chipping them and ruining their value?"

Jim held up his cup and snorted. "Teapots. I'm a coffee drinker myself, but I get your point."

There was one more thing that bothered him. A lot. "As you think this over, keep in mind that in the first six robberies, the thief or thieves went in, took what they wanted, messed the place up some and slipped out. In Melody's case, they completely trashed her studio." He folded his arms and leaned on the desk, recalling the chaos. "It seemed to me that they're getting bolder. Or else this one was personal."

"Maybe she should stay out at your ranch until you figure that out, son."

Of course Jim had been at the party and knew their history, and that sage advice was a direct reflection of

Tripp's opinion. He said neutrally, "I didn't want to put the cart before the horse, if you know what I mean. But maybe you're right."

"I'm old-fashioned." Jim's weathered face was thoughtful. "But I sure as hell, after all my years on this earth, am not naive. I'm going to guess that horse bolted out of the barn a long time ago. What's the second favor?"

Spence wasn't convinced he could sell the female trail ride, but Jim was surprisingly interested.

"Pauline might tag along if you don't mind. Don't think she's ever done anything like that."

"Perfect." Spence liked the idea of an older woman as one of the chaperones. Then he raised a brow. "Has she ever been in the saddle?"

"Nope," Jim said with a cheeky grin. "That'll be part of the fun."

MELODY SLID DOWN from Hadleigh's horse, feeling pretty good, but then again, the soreness usually kicked in later.

The ghosts of those unused muscles would appear soon enough; she had no illusions about that. Luckily, Sunset was a patient animal and had forgiven her rusty riding skills. Tripp met her at the barn and took the reins. "Nice morning. Enjoy the ride?"

"Absolutely," she answered. It was indeed a lovely morning, the breeze cool and clean, and the upcoming trail ride might be just what she needed. A break from her current woes, some time with Spence, not to mention Hadleigh and Bex. It sounded like a mini-vacation. She rubbed Sunset's neck, saying, "She's an extremely well-mannered horse."

"That she is." Like Spence, Tripp was calm and relaxed with animals, so they were comfortable with him. He slipped off the mare's bridle, and she nudged him affectionately. "The minute I saw her, I knew she'd suit Hadleigh."

"Yeah, it was definitely love at first sight."

He fended off another affectionate nuzzle. "Speaking of which, how's everything with Spence?"

Faced with such a direct question, she felt she'd been put on the spot. It wasn't as if she and Tripp weren't friends, but he was more in Spence's camp than hers. "I, well…I don't know," she managed to stammer out under his discerning gaze. She met it squarely. "I don't know how serious he is, so I'm going to stick with that answer. I just don't know."

Tripp began to loosen the girth as he spoke. "He'll tell you eventually. That's how he works. It all has to be settled in his mind before he takes a step. That makes him a great cop and a great chief."

Melody nodded then stepped forward, eager to change the subject. "Let me take the saddle. You don't need to coddle me."

He deposited it in her arms. "Here you go. It's true. On the trail you'll have to handle yourself and your horse. Put your own tack away."

She managed to heave it up onto the post. "It's been a few years, but I hope it's like riding a bicycle."

"Except with legs and occasionally a temper."

"Yeah, I guess horses are unpredictable."

"So is Spence," he said with a laugh. "I was talking about him."

She blushed. "You're as bad as your wife."

"Worse." He winked.

She shook her head, playing along, pretending to be shocked. "How does Hadleigh put up with you, anyway?"

"God knows. I've wondered that myself."

She nudged a pile of straw with her toe, not meeting his eyes. "She loves you. That's how she does it."

He hung the bridle on an iron hook. "You don't love Spence?"

Loaded question there.

"I tried that once. It didn't work out so well."

Tripp swung around. "Try it again, Mel."

"Whatever I tell you, you'll tell him, so can I just exercise my right not to respond?"

His mouth curved in another grin. "I think you're confusing our little talk with the amendments to the Constitution. I'm asking because he's like my brother. Look at it this way. If you thought I might hurt Hadleigh, you'd come after me like a rabid wolverine on steroids, right?"

True, although she'd never seen a wolverine, rabid or otherwise.

She left shortly after that conversation, not precisely unnerved, but certainly unsettled.

It only got worse.

Mrs. Arbuckle's sleek Jaguar, complete with chauffeur, sat in her driveway, all polished silver exterior and immaculate headlights.

Melody got out of her little yellow BMW and summoned her best smile, even though she smelled like horse; it was impossible to ride a horse and not smell like one. Added to that was the odor of dogs, because Muggles and Ridley seemed to be her biggest fans. Their greetings involved a great deal of leaping around, and she never emerged unscathed. "Mrs. Arbuckle. How are you?"

The lady emerged from her vehicle, placing one expensive but practical shoe in front of the other. Her gray hair was perfectly coiffed, and her slacks and blouse pressed. Roscoe, her terrier, followed, naturally. "Busy," she announced, as if Melody's tardiness was an affront, although she'd made no appointment or given any indication that she planned to drop by. Then she softened her response, saying briskly, "I suppose I bring that on myself. Now then, I heard what happened."

Melody herself might not be pristine at the moment, but she and Hadleigh had spent a lot of time scrubbing away every trace of the intruders in her home, so it was tidier than usual. For that, at least, she was grateful. "The stones for your necklace were in the safe, and the thieves didn't even try to get into that, according to the police," she informed her unexpected visitor as she unlocked the door. "Please come in."

Mrs. A. sniffed as she accepted the offer. "I was worried about *you*. Come, Roscoe."

That was gratifying. She hadn't felt she was high enough on the list to warrant concern. "Thank you. I wasn't here, so the danger was more to my possessions." She sighed and decided just to fess up. "I assume you got my message about the diamond. It's my fault—I'd left it out on my worktable, since I was still working on the design, and the thieves took it. I'll start looking for a new one right away. My insurance will cover it. Um, can I get you some tea or coffee?"

"I'll take a glass of wine." Lettie Arbuckle eyed the sofa, apparently felt it was worthy and sat down. Roscoe hopped up beside her and stretched out, head on paws, taking for granted that he was allowed on the furniture. "None of that sweet swill, please. I like body and actual taste."

By now it was past noon, Melody supposed, although the assumption that she had decent wine on hand was a little ambitious. But in this case she actually did. She went into the kitchen and found that bottle of expensive chardonnay she'd bought a few days ago and hadn't ended up opening. It was nice and chilled. She poured a glass for Mrs. A. For herself, she grabbed a bottle of water. She took both into her studio/living room and noticed that the cats were nowhere in sight. Stranger with dog equaled an instant vanishing act.

The way she'd arranged her house was fine for her purposes, but it did make entertaining awkward, since her worktable was more practical than elegant. She could've used one of the bedrooms as a studio, but she liked the light in here and needed the space. Besides, Mrs. A. had visited before, so she refrained from apologizing for the decor.

"What does Spencer Hogan say about the investigation?" Mrs. Arbuckle asked after taking a genteel sip of wine. "This is turning into a veritable crime spree. Quite shameful."

"I feel confident he's doing his best." That was the truth. "He's hoping maybe some of the pieces they took from me will surface online and lead to the thieves."

Melody mourned the loss of her mobile in particular. She'd made it with pieces taken from a lamp with a stained glass shade her mother had accidentally knocked over while dusting; it had been inherited from *her* mother. Melody recalled the tears that had followed, and even though she'd been a child at the time, she'd carefully collected the pieces and put them in a box. Much later, while moving into her own home, she'd come across the shattered glass, and inspiration had struck. To have it stolen was like having someone rip part of her life away. Luckily she'd made two, one for her and one for her mother. Still, it hurt.

"They are unique, true." Mrs. A. looked thoughtful. "Clever of him."

"I understand there's some sort of forensic division at the state level to monitor things like that." Melody wished she'd taken the time to pour her water into a glass because chugging from a plastic bottle was really rather graceless. But then she still smelled like horse and dog and dust, so why worry about it? She took a swig. Her throat was parched. On the trail ride, she'd make sure she brought along plenty of water. Riding was thirsty work.

"I imagine his resources here in Bliss County are limited."

Why did Melody get the impression that Mrs. A. had dropped by to discuss something other than the robbery? In all her glorious grubbiness, Melody sat back and waited, saying nothing more than, "I imagine so, too."

"He's quite an attractive young man."

That was undeniable. Far too attractive, but the expectant way her guest was looking at her made it hard to keep from bursting into hysterical laughter.

Was the elite Lettie Arbuckle, queen of Mustang Creek society, such as it was, matchmaking?

"He has his moments," she confirmed in a neutral tone. "Nice to look at, but not always easy on the nerves."

Mrs. A. waved a hand airily. "All men are irritating, my dear. The balance between positive and negative attributes is what matters. That, and the man's smile. I must admit that what I first notice about a man is how he smiles. Chief Hogan's smile is exceptional."

Melody wondered if she'd been transported to another galaxy, one in which rich matrons dropped by to extoll the virtues of a man who'd slung her over his shoulder like a barbarian just a few nights ago and carted her off. It seemed to be a habit of his.

She set her bottle of water on the floor. "I don't disagree." Enough about Spence's sexy smile; she thought about it entirely too much as it was. "Like I said, my next move is to start looking for another stone for the ring. I can't count on the original being recovered, so I assume you want me to move forward."

"Please do. As soon as possible."

Then she pulled a typical Mrs. A. move. She finished her wine and got up to leave without saying goodbye, Roscoe trailing after her.

Bemused, Melody rushed to the door, whipped it open in the nick of time, and watched them exit. They both got into the car, which backed out of the driveway.

What had just happened?

She didn't have the faintest idea.

SPENCE ENTERED THE shop with teapots on his mind.

Ronald was unpacking a box full of old dishes, humming to himself, and a genuine smile broke out on his thin face when he glanced up. "Howdy, Spence. Nice day, isn't it?"

Yes, but chatting about the weather wasn't why he was there. "Sure, yes, very nice. I was wondering if you could help me out."

Ronald brushed packing material from his hands. "Of course. If I can."

Spence sent a fleeting glance over shelves of antique dishes and musty books then focused on the glass case in front of him. It overflowed with various pieces of jewelry in various styles and from various decades, the most valuable kept in a locked section. Spence saw any number of period pieces, including diadems, and knew he was out of his league. He needed some expert advice.

He went to lean on the glass counter then thought better of it. The case looked as old as the contents, and he wasn't a small man. "So here's my question. If you wanted to sell a stolen bunch of old teapots or an antique diamond ring, how would you go about it?"

"I'm sick about that ring. I called Melody when I got it in because I knew she'd *appreciate* it."

Spence believed him.

Ronald wasn't slow on the uptake. He nodded. "Narrow market. I wouldn't buy a collection like that, not to sell around here. Wrong place for it. Antique guns, sure. They'd sell. Those teapots would just collect dust. I mean, I can sell platters and gravy boats and such, but not a collection of high-end, extremely valuable teapots."

"So where *would* you sell them?"

"Online auction probably. With a minimum bid. There are fanatic collectors who'd pay a fortune for them."

"From what I understand, the diamond ring is worth a lot less without the history."

"The provenance," Ronald corrected. "Oh, you'd be right, but think about it."

The bell jingled as a couple came in, obviously tourists. Ronald rested his knuckles on the case and after he'd nodded at them, said drily, "When you get it for free—because you break into someone's place and help yourself to it—provenance isn't as big a concern, now, is it? A nice rock will still fetch you some serious coin. Same goes if it's a black market sale. I'm really careful not to buy anything that might be stolen, but I'm not the only dealer in these parts. If a good deal comes along, and I have no reason to be suspicious, I'll bite. I know Mrs. Rayburn, so no one's going to ask me to buy those teapots. The diamond won't come my way, either, not unless the person who stole it is an idiot. Since you haven't caught anyone, I assume he's not. Or they, as the case may be."

It made sense, of course.

"Thanks. Keep an ear out, will you?"

"You bet."

To make it worse, when Spence went to leave, the first person he saw was one of the women he'd briefly dated entering the store. Not surprising in a town this size, but the way she looked right through him didn't improve his day. He held the door for her. He didn't get a thank you or, in fact, any acknowledgment at all.

He didn't know if she was here because she had business with Ronald or as a customer...

The trail ride was starting to look more and more promising. Just getting out of town appealed to him.

He was considering fast-food options when his phone beeped.

Melody.

Yeah, he'd take that call even if he was standing on the top of Mount Everest.

"Sir Edmond Hillary."

There was a lengthy pause. "I'm pretty sure I don't have the wrong number—and it sounds like you, Spence—but I don't get the joke."

"He climbed the world's highest mountain in 1959."

"I know that, thank you. Why would—"

He cut her off. "What's up?"

"I wondered if you'd like to have dinner," she said.

"You're asking me out?"

"No, not really. Just dinner. That meal we eat in the evening."

"My grandmother referred to lunch as dinner, and supper was in the evening."

Her sigh was heartfelt. "Forget it. Talking to you is—"

Before she could hang up, he said swiftly, "I'd love to, but my place, okay? Is that too much trouble? I have to take care of Reb and there's Harley, too. I'll pick you up."

He understood that she was nervous about staying alone, and he was nervous about letting her stay alone, so it worked out.

"I'll cook," she said, quiet but firm. "And I'll drive myself. Your place is fine. I'll bring the ingredients and be there by six. Now that the window's fixed, the cats should be fine. I have nothing left to steal, so no one will break in."

He winced to hear the disillusionment in her voice.

"Six it is. If you need a fancy pan of any kind, you might want to bring one because my kitchen has two cast iron skillets, and that's it. I should have enough dishes, though."

"See you then."

When the call ended, he hit the pavement, walking back to the station with a purposeful stride. He kept the house decent, but he couldn't swear he'd done the dishes—and how long had it been since he swept the front porch? Too long, probably.

The elation he felt was like that of a high school kid who'd just managed to snag the prom date of his dreams.

Melody wanted to cook for him. That was progress.

"I'M AN IDIOT."

Melody said it out loud as she drove down the long lane to Spence's house, because her pulse had decided to pick up its pace despite her resolve to approach this evening like a mature woman and not some starry-eyed adolescent.

Fine. They'd slept together.

And then just *slept* together.

She wished that hadn't happened. Not the first time, but the last one. That he hadn't held her through the night when she was vulnerable and unhappy and alone. In truth, he'd been sweet. No touching, no whispers, just his arms around her when she really needed it.

It was hard to think of a man so virile and masculine as sweet, and yet there it was. Not that she didn't believe he could be kind and considerate, but *sweet* had shaken the foundations of her resistance, leaving a crack in the wall.

She needed to do all women in the world a favor and start a blog or something. *Beware of Sweet: It'll Hook You Like a Trout Swallowing a Lure.*

Harley dashed off the porch when she pulled up, barking his fool head off with joy, and she was smart enough not to get out the groceries until they'd greeted each other properly. It was nice to be loved, but in the process her jeans had acquired some attractive paw prints.

Spence was nowhere in sight, which probably meant he was still at the barn.

She hauled out the sack of chopped vegetables and marinated chicken she'd spent quite some time preparing and went up the porch steps and into the house, Harley at her heels.

And stopped short.

Mouth open in surprise, bags clutched in her arms.

There was no question the man had gone overboard.

The small dining room was between the living room and the kitchen, and he'd set the square table for two, complete with attractive dark blue placemats and matching cloth napkins, silverware, simple white plates and water goblets, but that wasn't the real surprise. He'd taken the time to gather a bouquet of wildflowers as a lavish centerpiece, just for her. She was almost certain he didn't usually eat with a vase of flowers on the table. More likely it was dusty boots in the corner, the television on ESPN, his plate on his knees as he sat on the couch.

As an artist, she had to admit he had an eye.

They were wildflowers of almost every variety blooming right now—red, violet, mustard yellow, and there were green spikes of leaves through it all, too.

Arranged very effectively. He could give the flower shop in town a run for its money should he decide to leave law enforcement.

More sweetness. She was a goner. A lost cause. Just write her off.

She texted Bex and Hadleigh.

Spence picked wildflowers for me.

She had to laugh when they both texted back the same thing.

Uh-oh.

It wasn't as though she disagreed.

When he came through the door, she had her wok out, and the rice was already steaming, and the won-tons—a new recipe that didn't require frying—were in the oven. She glanced over her shoulder. "As you can see, I made myself at home. Blame Harley. He invited me in."

"Smells fantastic in here." He took off his hat and hung it on a hook by the door. "Sorry, it took me a little longer in the barn than I intended."

He was probably late because he'd been out gathering wildflowers before hitting the necessary chores that come with having a ranch, big or small.

That proved something she was fast becoming aware of—she was a sucker for a romantic gesture, especially from Spence. Didn't that just complicate things?

Melody poured some peanut oil into the pan and added garlic. "Dinner's not ready yet, anyway."

She liked his kitchen. No extra frills, but it had

clean lines and knotty pine cabinets, a state-of-the-art stainless-steel refrigerator she envied and a plank wood floor. The design was efficient, economical—not a surprise, considering whose kitchen this was. Some tin canisters sat on the butcher-block counter; she'd bet they were antique. The window over the farmhouse-style sink didn't face the mountains, but looked out on a meadow bordered by a fringe of Ponderosa pines, standing there like stately warriors. If a person had to wash dishes, and she didn't see a dishwasher, it was exactly the view to compensate for the task. She might dirty up some more pots and pans just to stare out at it.

"Can I help?" He leaned against the counter, watching her.

"Nope."

"Time for a quick shower?"

She turned, the pan sizzling. "I'm not going to sleep with you tonight."

His quicksilver smile was as compelling as ever, his dark hair ruffled. "That's not what I was asking. I was actually thinking that I just mucked out a stall and brushed down a horse, and I'd like to clean up before I eat whatever it is that smells so good. Have I got five minutes?"

She flushed. "Sure. Yes."

Idiot was exactly right.

Melody crossed over to yank open the refrigerator door and take out the plastic bag that held the marinated chicken for the stir-fry. She tried to remind herself that maybe he wasn't sitting around thinking about sex all the time. This was just dinner. Wait, no, supper. Oh, whatever!

The chicken hit the pan with a satisfying sizzle.

She used a wooden spoon to stir it then threw in some broccoli florets and let it cook with the lid on before she poured in the sauce.

When Spence strolled back in, hair wet, in clean jeans and a denim shirt, he sniffed the air. "I'm upgrading this meal from good to great. What are we having, and do you want a glass of wine?"

"Garlic chicken with broccoli, and yes." Reckless move, but she'd spotted that wine already chilling, and if he'd gone to the trouble of buying it, she didn't mind having a glass. She'd follow Mrs. Arbuckle's example. The sun was well over the yardarm, wasn't it? Not that she could have explained what a yardarm was. Something to do with sailing, she thought...

"I'm off duty. I'll have one, too." He removed it from the fridge and opened a drawer to get a corkscrew. "This particular week I've done my civic duty. What's in the oven?"

Cowboys were notorious for always being hungry. Lawmen, too, she supposed. "Crab wontons."

"Music to my ears." He uncorked the bottle with a soft popping sound. He had to search several cupboards, but in the end produced two wineglasses that didn't match. Melody felt a sense of enjoyment as she watched him take a tentative sip, long fingers curled around the stem of the glass.

Surely not his usual tipple. On the rare occasions when he drank, he was strictly an ice-cold American-brewed lager kind of man. Judging by what she'd observed on the rare occasions they'd been at the same social event.

"Not too bad." He eased onto a stool by the counter.

"You seem to have things under control, but is there anything I can do?"

Just sit where you are and be part of the scenery. She didn't say that out loud but he looked like a guy on the front of a *GQ* magazine—if they dressed their models in boots and a denim shirt, which they usually didn't but maybe should. Even the hint of a fine beard creeping along his jaw worked in a rakish sort of way. There went the romance novels again. But she supposed if anyone in this neck of the woods qualified as a rake, he was the one.

Melody shook her head. "I'm fine."

"I like having you in my kitchen."

"You like someone else cooking for you." She sprinkled in chopped green onions.

"For once, no argument. Both statements are true."

"No argument? That would be a milestone."

"For us," he agreed, "sure would. But I'm glad you're here. Tell me that counts for something."

It did, and she was afraid of it, so she changed the subject. "I don't suppose someone kindly returned my diamond today and said, 'Aw shucks, officer, I'm sorry I robbed the nice lady.'"

"No. That isn't, by the way, how it usually works."

"I know." She continued chopping, which was therapeutic for taking out her anger. "Tell me you like ginger."

"I do."

"Do you want kids?"

She heard an inner voice screaming, *Where the hell did* that *come from?* two seconds after she opened her big mouth. She hadn't seen it coming. Maybe it was because of Hadleigh's possible pregnancy, maybe it was the robbery, but it all resulted in a desperate need to get her life in focus.

Spence looked down at his glass of wine and then at her. His blue eyes were direct. "Yep."

Nothing more. No dissertation on why, or any hedging, just a confirmation. She'd be pushing it if she asked how many, so she went back to stirring the chicken. She didn't really know how many she wanted, either, so that was a discussion better left for another time.

That was the moment, the very moment, she decided she was going to marry one headstrong police officer who'd never even pretended to propose to her.

She glanced at the charm on her bracelet and made a silent wish.

CHAPTER FIFTEEN

BEYOND A DOUBT, Spence thought happily, the meal was off the charts.

Tender chicken and fluffy rice and some sort of spicy sauce that was sort of Asian and yet unique enough that he asked her what was in it. When it came to cooking, he was mostly a meat-and-potatoes man, with the obligatory veggie chucked in.

Melody just smiled at him in that way she had, which always did something interesting to his composure, and promised to give him the recipe. She wore another one of those clingy blouses tucked into perfectly fitting jeans, and her usual understated makeup. When a woman looked like Melody, she didn't need to doll herself up.

He wasn't all that interested in the recipe. What he really wanted was to ask her to make it again. For him. Just for him.

He did his solid best to not devour her stir-fry like a starved madman.

The *madman* description applied in more ways than one, particularly when he remembered her question about kids—and his answer.

Yep. That was what he'd said.

He'd meant it, too.

When he put down his fork after his second helping, telling himself that thirds was going a bit far, he picked up his napkin. "That was way good. Take good and make it ten times better."

Melody managed amused and appreciative pretty well. "I got the impression you liked it."

"I swear I ate lunch. Although it didn't compare to what you just made. Not even close. I'd eat this every single day."

"Spence." Sitting across the table, she held her head in both hands. "I swore I was not going to sleep with you."

"But now you're tempted?" A man could hope.

"No."

Ah, shot down again.

"Yes."

A light glimmered at the end of the tunnel. "No *and* yes? If you want to confuse me, that's the way to do it."

"I want to."

Valuable information to have. He raised his brows. "I sense a 'but' coming."

She fiddled with the stem of her wineglass. "But... I recognize that a relationship involves a lot of different things. There's companionship and romance—like moonlit walks on the beach or sharing a hammock on a sunny afternoon. There's the everyday stuff, the triumphs you share, and the problems you cope with. And, yes, there's sex. What I'm saying is, I don't want ours to be based *primarily* on sex. People spend time in bed, but as a percentage of the average day, it's small potatoes."

"I think I've just been doubly insulted. Were you implying that I'm a little fast on the trigger? Nor do I like being compared to a fairly bland root vegetable, either."

Melody shook her head, laughing. "Neither one, as you very well know. I'm just saying great sex isn't enough."

"Okay, that's better. I like the *great* part." He lifted a placating hand. "I'm sorry, I'll be serious. I understand what you're saying. I don't even disagree. Let me help you clean up, and we'll go sit on the porch."

If she wanted moonlight, there was nothing like watching the moon rise over the mountains, no matter what phase it was in. He'd trade a rocking chair on his porch, a horse grazing in the background and a tangy breeze over a beach any day of the week. Nothing wrong with an ocean view, but he was more of a Wyoming man.

They worked companionably together to clear up the kitchen. He dried, since he knew where the dishes and utensils went, and she washed and rinsed. When they were done, he picked up her wineglass and refilled it—she wasn't driving anywhere tonight—and escorted her to the best place in the world.

As they settled in their respective chairs, he took in a breath of clean, fresh air. "I know it isn't a city view of skyscrapers with all the lights, and I can appreciate that, too, but I think I need…quiet."

On cue, a pack of coyotes began to yip in a western chorus.

"Or such as it is," he added ruefully. "Critters aren't quiet. The elk bugling in the fall wake me up in the middle of the night. But it's a good kind of noise. Not cars on a freeway."

Melody's profile was soft in the moonlight as she settled back, her gaze focused on the view. She crossed her ankles. "I haven't really wanted to live anywhere else. There are people who roam the globe, addicted to always being in new places, but I wasn't born with that gene. Oh, I took a semester in Glasgow at the University of Strathclyde my senior year in college, and I loved it. And I went to Italy once and enjoyed the beauty and the history, but my roots are here."

He knew she'd studied abroad. This was Mustang Creek; not everyone from around here went to Scotland for six months. "What else?"

"It's your turn. Tell me something I don't know about you."

He'd lived in this town his whole life. The book on Spencer Hogan was wide open, except for one thing. "My mother sent me a card the other day," he said slowly. "Just like that, out of the blue. After all these years. Why?"

The fact that he'd even admitted it surprised him. It wasn't a part of his life he talked about. Melody knew, of course. Everyone did. His mother had dumped him with his aunt Libby and walked away. None of that was news.

Of course she asked him, "What did it say? The card or letter, whatever it was."

"Don't know." He looked over at the mountains. Peaceful. Serene. A timber-ridged silhouette against a darkening sky. There were wolves in those darkened ridges, mountain lion and plenty of bear, other dangers, too, but no people.

Melody stared at him. "Don't know? You haven't opened it or did you burn it?"

He shifted in his chair. "Burn it? Let's not get dramatic. Though I have to admit it occurred to me to just throw it away. It's in my desk at the office. I'm trying to decide if I want to hear anything she has to say. I'm leaning toward not."

She didn't go all female on him and tell him he should open it. Melody sipped her wine and studied the glorious scenery. Harley had it bad. He'd come out with them and was asleep at her feet.

He and that dog sure understood each other. He'd worship there, too.

"I take it my opinion is welcome."

"I haven't told another person on this planet but you. Not even Tripp. Feel free."

She gave him an unfathomable look. "You haven't told Junie?"

"Oh, jeez. We work together, and we're friends. Have been since childhood. That's the beginning, middle and end of it."

To his relief, Melody seemed to accept that and settled more comfortably against the back of her chair. "I honestly don't know what I'd do in your place. Atticus Finch says, well Harper Lee does, anyway, in *To Kill a Mockingbird*, unless you've walked in another person's skin, you don't know what he's put up with, what he's gone through, and I think it's a valid point. Although I'm trying to imagine what would make me abandon my child, and I just can't come up with it."

"Me, neither." Spence sighed and rubbed his jaw. "So I can't decide if I should even waste my time reading it."

After several minutes of silence, she said the most unexpected thing.

"It hadn't occurred to me before, but women are sort of like cats."

He turned his head to look at her. "Okay."

Melody had a quirky smile on her face. "I just mean we are so inquisitive. Men are different. They're more like dogs. They take everything at face value and deal with it and move on. There's not a cat on this planet who could leave that envelope on your desk alone. If it was from my mother who'd been gone since I was nine years old, I would've torn it right open. Now, I see your point, she deserves nothing from you, but I still would have opened it on the spot. I couldn't have stopped myself."

"Being designated a canine," he said wryly, "I thought I might take it over to my aunt and let her look at it. Since she's the one who raised me, maybe she should make the call as to whether I reply or not."

"Your aunt is fantastic. She definitely deserves a lot of credit."

She sure did deserve credit. She'd welcomed a confused nine-year-old boy into her home, her life. No hesitation. He'd been a handful in high school, too, and she'd taken it in stride. "I don't know that it's a plea for forgiveness. I don't know that it's a plea for anything. It's a card, judging by the feel of the envelope. That's it. My birthday's in March. Maybe it got lost in the mail or something."

"How many has she sent you?"

"Cards? My mother? This would be the first."

"I kind of want to wipe the floor with her."

That muttered comment made him choke on a sip of the wine he'd been trying to drink all evening. One glass, and he still wasn't finished. Apparently, he wasn't all that cultured. A squat brown bottle was more his style.

Melody wasn't the kind of woman who engaged in

brawls. She was artistic and much too sensitive. He said quietly, "That impractical and rather improbable sentiment is duly noted. And appreciated. However, I'm not nine years old anymore. I don't understand her reasons for doing what she did, but I no longer *need* to. The day I worked that out set me free. She doesn't define me, I do."

She nodded slowly then went back to gazing up at the star-speckled sky. "That's a healthy attitude. It's clouding up a little. I heard it was supposed to rain."

She was perceptive enough to abandon his least favorite subject. "That'll keep the ranchers happy."

"Are we really talking about the weather?"

"Seems like it."

"You shouldn't drive home," he said.

"I came to that conclusion myself a while back." She gave a small shiver. "Right now I'm spooked. If you want to see someone leap over those mountains in a single bound, break a window."

He thought about Tripp's suggestion—seconded by Jim—and tried to sound detached, as though his offer was motivated strictly by concern for her. "I'd feel more comfortable if you'd consider moving out here. Bring the cats. I have that back porch. It has no furniture, and it's screened. For the winter, I've got glass panels to put in, and there's a woodstove. You could use it for your work space."

MELODY WAS TAKEN off guard.

Not just a little.

A lot.

Was he asking her to *live* with him?

Sounded that way.

"It would make Harley really happy," he said in a mild tone. "He has a serious crush on you." And that nearly sealed the deal.

They really needed to work on their relationship skills, but she had to admit that was one persuasive argument. The dog snored softly and snuggled closer, as if it was a perfectly orchestrated moment planned between man and dog.

She checked to see if he had one eye open, but the critter in question did appear to be genuinely asleep.

"I don't...don't know what to say." He'd certainly managed to fluster her.

"*Yes* would be my preference, but you can think about it. No instantaneous decision required." He yawned. "I might go to bed soon. A good meal and a long day sure make a man sleepy."

She must be touched in the head, or she had the backbone of a weeping willow branch. Before really thinking it over, she asked, "Too sleepy?"

He stared at her, the night breeze blowing a lock of dark hair across his forehead. Rakishly, of course. She was going to kill Bex for ever bringing that up. "Too sleepy for what?"

"Spencer Hogan," she threatened, "if you make me say it out loud, forget it."

In response, he did what he did best. Stood and scooped her up, tossing her over his shoulder, and told Harley, "Come."

He walked through the house to his bedroom, depositing her on the mattress of his bed, looking into her eyes. "Suddenly, I'm awake."

Melody found that laughter was at war with desire. "You enjoyed that way too much."

He grinned and sat down to take off his boots. "It's corny, I know. But it works like a charm."

That choice of words made her eyes widen.

The pact.

"You happen to be right where I want you." He undid three buttons and then pulled his shirt over his head. "This is a private party," he told Harley, shooing him out of the room. "Go sleep on the couch. I know you do it, I just never catch you at it."

"He's smarter than you are," Melody informed him, enjoying the view of his muscular bare chest as he shut the door. "Goes without saying."

"I wish I had a good argument in my favor, but I don't." As he walked back to the bed, his voice dropped to a whisper. "I'll just leave it that I'm damned glad you changed your mind."

He unfastened her blouse, button by button, his fingers brushing her skin.

She unzipped his jeans.

One thing led to another.

So much for her earlier argument.

Their lovemaking was more intense than ever before, every kiss longer, every intimate touch lingering and when she trembled against him before he moved to enter her, she almost didn't hear his whispered question. "Condom or no?"

It wasn't as though he was giving her a lot of time to think about it. She was already caught in the upward spiral, her control slipping.

"No," she said against his mouth.

He made a low sound of assent and slid deep inside her. As lovers they'd always been well-matched, their bodies naturally attuned to what they both wanted, and she climaxed almost immediately. He didn't follow until it happened for her again.

Some time later, as his breathing eased into the pattern of sleep, his arm possessively around her, reality came jolting in. Melody wasn't sure if she was more surprised by her own reckless behavior or by his. "I thought," she said with as much composure as she could manage, "that you told me you'd never ignore contraception with any woman. Not without a serious discussion first. And by that I don't mean…" She stopped, too embarrassed by her unrestrained reaction to continue.

Gorgeously rumpled, Spence urged her closer. The scythe of a moon hung in the window, throwing its silvery light on the room, on them. "First of all, you aren't just any woman. And we did discuss it. You asked if I wanted kids. I said yes."

"Now?"

"Last I knew, it took about nine months."

"Every time you try to be funny, I want to punch you in the nose."

"Let me remind you that I gave you the option. I asked whether you wanted to use protection or not. And you said *not*."

"Yes, but—"

He nuzzled her neck, something he did very, very well. "I want you to live with me. I'll take on the cats, although they're weird. My dog likes you better than he likes me, which kind of hurts if you want the truth. Listen, Melody, I'm right here. Always will be. Don't panic. As old as those condoms are, I doubt they work all that great, anyway. I didn't get around to buying more because you told me I didn't have a hope in hell with you. If it happens, it happens. Can we leave it there?"

"Easy for you to say! You don't have to have the baby."

So wrong, so wrong, but she realized she *wanted* to get pregnant.

He nudged her. "Yes, I do. We'd have it together."

She relaxed against him.

He started to snore about two minutes later. It wasn't loud, but a comfortable sound in the dark, just a gentle hint of respiration, and Melody fingered the bracelet around her wrist.

Maybe she could market the charms.

Not a bad idea.

CHAPTER SIXTEEN

HE PACKED UP the horses, fastening the last saddlebag.

Reb was restive at the rein, but then he was always ready to run. When he was a two-year-old, Spence had considered keeping him a stallion because he was such a great-looking horse, but gelding him was the more prudent course of action, and he didn't breed horses, he just wanted a good riding mount, and that was what he'd gotten.

"Easy," he said, rubbing Reb's neck. "This isn't going to be that kind of ride. You'll get to lead, so settle down. This is a walk, not a race. There are children involved. Behave yourself."

The horse stilled and nibbled at his sleeve; apparently his explanation was a satisfactory one.

"Saddle up." Moe sounded pretty official, but this was his project. "We're going to hit the river and make camp by nightfall. We're burning daylight."

This wasn't a John Wayne movie, so Spence hid his laugh as he swung onto his horse. He probably should've called out *Westward Ho*, but he'd spent part of the early hours checking in—boys and their parents, all of whom wanted reassurance that their darlings would be safe, and he was out of smiles.

He would have invited Harley along. Instead, he'd left him with Melody. Any excuse to make her more open to moving in with him. Plus, that mutt was a sight more canny than most people, and Spence liked the idea of her being protected. Harley was the single best alarm he could think of, so if someone came around the ranch, Harley would let her know, and loudly. They'd probably be able to hear him in the next county.

No progress with the robberies. It was the worst possible time for him to take off, but he'd committed to this. There really was no convenient agenda in his line of work.

The investigation was stagnant. Dead in the water. Not a bubble on the surface. No one even *under* the surface gasping for breath.

It wasn't only because of Melody that he wanted to solve this. It was happening on his watch, and he took that seriously, didn't like it one bit. Mustang Creek was a small town, he knew just about everyone, and yet he didn't have a single clue.

Well, he thought as he swung into the saddle, *maybe one*.

Before they were too far out they lost signal, he called Junie. "This is a little off the wall, but do you mind doing something for me?"

"Huh, I figured that's what I got paid for. Like what?"

He pictured her with a pencil tucked behind her ear, sitting at her computer. "Can you run a background check on someone for me?"

"This dispatcher wears many hats. Can I have a raise?"

"No, ma'am. Just my undying gratitude."

"We'll see about that. Give me the name."

A few hours later, he was toasting sandwiches for

hungry boys on a campfire. They swarmed in and grabbed the grub with more enthusiasm, perhaps, than the simple cheese-and-tomato sandwiches warranted. Even Moe said, "Dang, I hope there's some left for us."

"Remember that age?" Spence did with some nostalgia. "If it was there, I ate it. When my aunt wanted to clean out the fridge, she used to shove whatever was left over—lasagna, a chicken leg, potato salad—on a plate. Then she'd come knock on my bedroom door. I'd take the plate and scarf it all down. It was food. Life was good."

Moe hung his hands between his knees, sitting on a camp chair. "I suppose my life was the opposite in some ways. With my mother, everything was planned and organized to the nth degree. She always wanted us to sit down and talk about our day. What day? What the heck was that? I got up and went to school. End of story. Eventually when I hit my mid-teens, I started to rebel—against all the expectations, I guess. I got into trouble. Now I'm boring but predictable. I have a job I like and a wife I love. That's how I keep everything going." He paused. "That's *why* I keep it going." An hour later they were riding again.

The boys were following behind them in single file. Tripp had selected placid horses for this ride. Older trail horses tended to know the drill and didn't need much direction. They also knew their way around human beings, while younger horses were sometimes skittish.

"I'm planning on burgers and camp fries tonight, and eggs and sausage in the morning. We didn't promise meals with a lot of extras, right?"

"I brought some fruit salad."

"Good idea."

"My wife's idea."

"Genius. Tell me it isn't the kind with coconut in it."

"Boss, I have no idea. How it works at my house is if she makes it and sets it in front of me, I eat it." He paused. "Sort of like it was with your aunt."

"I have it on good authority that women are like cats and men are like dogs," Spence said sagely.

"Huh?" Moe looked confused.

Spence had to laugh. "Never mind. I'm sure they'll be hungry enough to eat everything we've got to offer, but I'm not going to insist. This is supposed to be fun. Nutrition's an iffy thing for loads of kids, especially guys, until you're in college, anyway. By the way, I packed some apples and oranges, so there's lots of healthy stuff for anyone who wants it."

Melody had also wisely suggested celery sticks and peanut butter and had even washed and cut up the celery. Moe's friend in the forest service, an earnest young man named Steve Whitehall, who was riding at the back, making sure they didn't lose anyone, had brought good old-fashioned trail mix for snacking. No one was going to starve to death, that was for sure.

The trip with the girls was going to be a whole different matter. He'd let Hadleigh, Bex and Melody handle that menu. Tripp had told him there was some discussion of white-chocolate-chip cookies with macadamia nuts, Black Forest brownies—whatever they were—and chicken with penne and alfredo sauce. At that point, his best friend claimed, his eyes had started to glaze over. Sounded good, and he was pretty sure he'd enjoy it, but that kind of meal over a campfire might be a little tricky. The fancy outfitters who handled rafting trips cooked up some gourmet trail grub, or so he'd been told, but they didn't do it volunteer-style for a group of boys aged 12 to 16. Still, the women were pitching in, so he wasn't going to mumble a word about their impractical menu.

Spence had decided he'd saddle horses and pitch tents on the girls' trip, and otherwise stay out of it. He had visions of slumber parties with a lot of whispering and giggling, but he could sleep through just about anything, so surely he could weather that. He'd have Jim to talk to, and if he couldn't share a tent or better yet, a sleeping bag, with Melody, at least he'd get to see her all day long for three entire days.

Her new work tools had arrived to replace the ones taken in the robbery. Tomorrow she'd be attending several estate sales in Bliss and the surrounding counties in search of a diamond to replace the one she'd lost. Not that it could actually *be* replaced, she'd said with heartfelt regret, but maybe she'd find a substitute for Mrs. Arbuckle's nephew and his soon-to-be fiancée.

"Steve suggested Hack's Ridge for camp tonight," Moe said. He was on a paint gelding he'd broken himself, a spectacular animal that was so well trained Moe's hands almost never moved the reins. He pointed to a line of timber. "Right up there. Level spot, small mountain spring, a clearing that's safe for a fire. He went up and chopped wood yesterday. Tomorrow I think we're going to wing it."

"The three of us know this area pretty well." Spence guided Reb around a washed-out spot on the trail and trusted that the other horses would go around it, too. He sent his deputy a sidelong glance. "I know you spend most weekends fishing and camping. Does Sherry ever go with you?"

"Oh, no." Moe shook his head with a slight smile. "You should've seen what it took to get her to move here. City girl. I figure we'll have a stable marriage because we don't need to spend every second together. During the summer, she can have her weekends to shop and go out with her girlfriends, and I can do my outdoor thing. Match made in heaven."

There was something to be said for diverse interests, and he was hoping for a match made in heaven himself.

"Hey, Chief, has it occurred to you that with half our department out of town, we might have more trouble over the weekend?"

"Sure has."

The trail ride was no secret. Or who was sponsoring it.

He hoped the thief would be bold enough to hit again. If Junie and Estes delivered, he'd have a solid suspect. Suspect, singular. Because he was beginning to think there was only one person involved.

MELODY SURVEYED SPENCE'S back porch and thought it over.

Spence would be the first to admit he wasn't an artist, but he'd made a valid point about the light. In three of the four seasons it would be better than good, and in the winter, with a woodstove, it should still work.

She had no idea what to do.

For one thing, she liked her cozy house. It was hers alone, and it was comfortably set up to her exact taste and specifications. The cats could reign over their sovereign kingdom with iron-clad paws.

But…Spence's house was spacious and could use a little TLC. For a bachelor, he managed to keep it pretty clean, although she did find a shrunken bar of soap in the bathroom off the master bedroom. There were only three rather threadbare towels in the linen closet; laundry didn't seem high on his to-do list. And while Harley had plenty of food, and she had no doubt he looked after Reb with the greatest diligence, he had almost nothing in the fridge *or* the freezer.

This urge to take care of him...where did that come from? If anyone could take care of Spencer Hogan, it was the man himself.

The auction over in the next county was scheduled for noon, and she had a quick shower then headed out, not really hopeful, but you never knew. There were treasures out there. It was all about being at the right place, at the right time. She'd made a whimsical mobile once from antique spoons, and it had been snapped up by a storekeeper who'd called to tell her it had sold the next day.

At least the weather was nice. Neither Bex nor Hadleigh was free to go with her, so she went by herself and sat with her number card in a folding chair, hoping for the best. She wasn't going to get another Rochester Pierce diamond, but something might inspire her.

She had a vision, too, of something for Spence's house.

She had an idea, and a design in mind. What she wanted to create for him was a clock, a very special one.

And then she found the perfect piece.

It was part of an antique urn, and it had a unique patina, which caught her eye, and she placed a bid on it. This clock would have numbers that were all subtly different from each other and a picture of the ranch as its background… She'd have to cut out the numbers from the thin metal of the urn and create the face. She'd get Tripp to help her use his power tools for that. She was a jewelry maker, not a clocksmith, but she'd stowed away the old workings from a Seth Thomas piece.

The picture would be hand-painted and just for Spence. She'd have to find the right perspective, figure out the perfect medium. Water paints? Oils? The more she thought about it, the more she wanted to do it.

Whatever happened between them, he'd remember her every time he looked at it.

She wanted to make him a beautiful clock that would hang on the wall for the rest of his life, because she was sure he'd spend it in the house he'd invited her to live in. With him.

No mention of marriage.

She needed a discussion about this.

"I could use some girl talk. Call me."

One simple text sent to two people.

Bex called her immediately. "My house or yours?"

"I'm thinking Tripp and Hadleigh's. I need to ask him a favor. Wait, she's beeping in."

"Call me back."

"Will do."

"Okay, what's up?" Hadleigh asked. "Guess what I'm doing? I'm making a brisket. I'm trying it out on Tripp first and then I plan to make sandwiches for the trail ride. He keeps coming into the kitchen and hovering, so it must smell good. I'm about to kick his ass. Come on over and save him."

"Potatoes?" Melody asked with resignation.

"He'll be heartbroken if you don't bring 'em. They were gobbled up so fast the other night he hardly got any, or so he claims, although I could swear he had two helpings. Do the extra-cheese thing again and bring a swimsuit. We'll be real pioneer women and sit in the hot tub for our girl talk."

She did need to ask Tripp a favor, so if he needed extra cheese, she could handle it. "I'm not sure pioneer women sat in hot tubs, but it's a go for me."

"They would have if they had any."

Two hours later, she found herself sitting in warm bubbling water on the back deck, with two pairs of inquisitive eyes focused in her direction. She stuck her foot out of the water and wiggled her toes. "Like my new nail polish? Sunrise blush."

"Very nice," Bex agreed. "I want that job, you know, the one where they make up names for nail polish. I'm sure they say, 'Hey, we could just call it pink, but let's come up with something different and then we can charge a lot more.' Anyway, forget your tootsies and give. Girl talk time."

"Yes, give," Hadleigh echoed.

Might as well. It wasn't as if they weren't going to hear about it, anyway. Melody reached over and pushed a button to quiet the jets. "Spence asked me to move in with him."

"Do it." Hadleigh.

"Don't." Bex.

She'd expected a united front one way or the other, but not differing opinions.

"Oh, you two are helpful. Thanks a lot." She swept a froth of bubbles across the water. The hot tub was relaxing, and her muscles began to loosen. She let out a frustrated breath and held up her wrist, displaying the bracelet. "Apparently, my charm has lost its mojo. I want to hear your arguments, one at a time."

Hadleigh, who had the unfair advantage of having a light tropical tan so she looked fabulous in her suit, went first. "I don't think it's a bad idea to find out if you can stand to live together, day in and day out, before you take the plunge. The two of you have a rocky history, so maybe taking a stab at living together makes sense."

If there was going to *be* a plunge. Spence hadn't given any indication that he was poised to dive into those waters. So to speak… Maybe it was more appropriate to say *dive off that particular mountain.*

Bex argued, "I understand the robbery shook him up. It upset and worried me, too. But I think you deserve it *all*, Mel. The ring, the proposal, the wedding, the *love,* we all promised each other we'd wait for. He wants to protect you, and I'm glad, but we swore we'd hold out for *everything.*"

They both had valid points, and on a scale of one to ten, her confusion level was about a twenty.

"I need to talk to him," she said. "Marriage—yes, I want it. But I want *him* to want it, too."

Both of her best friends were so obviously, so transparently, relieved, Melody just had to respond. "What?" she asked. "You thought I didn't?"

They looked at each other and then back at her. "No," Bex replied. "More like we knew you did, but we weren't sure you'd ever admit it."

She supposed it was no secret that she was in love with Spencer Hogan. Always had been.

"The thing is, I can't make him talk about it." She

skimmed her hand over the shimmering water. "It's truly his choice. And it's not as if I want to risk asking him again, do I?"

"Why *not* ask?" Hadleigh had that singular glint in her eye. "I say if the time is right, go for it."

CHAPTER SEVENTEEN

THE HORSES WENT through the canyon in single file, well behaved. It sure didn't hurt that the weather held, with nary a drop of rain, cloudless blue skies and constant sunshine. Although the boys were a little rowdy, they'd been pretty good so far.

At night there'd been some serious playing with electronic devices in their tents, but Spence couldn't care less about that if they stuck to the rules the rest of the time.

No cell phones. There wasn't a tower nearby, so that didn't require a lot of discipline.

No fighting. He really meant that one. He could break up a brawl with the best of them, but he'd rather they found their own peace if there was an argument. Every testosterone-laden male needed to learn self-control, not to get his back up over every little thing.

Life lesson. He hoped they'd go home with a positive attitude toward not just law enforcement, but also the nature all around them. Many kids, maybe most kids, didn't have access to that. If this trip continued to go well, maybe next year they could extend it to Casper or Cheyenne.

He missed Melody.

Not just the physical part of being with her—oh, he did miss that—but the quiet stir of her breathing in the dark, and her soft warmth when he rolled over in bed and encountered her tempting body. The night before, he'd had a dream in which he was walking along a road alone, getting nowhere fast, no houses in sight, nothing but prairie. In his dream, he'd been searching for something—someone—but he'd seen nothing, no one. He'd started to run in a panic until he woke up sweating.

He didn't need a psychologist to interpret that one. Maybe what he should do was just buy her a regular ring, although his confidence in picking out the right one was null and void. Not to mention that proposing wasn't exactly without challenges.

She could say no.

That would be bittersweet revenge. Once, she'd proposed to him, and he'd declined. She'd never forgiven him.

Oh, good, a double play, with his heart in the balance. He probably deserved it, but he didn't want it to go down that way.

An eagle disrupted his thoughts, soaring overhead in a graceful and powerful glide, its high scream echoing off the rock walls. Behind him he could hear Steve Whitehall lecture the boys on raptors, and whether the information registered or not, the sight was undeniably beautiful.

HE PULLED OUT his phone. Still no signal, which he'd expected, but he'd love to know if Junie had found out anything that might help him.

Two clues stuck in his mind. The antiques store and the unusual wreckage at Melody's house. He didn't like either one of them.

Maybe the thief hadn't known the diamond was

there, but Spence was starting to think differently about that. It was clearly Melody's mistake not to put it away, but, unlike some people, she operated on the assumption that the world was a nice place, and people were basically good.

One of the things he loved about her.

They were setting up the tents, crouching in the pine needles and dirt, when he asked Moe a serious question. "So we have seven robberies now with fairly consistent methods of entry. Melody's smashed window is the most drastic. The theft at her place was also the most extreme. Is the thief accelerating the action and if so, why? I keep groping around that and wondering what's going on. All thoughts are welcome."

The true test of a deputy.

Moe moved to pile wood on the communal campfire. Steve was out guiding boys through the woods, giving them a tour of the coming fall wildflowers. They probably didn't give a rat's ass about wildflowers, but it was educational. Teach them about nature in all its beauty and diversity. Wasn't that one reason they were out here?

"Our thief—and I notice you're referring to *a* thief rather than thieves—is very focused on the community." Moe handed him some tinder, tiny cedar sticks from saplings. "Observant. Knows his stuff when it comes to schedules, and he's got testicles as big as canned hams."

Spence was amused by that last bit. He lit a small twig, and it started to burn. "Interesting choice of words. How so?"

"Robbing a man of his trolling motor is not a good idea. Robbing a woman of jewelry is a *really* bad idea, and if it's her livelihood, you've really gone and done it."

Melody had been mad as a wet hen. He didn't blame her.

Moe tossed a pile of leaves onto the fire, which Spence wouldn't have done, but he hadn't taken part in any extracurricular activities, like organized camping trips. Not with his upbringing. His aunt Libby had been taxed enough just getting him to school on time. He'd learned his way around a campfire or two by experience. Moe finally said, "I think he's done his homework and figured out that Mustang Creek works a certain way, and it's possible to take advantage of people who might not see it coming."

"Like Melody Nolan?"

"Yeah."

In the flickering light as the campfire caught, Moe's face was set. "All easy targets. No huge heists or anything. Women and older men. The thief knew about their valuables."

"How?"

"I'm still working that out." Moe got up and grabbed a pine log to add to the fire. In the background the boys were laughing as they unsaddled the horses, and Spence was one hundred percent positive he'd have to make sure they were all rubbed down properly, but these kids were learning pretty fast. They grumbled about cleaning the tack. In general, however, they'd been compliant and seemed to be enjoying themselves.

The first morning, when he'd shown them how to put a bridle on a horse, warming the bit in his hands so the metal wasn't cold as you slipped it into the animal's mouth, some of the boys had really stepped up.

Horses were big animals, no doubt about it, and when you were a kid, they seemed even bigger. Some had been intimidated, but he was fairly confident that by tomorrow morning everyone would be able to saddle his own horse.

Progress.

He was as new to this as they were in some ways and could sympathize. These kids weren't exactly city boys, because Bliss County was fairly rural, but not everyone had the same advantages.

He'd had very few, since his aunt really couldn't afford it. But she'd loved him and done what she could, and that was so much better than going into the child services system, which might have been the only other option. He needed to drop that card or letter from his mother at Libby's place, but one thing at a time. Obviously he was putting it off, but for now he was going to concentrate on the investigation and the trail rides. That had to come first. After all these years, his mother could come in a slow second.

THE FIRE WAS burning well. The promise of food made the boys gather around, and when Spence checked the horses he discovered that they'd all done a decent job. Moe did the grilling—it was his turn—and after they'd eaten, Spence did the cleanup and declared it a night. He claimed his bedroll, which he spread out some distance from the tents.

He'd chosen to sleep under the stars, except that he couldn't sleep. Instead, he looked up at the skies and thought about life. This trip came at an interesting time for him.

Was he ready to become a parent?

He had not used a condom the last time he'd made love to Melody, and she hadn't asked him to. They'd both been carried away, yes, but the decision had been mutual, even deliberate. He had the unreasonable hope that she'd turn up pregnant. Where did *that* come from?

Marriage was a big step, not that he'd asked her yet. But becoming parents—that was monumental.

He was ready. For all of it. Marriage *and* becoming a father. It might have taken nine years, but he was finally ready.

Tripp and Hadleigh were trying, he knew that. They'd make wonderful parents when the time came.

He looked around at the tents in the clearing. A couple of the boys were clearly still awake, cutting up and laughing and shushing each other when it got too loud. In the distance a wolf howled, which shut them up pretty fast, and Spence had to smile at the ensuing silence. The clean scent of the forest embraced him. The first night he'd heard that lonely sound he'd been tongue-tied, too, a frightened kid in a sleeping bag, but it was an exhilarating kind of primal fear.

"What was that?" It came from the closest tent, with the youngest boys.

"Wolf, dummy."

"It sounded close."

One of the boys snorted derisively. "You scared? How many people do you know who've been killed by wolves? Let me guess. Zip."

"I don't want to be the first one!"

"The chief isn't even sleeping in a tent. Just cool your jets. If it was dangerous, would he do that?"

"Yeah, well, at least he has a gun."

"You are such a wuss."

The wolf howled again, and another one answered. The twelve-year-old muttered a word Spence was sure he'd never say in front of his mother.

He stifled a laugh.

He didn't go camping often, now that he was older and had so much responsibility.

He definitely wanted a son, or a daughter to take on outings like this.

He just needed Melody to be part of it all.

He said clearly, "Boys, go to sleep. It'll be light soon enough. Besides, those wolves might hear you and know where we are."

The silence that followed was peaceful. He drifted off.

FIVE O'CLOCK IN the morning. Too early to be up.

Harley was still snoozing on her bed, but now that she had her replacement tools it was as if an irresistible force had awakened her. She could work again!

So she got up and did exactly that.

She had soft music playing in the background, a combination of Bach concertos and then some Kenny Chesney, rounded out by Brandi Carlisle. She sat at her worktable and drank two cups of coffee and made some real progress on the bib necklace.

It was always a gratifying moment when she knew she was hitting her stride. This piece was going to be gorgeous. A lot of the credit went to Mrs. Arbuckle because the semiprecious stones were superb, but Melody was very pleased with the design now that it was coming together. Mrs. A. could wear it at any of her fancy events and be a sensation.

The ring would have to wait. Her heart just wasn't

in it, not without the right stone. Despite the fact that it was unlikely, she held out an unrealistic sliver of hope that the Pierce diamond would be recovered.

She needed to get past that fantasy, but art wasn't an on-demand sort of profession. Inspiration came when it came, and sometimes it went on an unexpected vacation. Her muse, the one she needed for the ring, was currently on the Riviera, soaking up sun, not answering calls or email.

Speaking of vacations… Spence and his troop of boys would be back today. It was going to be interesting to hear how it'd all turned out, especially since she and Bex and Hadleigh were about to undertake the same kind of adventure.

That one ride on Sunset wasn't enough to prepare her for the trail, but it did remind her of forgotten skills. That was something, anyway. Bex was the fittest person she knew, with a killer body and toned everything, and Hadleigh often rode with Tripp. All of which meant that Melody wasn't likely to be voted queen of the trail ride.

Her questionable riding skills could be addressed later. She had something else on her mind.

The design for the clock was rough, but Tripp had agreed to help her cut out the numbers—and to keep it a surprise. He'd offered to mount the clockwork, too. She'd immediately accepted that very generous offer, because this was definitely not her area of expertise.

When it was light enough, she fed Harley then said, "Come on, boy."

He obligingly hopped in the car, his canine grin endearing.

Her expertise was much more geared toward the

clock's background picture. Today she'd try some sketches, see which worked the best for the design she was planning.

The house, the barn, the corral... She sat in the grass, Harley next to her. Biting her lip, she concentrated on the scene before her, sketching until lunchtime, starting to get a feel for it. That was where she was, what she was doing, when she heard the sound coming up the drive.

Hoofbeats.

Hm.

She'd known they were supposed to return the boys around eleven, so she'd packed a picnic basket with several chicken salad sandwiches, tossed in the leftover potatoes and included some of Hadleigh's famous cookies. She'd even put in some dog treats in a plastic bag for her new best friend and loyal canine companion. When Spence trotted into sight on Reb, she would have shouted, but Harley took care of that for her, barking and dashing down the incline toward the house to greet him. She merely waved and went back to her task at hand.

He would come to her. She knew it.

He did.

Not for another twenty minutes, though. He walked toward her, his hair still wet, and she could see that a shower had obviously been at the top of his list. He didn't bother with hello, but dropped down beside her and pointed at the basket. "I'm really hoping that's the lunch you promised."

She'd left him a note.

"It is." She closed her sketchpad and set it aside. "Harley missed you."

"Just him?" He reached for her and pulled her close for a memorable, lingering kiss.

When it was over, she said mischievously, "Yep, just him."

"Maybe I don't need lunch, after all," he whispered, his fingertips caressing her shoulder.

She sat up and pushed him away. "I'm starving. I suspect you are, too." She opened the lid. "How was it?"

He relaxed on the grass, all long legs and hungry male. "The trip? Pretty good. The boys were remarkably well behaved, and so was the weather. I can control the boys, the weather not so much. I was happy with the nod from above. Those teenagers are bursting with energy. Stick them in a tent for too long, and you're asking for problems. Luckily, we had beautiful days and clear nights, so they all got along."

She handed him a sandwich, chicken salad on bread from the bakery downtown. "Here you go. I didn't bake the bread. I wanted to. Hadleigh made the cookies, though. I like baking, but I've been too busy." She gave a self-conscious shrug. "I'm not positive I even combed my hair this morning."

"Doesn't make any difference to me. From my viewpoint, you always look great." He took a moment to make his point, studying her from head to foot with obvious appreciation before he unwrapped his lunch and dived in. Operation Sandwich took thirty seconds flat.

Luckily, she'd anticipated his hunger and gave him another one, plus some of the cookies. "Hadleigh will want to know if you liked them. Milk chocolate and dried cherries."

"Dried what? Cherries in a cookie?" He frowned at

the red spots sprinkled in the dough, but then quickly ate one. "Good," he said with enough decisiveness that it sounded genuine. If she'd handed him a stale Fig Newton from the cookie aisle at the local grocery, she suspected he would've said the exact same thing.

She wouldn't tell Hadleigh she'd probably agonized over that recipe for nothing, as far as Spence was concerned. Maybe the girls would be more discerning. After all, he'd just spent the past three days in the saddle and cooking over a campfire.

Melody thought they were delicious. If this was a bake-off, Hadleigh would've won the first round. For her part, she was going to whip up some Hot Brown sandwiches invented—and named after—the famous Kentucky hotel. They were made with garlic toast, turkey slices and a mornay sauce, although she'd have to figure out how to broil them for the finishing touch.

Wave a stick of flaming wood over the top? That would be the pioneer way.

Meanwhile, Spence was looking at her with a certain speculative desire in his eyes, and even though it was a sunny afternoon, even though they were completely private—except for Harley—and getting naked with him sounded like exactly what she wanted to do, she was going to stand firm. This time.

The breeze moved his wavy dark hair.

Melody refused to be swayed by that appealing image. "We're divided on your invitation to live here," she told him frankly, taking another cherry-chocolate cookie. "Harley, of course, votes yes. Hadleigh's on your side, but Bex and I aren't so sure. The cats are also pretty comfortable at my place and would prefer to stay where they are."

"Their opinions are paramount, of course."

She ignored that wry comment. "That's five to two."

"Um, my vote doesn't count?"

She modified her response. "Okay, five to three, but you're still outnumbered."

"Reb says it's the best idea he's ever heard. Now we're five to four. Can I do an office poll? I'm pretty sure Moe and Estes would give you a big thumbs-up as a roommate. There. I just won. Junie would agree, too, come to think of it. She'd want me to be happy." He tumbled her over and took the cookie away. "That was some great chicken salad, Ms. Nolan. I liked the cookie but can I have another dessert?"

She touched his face. "I need some space to work this out. Give it to me?"

Spence didn't argue. He could seduce her, they both knew it, and she fell even more in love with him when he didn't press his advantage. He rolled away, staring up at the blue sky, then got to his feet and offered his hand to help her up. "Thanks for a fantastic lunch."

CHAPTER EIGHTEEN

"SO THE NAME didn't come up in Mustang Creek?"

"Nope." Junie shook her head, frowning over his shoulder at the computer screen. "I tried it a dozen different ways. I checked it out on the internet with search engines, and contacted all the state law-enforcement agencies."

"So this person doesn't exist."

"Mary Allen? Oh, heck, yeah, she exists all over the place, but not here." She eased a hip onto his desk. "I'm insulted no Mary Allen ever moved here. What's wrong with this town?"

"Nosy dispatchers would be my guess. It blows our entire tourism campaign." He waved goodbye as he started to read the information she'd unearthed. "Thanks for checking. You go have a good evening. Headed to Bad Billy's?"

"Of course. It's dollar beer night." She winked and stood up then sashayed off. "Glad the trail ride went well."

He nodded absently, unsettled by what he was seeing.

Mary Allen had no existing address in Mustang Creek, which might explain why she'd never wanted him to pick her up but always suggested they meet somewhere on the few dates they'd had. There hadn't been much chemistry, and he was doing his best to remember what she'd told him about her past.

Pretty much nothing.

She claimed to be an appraiser specializing in antiques.

He'd seen her entering the antiques store a few days ago, and it was bothering him.

He picked up his cell and called Melody. "When you bought that ring from Ronald, who waited on you?" Was "Mary" working for him now? And if so, in what capacity? As some sort of "consultant"?

"He did." She sounded puzzled. "It was a big-ticket item. Surely you don't think he—"

"No." He scratched his chin. "I'm thinking about teapots."

"*You're* thinking about teapots? Why? You aren't making much sense to me at the moment."

"I'm going down a rabbit hole. I don't make much sense to me, either, but I'm working on it. What are we doing tonight, by the way?"

"That's quite an assumption, Chief Hogan. Who said we were doing anything?"

Maybe he hadn't been too smooth there. Time for a quick drop on the fumbled ball. "I meant would you like to have a pizza and movie night? You get to choose the movie. I don't need action-packed, but let's leave the box-of-tissues kind out of the equation. I'll pick up the pizza and meet you at the ranch in, what, an hour or so?"

"I'll compromise on the movie," she agreed with a laugh in her voice, "if you'll include at least one vegetable on the pizza you order. Not just double pepperoni and heavy on the sausage. Two vegetables, and you'll win my heart."

"Done."

They ended the call, and he sat and thought about the resources he had. He did have a buddy in Cheyenne who might be able to help him out. He could call, get a second opinion even though Jack Pearson was a homicide detective, and this wasn't exactly his area, but he did in-depth investigation a lot more often than Spence did.

Jack was out of the office.

Figures. He left a message, called Mike Mule's Pizzeria, asked for a large thin-crust with the works, and logged off for the night. Estes, who was at the desk, gave him a cheeky salute. "Have a good night, Chief."

"I'm hoping to."

"Second trail ride this weekend. We're taking bets that you come back pretty cranky from that one."

The ride for the girls had filled up faster than the one for boys, if that was possible. Teenage girls and horses. No wonder the parents had been so upset when it was a no-girls-allowed event. "Nice to know my mood's a source of humor in this office."

"Oh, always." Estes chortled and went back to his computer.

MIKE MULE'S WAS packed, of course, and even though he'd already called in his order, he had to wait in line. By the time he was back in the truck with the pizza, he was running late. As he drove up the lane to the ranch, he could see that the lights were on.

Warmth. *Home.*

Melody and Harley were curled up together on the

couch. He'd done his best to get that dog not to sleep there, and his authority meant something in this town, but in his own home, apparently not. The dog even wagged his tail as he came in the door.

At least Harley usually tried to pretend he hadn't been there. Spence walked past them to put the box on the table. "You're a bad influence on that critter. For your information, he's not supposed to be on the couch."

"He's slept on my bed," Melody countered, looking cozy in worn jeans and a faded T-shirt with plaid socks on her feet. "The couch seems a lesser sin. Mmm. That pizza smells *really* good. Please tell me you have paper plates. Then we won't have to interrupt the movie to go wash dishes afterward. I've got it ready to go. All I have to do is hit Play."

She'd chosen an old classic he'd never seen, *Father Goose* with Cary Grant. He laughed all the way through while demolishing more than his share of the pizza, and at the end of it, with Melody curled in the curve of his arm, Harley snoozing like it was his job, he must have drifted off.

A gentle elbow in the ribs brought him back to awareness of the world around him.

Melody handed him his phone, which he'd placed on the coffee table. "For you."

Jack.

"Hey." He did his best not to sound as if he'd been on the verge of the first sleep he'd had in days.

"Too late to call? I got the message, but I was out on a case."

"No, not too late at all. I just have a question or two." Spence was very aware of Melody listening in. "I think we might have an antiques theft ring operating right here in Mustang Creek. I've talked to the state police about it, but it appears to be strictly local. The thefts are interesting, to say the least. Steal the pieces and then as soon as they sell, steal them back—that's my theory. Do you have contacts who might specialize in this sort of crime?"

"I wish I could say no, but I have contacts who specialize in *every* sort of crime." Jack sounded intrigued. "Lucky me, eh? Let me make a few calls. I'll get back to you tomorrow if I come up with anything."

"Appreciate it, Jack."

Melody gave him an accusing look when he clicked off. "It has nothing to do with Ronald," she insisted. "I love that man. He's a sweetheart. I refuse to believe it."

"I must have missed the part where I accused him of something." He urged her to lie back against him. "To my mind, he's not a suspect, if that makes you feel better. I'm just asking around."

She was silent. He'd almost fallen asleep again, when she suddenly asked, "Is this what life with you will be like?"

He opened one eye.

She elaborated hastily as color crept into her cheeks. "I meant *would* be like… Oh, heck. You're obviously tired. Let's just go to sleep."

Harley jumped up and headed for the bedroom.

It was a clear sign: he wasn't supposed to say—or do—anything. He was supposed to stay where he was. On the couch. Not like Harley. Spence got it loud and clear.

That was one smart dog.

IF YOU WANT to catch a thief, think like one.

She wasn't a sleuth by any means, but Melody did know her way around antiques stores, and if that was the theory Spence had come up with for the robberies, she really had to go over it. Give it some thought. She was smack in the middle of the whole mess, which gave her a certain right, didn't it? It meant she was already involved. And maybe something useful would occur to her...

Oddly enough, she knew the perfect person to help.

Junie glanced up when she walked into the police station just a shade after two o'clock, and her smile seemed genuine. "Melody, hi. Sorry, the chief is out."

"I know. I came to see you. Can we talk for a minute?"

The dispatcher looked startled, but she didn't seem upset. "Sure. A call might come through, though, so excuse me if I have to take it. What's up?"

"My house was robbed."

"I know. I'm the one who called Spence to tell him about it."

"Yes." Melody took a chair by the desk. "Thank you for that. Otherwise I wouldn't have found out until I arrived home to a bunch of police officers standing in my yard. It was a lot easier with Spence right there—and that was hard enough."

"He's the nicest guy in the world, but since he's like my little brother, I could be biased."

Spence was hardly little at about six-two or so. That was irrelevant, Melody told herself, relieved that she saw no hint of jealousy. All good. "I don't disagree. I came here to ask you a favor, so can we keep this between us? As much as possible?"

"I love secrets, are you kidding? I work with males. They tell each other when they go to the bathroom." Junie shook her head and rolled her eyes. "Such complicated creatures—not. Now, there's a secret they *should* keep." She sighed dramatically, "If I could even begin to make jewelry, I'd gladly switch places with you, but I'm about as artistic as a garden snail. How can I help?"

"Spence said something last night implying that he thought the robberies could be linked to the antiques store on Main. Ronald's place. Isn't Cassandra your cousin?"

Junie looked at her sharply, eyes suddenly cautious. "Yes."

"She works there part-time, right?"

"If you'll pardon me, I'd love to know where this is going. Cassie's private life currently stinks. I'm sure you've heard about the divorce. Never divorce a lawyer. The odds are not balanced in your favor, but she's a nice person."

Quickly she explained, "No need to worry. I'm not accusing her of anything. I'm just wondering if she's noticed any people who've been dropping by the shop a lot. Spence was talking about a potential antiques theft ring, and it caught my attention, especially since that's what was taken from my house. Is Cassandra someone you could trust to pay attention? We know each other from high school, but not well enough for me to ask it. Tell her I'd pay a reward for the return of that ring. Insurance will cover the loss, but I want *that* stone."

"Seems like you do. Of course I'll ask. I should mention that Spence has probably already thought of that."

"Probably, but he won't talk to me about it. I don't think he's interested in me being any part of this."

Junie shook her head. "I'm sure he isn't. He's crazy about you, and you must admit that people who break in to other people's houses might be dangerous in other ways."

Crazy about you had a nice ring to it.

Junie went on, her twang pronounced. "I've known all along that he was going to pick you—as if he had a choice. The blonde one's for you I told him years ago when you first dated. I'm a little older, so my mature wisdom made my opinions superior. Still does."

"He didn't listen." Melody still remembered that botched proposal of hers, the suggestion that they elope.

Junie leaned her elbows on the dispatch desk. "Oh, he heard me. That's why he ran in the other direction. Spence is so gun-shy when it comes to commitment, it isn't funny, but he has a few more years on him now. His ability to trust is about two hundred percent better than it used to be, and keep in mind that his job does not inspire belief in the milk of human kindness. Stick with him. He's worth it."

One of the deputies strolled past, tipping his hat politely. "Ma'am."

Melody smiled back. Spence was going to find out she'd been there. That thought was confirmed in Junie's next comment.

"I bet Moe's on his cell right now," Junie observed with amusement as she watched the young man walk down the hall and go around the corner. "I love it. Nothing makes a man sweat more than two women talking about him. Even if they aren't, he worries about it, anyway."

Then and there, she decided that while she was still envious of their long-lasting relationship, Melody liked Junie and understood why Spence did, too.

"Thanks for your help."

"No problem. Just promise me you won't look into anything without talking to Spence first."

"I won't have time to do any sleuthing," she said. "That trail ride thing is on the horizon, and I've got a few pieces to finish before we take off."

"I love that bracelet, by the way. I assume you made it. Any chance I could buy one? I think charm bracelets say a lot about people, but only they know what it is."

"I'll give you one." Melody was serious. If Spence was attached to Junie, so was she. "I'll make you a special charm. Think about what you want, and I'll do it."

"You'd do that for me? That's so nice." Junie's face lit up.

"I'd do that for *him*," she said with a smile, "*and* for you. My pleasure."

"I get it." Janie gave her a wink. "I know what kind of charm I want. Cowgirl boots. Spence always teases me that I'm a shit-kicker, and maybe I am. I have to admit I like a feisty Saturday-night rodeo."

"You got it. Call me if Cassandra has anything to say."

"Sure thing."

Her next stop was the supermarket to pick up the groceries for the night she was in charge of dinner on the trail ride. Roast turkey, parmesan cheese, Texas toast for her Hot Brown sandwiches. A few ripe toma-toes and why not make dinner for Spence tonight? Barbecue chicken and potato salad sounded like a pleasant way to end a summer day. She paid at the checkout and headed not to her house, but the ranch.

Could I live here?

As she drove in, she thought the answer was hardly a secret. It wasn't a glamorous house, just a comfortable one, but there were mountains in the background.

Ranch house with mountains. What woman wouldn't want that, especially if Spence was included in the deal?

And Harley. The dog ran out of the barn to greet her, following her car, and although she adored her cats, they conveyed affection in a different—and far less fervent—manner. Harley's unconditional adoration was funny and touching, and she rubbed the top of his head when she got out of the car. "Love you back."

He yipped and ran in circles, which was an affirmation that he felt the same way. She suddenly noticed he was favoring one leg.

Harley refused to even come up on the porch, stopping at the foot of the steps and staring past her, growling.

That was the definitive moment when she knew something was very, very wrong.

Maybe at some point Spence might want to start locking his doors. Because the front door was ajar. *Someone's been here.* She eased closer and peered inside.

Yup, Spence *really* needed to lock his doors.

The damage was similar to what had happened at her house. There was stuff strewn everywhere, including broken dishes on the living room floor.

She was standing there in consternation when she

heard Spence pull in. She turned around, her arms still full of groceries.

"This is a nice surprise." His smile faded as he stepped out and caught the expression on her face. He slammed the door shut. "Mel? You okay?"

She sank into one of the deck chairs and set down her bags. "I think you had an uninvited visitor. I wondered why Harley was in the barn instead of his spot out here. Even his bark sounded different, like he was trying to tell me something."

"A *what*? Are you serious?" He took the steps two at a time, halting in the open doorway, his face tightening with anger. "Son of a bitch."

Harley whimpered and lay down, licking his right front paw.

"And I think Harley might have had a run-in with whoever was here," she said, feeling the same sense of outrage. "He's limping."

The destruction inside was instantly overridden by their concern for Spence's tried-and-true companion. He ran down the steps faster than he'd gone up them and knelt next to the dog, his hands gentle. "Hey, buddy, let's have a look."

"Should I call the vet?"

"There's dried blood on his fur. I don't think it's his, but let's make sure," Spence said tersely but with some satisfaction and held out his phone, his other hand rubbing the dog's head. "Yeah, good idea. Call Doc Richards, please. He's not a specialist in small animals, but he takes care of Reb. He'll come right out. Number's on my contact list."

Thankfully the horse was grazing peacefully in the fenced-off pasture by the drive. Robbery and rustling were two different crimes in the state of Wyoming. The law was adamant that you did not steal a man's horse.

She took the phone and discovered that she was quite shaken up when she went to make the call, explaining who she was and what had happened. The young vet said he'd be there as fast as possible and to keep the dog quiet until he arrived.

When she silently handed back the phone, Spence pressed a button and held it to his ear. "Junie, send Moe or Estes out to my ranch so they can file a vandalism and possible robbery report. Do me another favor. Call the regional hospital and local clinics and tell them to be on alert for anyone coming in to be treated for an animal bite."

After he'd hung up, Spence turned to her, those oh-so-blue eyes holding a grim look. "Do you mind sitting with him and making sure he stays put while I go check things out? This is starting to take on a personal edge I don't like. The first break-in and burglaries didn't involve any serious or malicious destruction. Just your house and now mine. I have an idea who's behind it, but I have to prove it."

That was interesting. She'd make him explain later.

"Of course I'll stay with him." She knelt on the ground beside Harley and rubbed his sides. "This dog is the only reason I put up with you."

While she and Harley waited together companionably, Spence searched the house. The antique canisters seemed to be the only thing missing, he declared once the deputies had come and gone, after taking the usual pictures, fingerprints and reports. The vet, too, had been by and his diagnosis had been reassuring.

They spent about an hour picking up pieces of broken glass, straightening the furniture and in general, repairing the damage.

Just like at her house, the damage had been superficial. And yet in both cases it seemed personal.

Maybe that had been the point of it all. Some kind of personal vendetta.

At least Harley wasn't badly injured. Dr. Richards had assured them that the limp might be because the escaping thief had stomped on the dog's foot, but that the mutt had held his own.

He'd called a while ago to confirm that the blood definitely wasn't Harley's. Good dog.

Great dog.

So maybe Spence would find a link come up with the connection he needed if the thief had gone for treatment. Across the table, Melody ate a forkful of some tasty potato salad—she'd put bacon in it, and she was a fan of the recipe, hoping the girls would like it, too. "So, who is it?" she finally asked. She figured she'd waited long enough.

She could sense that he didn't want to have this discussion, but considering everything that had happened, he owed it to her.

He sighed. "I briefly dated a woman who told me her name was Mary Allen. I just met her at the grocery store one day, struck up a conversation and we went for coffee. Had dinner once. She's attractive, but I think as a police officer you have an instinct for anything that's off about a person. I never asked her out again. Supposedly she lives here in town, but I can't find any evidence that she does, and I saw her at Ronald's antiques place the other day. She was going in as I was coming out."

Melody hoped her expression was neutral. "And you think it's her? Why?"

"By her own admission, she makes her living appraising antiques."

Now *that* made sense.

"I asked Junie if Cassandra could keep an eye out for anyone who came into the store frequently."

"I wasn't aware that you'd taken up detective work as a hobby."

"I want that diamond back."

His voice softened. "I know. And I want to be the person who hands it to you."

CHAPTER NINETEEN

CHECKLIST.

Harley staying with Tripp. *Check*. He'd have fun with the other dogs, even with his injured paw.

Horses saddled, packs in place. *Check*.

Same trail he'd just done, so that was a breeze. *Check*.

Jim Galloway was a few feet ahead of him, easy in the saddle, his horse a veteran who was so attuned to every movement, he probably didn't need anything but a halter. "Let's get this show on the road, son," he said.

On the one hand, he was glad he'd be able to keep an eye on Melody's safety. On the other, it chafed him to leave town again.

"Ready if you are." He turned Reb and pointed his nose in the right direction. Hadleigh on Sunset, Melody on a bay of Tripp's that he swore was reliable, Bex on a mare she'd borrowed from a friend. Pauline Galloway rode a well-behaved horse Jim had hand-picked from the ranch, and all the young girls, ready to go and chatting excitedly, were behind them.

Some had pink backpacks, but he wasn't going to even mention that, since he wasn't in charge.

He and Jim were just backup, hired hands to do the grunt work.

But…pink? On a camping trip? Fine, maybe he'd

have a daughter someday. The pastel color might even scare off wild animals. Still, pink backpacks felt wrong to him, but what the heck. The girls were laughing and joking, and all that fancy food Hadleigh, Bex and Melody had made would be better than the campfire fare they'd served the boys.

Black Forest brownies. He and Moe and Steve definitely hadn't whipped those up, whatever they were.

"Tripp's back there dying with laughter, right?"

"Dyin'," Jim agreed, his mouth curved in a fond smile. "Don't worry, we'll get him back. We'll come up with something inventive."

"Sounds good."

"I'm thinkin' on it. I've also been thinkin' about the robberies. No one local I can pull out of my sleeve as a good suspect, but maybe we can dangle some bait to trap 'em."

Entrapment wasn't legal because it equated to encouraging someone to break the law. But Jim wouldn't do anything remotely illegal unless it involved protecting someone he loved or an animal in danger. So Spence was listening.

Jim took a deep breath. "I have this old sword. I always believed it was from the War Between the States, but you know, I did some research and I think it's more likely that it came from about the time of the Revolution."

Riding next to him, Spence gaped. "What?"

"I looked up the person whose name is on the blade. Hanson. Turns out he was a silversmith who worked with Paul Revere. Who'd have thought?"

Spence turned to stare at him. There were days when you got out of bed and just didn't see something coming. He cleared his suddenly dry throat. "Let me get this straight. You have a sword that goes back to 1776? It should be in the Smithsonian if it's genuine, Jim. Where do you keep it?"

The older man glanced back at the women and girls following them and lowered his voice. "I used to stick it in the attic. What if I went around getting estimates on it? If nothing else, it's pretty showy."

"What if you put it under lock and key, instead? We can find a different way to handle this. Pardon me if I'm fond of you and Pauline, so I don't want to invite thieves into your home. That recently happened to me, and I didn't enjoy it."

"Um, well, I already started the process. Let's just hide it in a better spot. We'll pick one out. I brought it along."

"Where—"

"What do you think is in the long sheath strapped to my saddle? Not a rifle."

Spence could hardly believe it. Jim had brought a Revolutionary-era sword that might have been touched by Paul Revere. It was probably worth a fortune.

And they were going to hide it in the mountains. *Right.*

Swords. Pink backpacks. Black Forest brownies. This was unlike any other camping trip he'd ever taken.

The forecast hadn't been accurate, either. Although he knew better than to rely on a weather forecast. What happened in Mustang Creek wasn't necessarily what happened as you gained altitude.

NOT A SINGLE one of the females present was happy when it started to sprinkle. Hair seemed to be the main objection. At least it was summer, so getting soaked wasn't pleasant, but not as bad as it could be.

He pointed that out to Melody when he dropped back to see how everyone was doing. In return, she said coolly, "I invite you to explain that to girls who probably spent a lot of time getting ready for this trip. Good luck. Go for it."

He beat a hasty retreat, nudging Reb toward the front of the line. He told Jim, "The it-could-be-worse speech didn't go over very well."

"I told you not to worry about that, but I get it. You want to keep her happy."

"I want to marry her."

"I've known that for some time."

He shoved back his hat. The rain was increasing, which wasn't going to improve his evening. Droplets caught in his eyelashes. "I'm trying to figure out how to ask. It's a pretty important question."

Their horses moved calmly up the trail.

"Oh, yeah, it is."

"Pauline is a trouper."

Jim smiled contentedly. "She is. But let's keep in mind that she has the advantage of life experience. She understands that everything isn't going to go perfectly. She's faced real adversity and compared to that, this is just a little vacation with some rain."

Spence rested his hands on his saddle, thinking it over. "I don't really know what my own mother went through. I haven't seen her in years, but she sent me something recently. There's this part of me that just wants to walk away. That make sense to you? Shake it off like a wet dog and call it a lost cause. I want to give it to my aunt, let her deal with it, but you know, she's had to put up with enough of my problems. Should I do that? Would it be fair? I have no idea what this letter or card even says."

"Life ain't fair." Jim laughed, but it wasn't with humor. "Life is…well, it's life. All kinds of people out there are trying to explain every little thing. Can't necessarily be done. My advice is just open it, trust yourself and then respond to her or don't. Not complicated."

Good advice.

They rode on, and the weather did not improve.

When they stopped to set up camp, he was especially grateful that Tripp had recommended Jim for the trail ride. The man could put up a tent faster than Spence could—and Spence was pretty handy. Jim's genial smile also won over every one of the grumpy girls with damp hair.

Hadleigh, also, wasn't at all happy that her fancy alfredo meal wasn't going to happen.

It got worse.

The skies *really* opened. Rain pelted down.

He received accusing glares.

This business of apologizing for the weather was frustrating.

The campsite was fairly sheltered, but not sheltered enough to keep it dry.

"Sorry," he said about thirty minutes after they'd halted, all of them relatively dry in their tents, shaking his head as he peered into the one Melody, Bex and Hadleigh were sharing. "I'll stand over you with an umbrella as you cook. You brought one, right?"

Hadleigh, who'd seemed about to combust over their situation, instead burst into laughter, and Melody and Bex followed. She fell on her sleeping bag. "Yes," she gasped. "I want to see the chief of police standing over me with a pink umbrella while I cook chicken and pasta… By all means, Spence. You have a deal."

"It would work, right?" Dammit, he was trying to be helpful here.

Hadleigh collapsed in another fit of laughter. So did Bex and Mel.

"I'm willing to get soaked," he said, in what he thought was a reasonable tone, "so you can cook dinner. And y'all think this is funny?"

They did.

Jim was the one who saved him. He tapped him on the shoulder and gave him a plate covered in plastic wrap to hand to the occupants. "Pauline watched the weather report, didn't believe it—I swear that woman can smell rain coming—so she brought along some peanut butter and jelly. She made a few sandwiches for everyone. I've been passing them out. The girls seem happy enough."

He might kiss Jim right then and there, or better yet, Pauline, who was darn cute in a grandmotherly way.

Bex took the plate with alacrity and tore off the plastic. "I'm starving. Grape *and* strawberry? Be still, my heart. Girls, you'll have to arm wrestle me for the strawberry."

"Have at it. I want the grape, anyway. PB and J is exactly how I remember camping." Melody selected a sandwich and passed the plate to Hadleigh. She eyed Spence's dripping hat through the mesh doorway. "We'd invite you in for supper, but first of all, you'd take up half the space, and secondly, you'd get everything wet. This is the wilderness. Every man for himself. But…would you mind passing out the cook-

ies?" She handed him a bag and smiled with real mischief in her incredible eyes. "There are ones for each
tent in there in separate bags. Consider yourself the
cookie elf."

Bex and Hadleigh each clamped a hand over her
mouth.

"Hmmph." Spence straightened, feeling ridiculous. They were probably those dried cherry kind or
white-chocolate doodads, and while they tasted good, a
grown man walking around in the mountains, deliver-
ing cookies in the pouring rain, well, he might as well
turn in his male card.

He *was* soaked, and he still had to take care of the
horses and tack. Maybe the cloudburst would pass.

Jim was openly amused. Spence heard another
round of laughter from the three women as they zipped
the doorway to the tent. "You tell anyone about this,
Galloway," he warned, "and I'll steal Pauline away
from you."

"Son, that is a powerful threat coming from a
dripping-wet cookie elf." Jim, just as wet, was holding his sides now, guffawing up a storm.

"You do know you're a sadistic bunch," Spence muttered, stalking toward the closest tent.

Jim did help him with the chores after the bags of
cookies had been dutifully delivered to squeals of de-
light. The only real consolation was that, despite the
weather and the lack of a gourmet meal, there was a
lot of feminine laughter coming from each tent. Especially the one with the chaperones.

That was something, anyway.

His one-man tent was the last to go up, and while
Spence would normally just strip out of his wet clothes

before crawling in, that wasn't an option with a group of teenage girls around. So he had to finagle a way to get out of his sodden attire and muddy boots to ensure that he didn't sleep in a damp bed.

No one, he noticed, had delivered sandwiches to his tent. He ate a couple of the granola bars he always kept in his pack and washed them down with a bottle of water then munched on some nuts while thinking about Jim's sword idea.

It might work.

And if Jim had jumped the gun by asking around already, at least he'd brought the prize with him; it would take one hell of a thief to track them down in the pouring rain.

Without warning, the flap to his tent opened, and someone practically dived in.

Melody landed on top of him, since there was no-where else to go, and he whooshed out a breath as he caught her. Good thing he had excellent reflexes.

"I'm just a drive-by good-night kiss," she said, a little damp but not too bad, thanks to her rain slicker. The weight of her body felt so…comforting. And sen-sual, all at the same time. "I'm supposed to be a role model, so I can't be seen sneaking into your tent," she whispered against his mouth and kissed him.

Very nicely—with a hint of naughty thrown in.

He certainly kissed her back.

It was over far too quickly, and she scooted back-ward as she prepared to leave. But before she did, she pulled a bag from her pocket. "Cookies. I forgot to give you these."

He wasn't proud, he ate them, and decided that maybe he was more of a Renaissance man—on the cookie front, anyway—than he'd realized, because he was developing a fondness for dried cherries.

DAY TWO WAS worse than day one.

The rain had stopped, but it was drizzling, and the wind had picked up. Melody wouldn't describe herself as miserable, exactly, but it was close. She didn't know how they did it, but Spence and Jim managed to start a fire when they paused for lunch. Hadleigh's chicken dish wasn't going to work, since boiling water was out of the question, so she'd improvised and made fried chicken strips instead and served bagged salad with ranch dressing to complete the meal. The girls devoured every bite as they all sat there and tried to not get blown off the mountain.

The scenery was gorgeous, but it was hard to appreciate with the wind howling at about fifty miles an hour.

And, not to put too fine a point on it, Melody's rear end hurt, and she was sure almost all the females felt the same way.

Oh, Jim and Spence sat on their horses as if they'd been born on them, but the muscles she'd used the day before were beginning to make themselves known. There were aches in various strategic places.

By the time they made camp, at least not in the pouring rain this time, she was ready to trade her saddle for a comfy couch.

No such option available.

The relentless wind didn't help, and the tent rocked as the trees echoed with the sound of branches whipping around. There was an eerie whistle in the air. Melody had put together her Hot Brown sandwiches, tried to broil the tops with the small propane torch she used for crème brûlée, but she quickly saw that wasn't going to work. She didn't want to be responsible for a forest fire.

So everyone ate soggy turkey sandwiches.

"We could be the worst trail ride supervisors in the history of the world," she said, lying on her sleeping bag an hour later, after the lamest dinner ever, wondering if the tent was going to get picked up by the wind and whisk her to never-never land. "Jim and Spence have been taking care of everything. They don't mind the wet, the work, the horses, the wind... My thighs hurt so badly that I could give a whole new meaning to the term bow-legged."

Bex, also supine on her bedroll, sighed heavily. "I work out every day. If it's any consolation, my thighs sympathize with yours."

Hadleigh, who rode frequently, was in better shape. She sat easily, ankles crossed. "Like everything else, it takes practice."

Melody asked Bex, "Do you want to strangle Miss Sunshine, or should I?"

"We could do it together." They exchanged a look.

Hadleigh elevated her brows. "Hey, someone needs to stay positive in this tent of gloom and doom. Besides, it doesn't appear that either one of you—or both of you together—are capable of taking me out. So it isn't going perfectly. So what? I'm having fun. For one thing, when do we all get to spend time together like this? I miss it. It's like the slumber parties we used to have."

Okay, Melody had to agree that she had a point

there. She rolled over on her stomach. "I remember you used to tell the best stories. Go for it, H."

Hadleigh pondered a minute. "Okay, sure, got it. Once upon a time there was this beautiful princess…"

Bex made a derisive sound. "Here's an FYI. I think that one's been done before."

"Hey, give me a minute. There's this beautiful blonde princess who is incredibly stubborn, and she's in love—madly—with the sexy police chief of a small town in a place we'll call Wyoming. They're both really independent, and they break up and go their separate ways. But he's a hottie, and more important, a good guy, and they hook up again."

Melody raised her head so she could look at her friend. "You're hilarious. Hottie? I hate to inform you, but I don't remember the Grimm brothers using that kind of language."

"Well, this isn't a fairy tale." Hadleigh shrugged as the wind broke off a branch somewhere, the crack startling as it thudded to the ground. "This princess is pretty stupid and doesn't realize what she has right under her nose."

"Stupid? Oh, that's nice." Melody still had to admit that she'd love to know where this was going. "Oh, yeah, everyone wants a stupid princess."

"She *is* blonde," Bex, the brunette, pointed out, enjoying it.

Hadleigh piped up. "Hey, it's my story. Can I finish? So, the princess asked the chief—before he became the chief—to marry her many years before, but he was wise, and he said no."

"Wise?"

"Neither of them was ready. I know all about that." A blithe wave.

That was certainly true. Hadleigh's first wedding, had it happened, would have been the mistake of a lifetime.

"There's a happy-every-after, right? This is an inspiring story. I love it so far." Melody tried to keep the cynicism to a minimum. "I actually remember that day. Thanks for reminding me, though." Okay, she couldn't prevent a little sarcasm, after all.

"And I think the princess should ask him again." Hadleigh leaned forward. "Listen, this is a secret, but I happen to know *he* bought the diamond that was stolen from her house. He bought it for her. He commissioned that engagement ring, Mel."

Despite the shriek of the wind, the tent was suddenly quiet. Hadleigh, in pajama pants and a tank top, stared at her. "I shouldn't spoil it," she said in a low voice, "because it's his surprise, but I love you, and I love Spence, and you're just plain meant to be together. I see him look at you and…" Her eyes were glossy with sentimental tears. "It might be a little-known fact, but Mrs. Arbuckle is his godmother. Tripp told me Spence wanted you to design your own ring, but didn't know how to go about it, so he called her."

That explained a lot, but Melody didn't have any idea what to say.

She'd been waiting for any sign that he was interested in marriage, but of course, he wouldn't just *say* it.

And yet…he'd delivered cookies in the rain. Fed her cats. Taken kids on a trail ride.

All of those things meant more to her than the ring, believe it or not, and she was deeply touched. Some men couldn't say the words, she supposed; they expressed them in acts of kindness and generosity, instead.

"How should I go about this proposal?" She ran her fingertips over her eyebrows. "I blew it the last time, shall we keep that in mind? You already know I'm not good at this. I proved it nine years ago, and I have to admit that getting shot down makes me leery of trying again. I don't know how men do it. It's like slicing open your chest and presenting the other person with a beating heart."

"Oh, that's a romantic picture." Bex took a chocolate bar from her backpack and broke off pieces, handing them out. "Let's plan this. It seems like I'm the only sane one here. I'll go first."

"The *only* sane one?" Both Melody and Hadleigh took umbrage—and the chocolate, which was really good.

Bex leaned up on an elbow and nibbled, the light of the tent lantern reflecting off her face. "Well, it seems to me that all along, your problem with Spence has been that both of you want to be in control of everything in your lives, and what you have to get is that it's going to be *one* life. A shared one. Your main obstacle is that you've both been fending for yourselves for a long time. Neither of you can give up that role, so you clash at every turn. *You* want to run the relationship and so does he. I don't think it is a mystery to the rest of us, but the two of you don't see it."

This was true campfire talk, but a campfire was impossible, so Melody settled for her sleeping bag and snuggled in with her chocolate. "Oh, wise one, you are a font of advice. How *would* you suggest I go about it?"

Bex gave her a predictable Becca Stuart scowl of reproof. "Trying to help here, okay? I just think you should look him straight in the eye and say, *guess what, I don't mind moving in with you, but only as your wife.*"

"That's a romantic proposal?" Hadleigh obviously disagreed as the tent shook under another onslaught of wind. "That's an ultimatum. Men don't respond well to ultimatums."

"Just because you're the married one, you're the expert? You and Tripp didn't exactly get it right the first time. Hardly smooth sailing, if you'll forgive the cliché."

Warning: argument brewing. Melody could only think of one way to stop them, so all she did was say mildly, "I might be pregnant."

She'd always liked the word *flabbergasted* but had never had occasion to use it in a sentence. Now might be a good time. They both looked shocked, stunned, staggered—pretty much the definition. "I'm not saying I am," she amended. "What I am saying is it's a possibility."

"Spence was that irresponsible?" Hadleigh asked in disbelief.

"Spence? That isn't flattering. What about me? I was irresponsible, too, but *that* doesn't surprise you?"

"I'm kind of thinking you want to have his baby," Bex said in a soft voice. "So, what H is saying is that he feels the same way."

It was like old times—they were in their jammies, whispering together before they fell asleep—but these were much more grown-up topics. True, they were still whispering about boys, but now it was boys who'd turned into men. Different page, same subject.

Melody would probably have replied but at that moment their tent flap flew open, and three girls tumbled in, all of them out of breath. They started to talk at once, until Melody lifted a hand for silence. "Calm down, and just one of you talk, please."

"There's something out there." One of them, a slim dark-haired girl named Tina, said it with a shudder. "We can hear it. I think it…growled. And it scratched on our tent!"

"It did."

The camper influx didn't stop there. Within minutes the entire tent was full of frightened girls, and it was clear that panic was the order of the night.

The wind gusted. One of the girls shrieked. That helped matters not at all, since everyone else shrieked in response. Including Melody, Bex and Hadleigh.

Luckily, it brought Spence and Jim running.

Rumpled and obviously asleep before that moment, because he was wearing only a pair of jeans, Spence pulled open the door, saw the pile of girls and said, "Can someone tell me what's going on?"

"Scary noise." Bex was succinct, a trembling twelve-year-old in her arms.

"A scary noise?" He ran his hand through his dark hair. "You have to be sh—…er, kidding me. All this screaming and ruckus over a scary noise? What kind of scary noise? Anyone have more information? Describe the noise."

"They said it was a growl," Melody explained. "And something scratching at the tent. Scary noise works for me."

Behind him Jim said, "Well, son, they ain't making this one up. We've got a bear problem."

WHAT HE WANTED was some sleep.

Not much to ask. Forty winks.

Forget it. Unlikely to happen.

Bear problem. That was great news. Bears were pretty dang smart, and they were also tenacious. The only reason they ever bothered humans was if they needed to defend themselves or their young, or if they wanted food.

He didn't need to be a biologist to figure out what this bear wanted. Food.

He went back to his tent to get a shirt and could hear it crashing around. "What kind? Did you get a gander at it?"

Jim watched him yank a sweatshirt over his head, rifle in hand. "Looks like a brown bear to me, but it could be a young grizzly. Those silvertip cubs look full-grown even when they're young."

Grizzly? Now that would be perfect. How big did they get? Oh, they got big. *Big.* He'd met one face-to-face once when he was about fifteen and out camping. Thankfully it just gave him a contemptuous look and walked away.

"That .22 won't stop him."

"Might frighten him off," Jim said. "He's pretty well trashed one of the tents."

Spence let out a sound of pure irritation. "It's those damned cookies. Let's see. Mix something like berries and nuts with sweets, and guess what? Bears will like it. I thought I asked every camper if she had anything like that to give it to me. I promised she could have it back first thing in the morning, but for tonight I had to hoist it up out of harm's way. Dammit, that critter is spooking the horses. I can hear them moving around."

Jim handed him a small bag. "Here's Pauline's. With an apology. She's joined the others in that tent."

Oh, great, now he was walking bear bait. He turned, high-powered rifle in hand. "Tell me you don't think every one of those tents doesn't have some of those damned cookies in them. I was clear, wasn't I, when I talked about bears?"

Jim gave an unholy grin. He was taking it seriously, but still thought it was funny. "Yup, I'll bet all of those tents have cookies and God knows what else in them, and you were very clear."

Spence glanced around. "This is going to be interesting. So do you want to go search for the bear or do guard duty and keep an eye on the horses? I'm not leaving the girls alone. Especially since they probably have more cookies to attract bears."

Jim tilted his head. "I'll guard the tent. Since they're all piled in with Hadleigh and her friends, that makes it pretty easy on me. Can we exchange weapons, though? What you're holding there would make a statement, and I'll be guarding precious cargo, including my wife and my daughter-in-law. My gun is just a suggestion to move on. Most critters will do that, but not all, so it's your choice."

He agreed, of course, exchanging his weapon for Jim's, but he hoped the young grizzly theory was a case of mistaken identity. Bears tended to stay with their mothers for quite some time, usually two years. Young bear, fine. Young bear with a protective mother...not so good.

It didn't really matter. Black bears killed more people than grizzlies or brown bears; bees and wasps were a lot deadlier than any of them. Mother Nature abounded with critters that could do you harm, but usually weren't interested in people. The bear was after food, which it had found. Now they needed to encourage it to go foraging elsewhere.

"Make the girls tell you the truth," he warned, checking that the rifle was loaded and ready. "If I discover one of them hoarded a bag of cookies in that tent where they're all huddled together, I'm going to be really annoyed. Get Mel, Bex and Hadleigh on it."

"*No* food in there. You know how bears are."

"Yes, Chief." Jim saluted him. "Wait. Hold on." A moment later he was back. "Take this, too."

It was the sword.

He had to be kidding. The night just got better and better.

Oh, yeah, that would complete this delightful trip—staving off a hungry grizzly with a Revolutionary War sword. He could see that headline already: Small Town Police Chief Defends Girls By Skewering a Protected Species.

"See you later," he muttered. "If I'm not blown to Nebraska by this wind. Or eaten by a bear. Or impaled on this sword."

With a curse he went off into the darkness, and the bear wasn't at all that hard to find. For one thing, bears are large and without any natural predators, besides other bears and humans, so it felt no particular need to be quiet.

Brown bear, he figured out quickly, and full-grown. Although it had wrecked several tents, two shots in the air were enough to persuade the offender to amble away into the forest.

Then came the worst part of the entire debacle.

None of the girls wanted to return to their beds.

All twelve of them, it seemed, insisted on sleeping together, in the tent with the four adult women. Which was impossible in such a small space, and the girls wanted Jim Galloway and him to sleep in there, too.

Where? Sardines had more space in one of those cans.

Nope. Not in one million years.

The howling wind outside was preferable.

It was sprinkling again. Pauline had regretfully told him she thought it was going to rain all night as she and Jim finally headed back to their tent.

"I'll sleep across the doorway outside," he promised the group of wide-eyed females. "I have my gun and the sword, so you should all be fine. Wake me up if—"

"Sword?" Melody interrupted. She sat up and stared at him. "What are you talking about?"

"Oh, never mind. We'll talk about it later." He pointed into the darkness toward the tree where he'd put his tent. "I'm going to get my sleeping bag and camp out on your doorstep. Okay? He'll have to come through me to get to you."

The girls seemed placated—and tired. "Okay."

He was going to be wet again. Soaked. Maybe the bear would rip him to shreds in the night and end his misery, he thought as he dragged out his sleeping bag and adjusted the hood. He was sleeping with an ineffective .22 rifle and a sword that hadn't been sharpened in about three hundred years, the grand protector of a group of girls in a seriously overcrowded tent.

Spence made himself comfortable in his sleeping bag, or as comfortable as possible under the circumstances. Trying to ignore the rain, he closed his eyes.

CHAPTER TWENTY

As HEROES WENT, he was an impressive one.

When the horses trailed back to the Galloway ranch, Melody was sure there wasn't a single girl on that expedition who didn't have a crush on Mustang Creek's handsome police chief.

She certainly did.

As soon as they got within range of a tower, the girls had started calling their parents, and there was a line of cars along the lane to the house, waiting to pick them up.

The sun had the nerve to actually peek through the clouds at the very moment Spence brought Reb to a halt. He slid off in a single athletic move that showed he wasn't stiff and sore in the least, and began helping everyone dismount. Tripp had come out to deal with the horses.

Next to her, Bex groaned. "I'm going to have to borrow either Tripp or Spence to carry me to my car. Hope one of you will be generous enough to lend me your guy for ten minutes. I thought by the third day I wouldn't be sore. I've trained for and run in six different marathons, but *this* was something else."

Melody's backside agreed. "I'll never be the same again," she declared as her horse came to a halt. "I'm not even going to dismount, I'm just going to fall off."

Hadleigh said, "Stop your whining. Let's see, yes, we were wet the entire time, fifteen people slept in a three-person tent, ate soggy sandwiches and were threatened by a monstrous bear—but it was a great experience."

Bex and Melody looked incredulously at each other and then at her.

She amended hastily, "I meant for the girls."

It was really hard to not laugh.

Melody said emphatically, "All I know is that there's a hot bath with my name on it. A glass of chilled wine awaits and a nice soft bed will cure some of these aches and pains. I want a steak for dinner. A nice, juicy steak."

She didn't realize Spence had come to take her horse, but a queue of cars was already pulling away.

"That can be arranged." Spence's hands suddenly spanned her waist, and he lifted her easily from the saddle. He set her on her feet. "Do we have a date, then? My place or yours?"

She had steaks at home; she'd bought them on her last grocery trip. She wanted to be in her own place, wanted to see her cats. A friend had come to feed them, so they hadn't been neglected, but she missed Ralph, Waldo and Emerson. "Mine. Bring Harley. I think the triumvirate would be disappointed not to spend some quality time with him."

Spence winked at her. "Done. Six o'clock?"

Then he helped Bex out of her saddle, and walked along the line of remaining girls and their parents with that lanky cowboy stride. He spoke to a mom who had an anxious look on her face, probably due to the bear story. His quick smile was reassuring, and her anxiety eased almost at once.

"He's smooth," Bex murmured. "I'll give him that."

Melody didn't disagree. She said, "You know, I see Tate Calder's here helping out. That's nice of him. Get *him* to carry you to your car."

Bex blushed. Yes, she blushed. "We've only met once."

Tripp came over to help Hadleigh down, interrupting the conversation. "How was it?"

His wife fell into his arms. "Um, ask Spence and Jim first. I'll either confirm or deny what they say. Bex and Mel will back me up."

"I see." Tripp kissed her lightly. "All I know is that the girls claim they had a terrific time. I heard them talking to their parents as I got the horses."

All three of them stared at him. "What?"

He gave a masculine shrug. "They said it was a great trip."

Then all three of them stared at each other.

"I don't think that's what Spence would say, but it's good to hear. Pauline, by the way, is wonderful, and I've always been impressed with Jim, too." Melody wondered how long it would take her to limp to her car. She wanted the crowd to thin out first so there'd be fewer people to witness her current infirmity.

"They were robbed while you were gone," Tripp said in a low, regretful tone. "Just like at your house. Came in through a window someone busted out. A neighbor called me."

"Oh, no." Hadleigh looked distressed, and Melody felt sick at heart.

"Funny thing, my dad wasn't surprised when I told

him a few minutes ago." Tripp frowned. "He seemed almost happy about it. What's up with that?"

REB WAS GLAD to be home, and so was Harley.

One out to pasture, the other snoozing on the living room rug.

Spence was more content after a hot shower, and scrolled through the messages loading on his phone, not in order of delivery, but in order of importance.

Jack was at the top of the list.

He called back and managed to reach him.

"Pearson here."

"Hey, Jack, this is Spence, fresh off a hellish trip we'll discuss sometime over a pitcher of beer. I see you called. What do you have for me?"

"A potential arrest. Big one. Want details?"

"Are you kidding? I called *you*, remember?"

His colleague took a moment. "I'm looking through my notes…wait, here you go. There's a ring based in my fair city that operates through most of Wyoming and into Montana, and might even be responsible for some robberies in Idaho. They specialize in antiques, have buyers all over the place, and their method seems to be to get a foot in the door by doing appraisals—and then the items disappear. The woman who's fingered as the leader has a number of aliases and false credentials, but she does have a degree from Harvard, no less. Her real name is Marilyn Artois, and she really is an expert in antiques. The FBI has been sniffing around this since it crosses jurisdiction boundaries, but they haven't been able to locate her. Do you have any idea how much old stuff can be worth?"

The sword. If Marilyn Artois, aka Mary Allen, got

hold of it, he was sure it would never make it to auction. The thing was worth a fortune, and she'd almost certainly have a private buyer.

"I do, since an education on the subject is being forced down my throat. Can you send me a picture of this Marilyn Artois? I think I might be able to help out both you and the FBI, courtesy of one old crafty rancher. If she's still here in Mustang Creek, and I suspect she is, given what happened over the weekend, then maybe I can pick her up."

"I'll forward it to your email."

"That would be great."

"You'll look like a superstar if you pull off getting these guys. They've been in operation for a while. Several state agencies have them on their lists. Marilyn's the ringleader, and without her, they couldn't pull it off. From what I understand she's very personable and attractive and her credentials are impeccable. The group moves around and they fly under the radar because no one's been hurt yet, but they're raking it in."

Well, *hurt* was a relative term. He thought about Melody's panic over the cats and Harley's limp. And Jim and Pauline probably weren't enjoying their homecoming after a less than satisfying trip.

"I don't care about being a superstar. I just want to get a diamond back."

And his great-grandmother's canisters, which wouldn't be worth all that much to anyone else, but he loved them. He recalled that he'd once said something about them to "Mary."

"Diamond? Fill me in when we drink that pitcher."

"Deal."

"Good luck."

The picture came through, and he had no trouble identifying the subject. A bit embarrassing that he'd dated a con artist and well-known thief, even if it hadn't been more than two or three times.

He immediately called Tripp. "Tell your dad Operation Sword was a stroke of genius."

"Uh, mind telling me what the heck you're talking about?"

"Nope. I have a date, so I gotta go."

"Tell Mel I said hello. I was so busy greeting Hadleigh, I don't think I did earlier."

On his way into town, he stopped at the antiques store and found Junie's cousin, Cassandra, locking up. "Can you have Ronald give me a call? I was hoping to catch him," he said.

She reached into her pocket, produced her phone and flicked open a screen. "Any chance this is about her?" She held it out.

Definitely Marilyn Artois, aka Mary Allen. He must have looked flummoxed, because his dispatcher's cousin explained. "Melody asked if I'd watch out for someone who might know she bought that ring. I remembered she was in there when I was wrapping it up, so I took this picture with my phone. Mary floats in and out pretty often."

He took a breath and said a prayer. "There's no chance you have an address for her, is there?"

"PO box. My ex is a lawyer, and I used to work in his office as a clerk, so I know a little about how to do this. I looked through all our invoices. She bought something months ago and paid by check. The account is closed, but the PO box is still rented. I inquired about that on Friday and told Junie about it. According to her, this woman still collects her mail there, but under a different name. You know Terry, the postmaster? He noticed that she changes banks often or at least has a lot of different accounts."

His smile was genuine. "I don't want to steal you from Ronald, but if you ever need a job with the police department and we have an opening, let's talk."

He immediately called Moe. "Surveillance detail on the post office. I'll send the number and the picture of the suspect. If she shows up, detain her."

"Okay. How was the trip?"

"We'll have to discuss that next year. I'm reluctant to have a repeat performance."

"Word is, everyone had a ball."

"Not everyone."

A muffled laugh was the response. "I kinda heard about the bear when I saw one of the parents at the grocery store."

He put his truck in gear. "If you keep this up, I'll put you on third shift. Right now I've got someplace to be."

When he and Harley pulled in to Melody's house, the smell wafting out was fabulous. Melody answered the door barefoot, wearing a tan skirt and a pale blue sleeveless blouse. Her hair was smooth and shining, and she immediately bent to pet the dog.

"Good to know Harley's welcome," he joked.

Then she rose up on tiptoe and kissed him. Nothing complicated, just a kiss with her hands on his shoulders, but he felt weak in the knees when it was over.

She knew it, too. "Come on in. I'm hoping you'll agree to grill the steaks, because I have everything else going."

"I'm sure I'd agree to anything you suggest."

"Really? Glad to hear it."

She had a very nice backside, so following her into the kitchen was his pleasure.

When she turned around and rested against the kitchen counter, she brushed her hair back from her face. "So, not to waste any time, but... I did this once, and I need some sort of medal for trying again, but will you marry me?"

It wasn't how he'd pictured the moment. Spence was tongue-tied.

Wasn't he supposed to be the one on bended knee, holding a ring...?

"There's a condition," she said. "We're only going to do this if you love me. We aren't going to negotiate on that one."

"Mel, you know I love you."

"Honestly, I've never heard that from you."

He stopped and considered. She *could* be right. But...surely he'd said it. Hadn't he?

Maybe not.

"I'm not positive I've heard it from you, either." He figured turnabout was fair play—especially in love. Or war? He was confusing his clichés.

She looked endearingly startled. "Yes, you have."

"Name the date."

"Like I carry around a book to note those things down? Spencer Hogan, you know I've told you I love you."

That was progress.

He crowded her against the counter, his much taller body pressed against hers. This was one argument he wasn't going to lose. That decision nine years ago had been right—but it had cost him. "No, I don't think you have. When you wanted to elope, you suggested we go off and get married. Love was left out of it."

She put her hands on his chest and shoved. "Then why didn't *you* bring it up?"

He refused to budge, and his mouth brushed hers. "Maybe because I loved you so much, I didn't want you to settle for a man you didn't love completely. Even if that man was me."

Her eyes instantly clouded with tears. "What?"

"Just kiss me. My answer is yes. I want to marry you."

She buried her face in his chest. "Keep trying. You almost have it."

He ran his fingers through her silky hair. "I love you."

"There you go. I love you, too."

"I'm going to be so distracted this evening, I'll burn our steaks."

"I'll supervise. Besides, there's always peanut butter and jelly."

He laughed.

"Tell me about the sword, and I'll give you twice-baked potatoes and a spinach salad with a dressing you won't believe."

"That sounds like quite the deal. Done."

CHAPTER TWENTY-ONE

IT WAS AN unusual kind of day.

Mrs. Arbuckle, wearing a pressed jacket and tweed skirt, arrived on her doorstep before seven o'clock, with two cups of takeout gourmet coffee.

She'd taken the liberty of adding vanilla creamer to the coffee because she liked it that way, and breezed in as if Melody wasn't in her pajamas with her hair bunched up on one side.

"Good morning. Is this too early?"

At a loss for words, Melody stepped aside. "No… no, of course not. I was practically up."

Harley bounded out of the bedroom; all Mrs. A. had to do was lift an aristocratic eyebrow and he calmed right down and sat obediently. No words needed.

Mrs. A. should run a charm school of intimidating females, Melody decided as she followed her into the kitchen.

"You must meet my Roscoe sometime, young man," she told Harley. "I left him at home, I'm sorry to say."

Melody murmured something vague.

Her visitor held a bag aloft. "I brought blueberry Danishes. My favorite."

"Um, thank you." She was glad she'd taken the time the night before to tidy the kitchen. Spence had kept nudging her toward the bedroom, but she'd refused to leave dishes in the sink; in the end, he'd pitched in.

It was her fervent hope that he wouldn't wander out in his boxers some time during this conversation she was apparently destined to have, vanilla creamer and all.

"My precipitous arrival has a purpose." Mrs. A. slipped a hand into her pocket. "Here. This is perfect for the ring you're making for me. It was meant for you, anyway."

Spence had told her the night before that he'd planned on giving her the ring of her dreams, and Mrs. A. had agreed to help. She hadn't mentioned that she already knew, thanks to her loyal friend, Hadleigh.

She opened the box, and there sat the Pierce diamond nestled in white velvet. Her pulse skipped up a couple of notches. "Where did you find this?"

"Well..." Mrs. Arbuckle looked smug and took a sip from her coffee cup and confided, "I didn't find it. I stole it back."

If the sky had turned green and the grass blue, she couldn't have been more surprised. Although, when Melody thought about it, she'd always known that Lettie Arbuckle was a force to be reckoned with.

"You—what? How—"

"Who do you think was approached to buy it? One of my friends, of course. As soon as I found out about the robbery, I sent emails to everyone I know, asking them to contact me if anyone offered them a ring of any kind. A very elegant young woman calling herself Margot—she clearly likes names starting with "M"—approached my friend with an offer, although the provenance was forged. They arranged a meeting to look at it. My friend turned it down, and after that, I followed this other person back to Mustang Creek. I watched through the window of her—fortunately downstairs—apartment and saw her put the ring in a drawer. After she left, my driver opened her door for me. You see, he once had a less than respectable past and therefore some remarkably valuable skills."

Picturing Mrs. A. breaking into someone's house was beyond the realm of imagination. And yet the re-doubtable older woman seemed to expect praise.

Tongue-tied, Melody managed to murmur, "That was…clever."

"I thought so." Mrs. Arbuckle actually beamed, if that was possible. "And you can be sure I've passed Marilyn's address on to Spencer, so he has everything under control. Now, on to a more pleasant subject. I understand the trail ride was a great success."

"It was?" Melody took a hearty gulp from her cup. Maybe she was still asleep, and this was all a dream.

"Oh, yes." Mrs. Arbuckle nodded. "I want to spon-sor it next year."

Next year? *There* was a happy thought. "Another trail ride for girls?"

"I might even come along."

Oh…dear.

While she had a genuine fondness for the woman sit-ting across from her, Melody didn't find this suggestion appealing. In fact, the very idea of another trip like the one she hadn't yet recovered from made her shudder.

"And I'm very interested in your wedding. Do you need help planning it?"

That was a loaded question.

"I, er, well…"

"Think about it, my dear. I'm very good at that sort of thing, if I do say so myself. Now, I must be running along, but we'll speak soon."

Melody was sitting there alone, except for all three cats and Harley, devouring a Danish when Spence wandered out of bed half an hour later, his hair standing straight up. Somehow he managed to pull it off. She was sure she'd never looked that gorgeous first thing in the morning.

"I smell coffee."

"There's vanilla creamer in it."

"Fine."

Melody leveled a look his way. "The last time I asked, you weren't very cooperative, but can we elope, please?"

"Pardon me?"

"I have a good reason for asking."

He paused. "Before coffee?"

She smothered a laugh. "No, but if you refuse me this time, Mrs. A. is going to plan the whole wedding. Also…I know you're much more familiar with the law than I am, so can she get in trouble for this?"

When she extended the diamond ring, he finally woke up completely. His fingers raked his hair into a new degree of dishevelment as he stared at it. "Is that what I think it is?"

"The Pierce diamond. It sure is."

"Where the hell…I mean, that's *evidence*."

"But a very nice gesture."

Melody offered him her cup in sympathy. He took it and downed the contents, although it had to be luke-warm at best. "Where'd she find it?" he demanded.

"No idea. I didn't ask."

"You didn't *ask*." He tossed the paper cup in the trash can.

She shook her head. "Nope. No way. Now, this elopement thing—are we doing it, or should we let Mrs. A. have at it when it comes to the wedding?"

He shuddered and dropped into a chair. "No, no. We're going to Costa Rica or someplace suitably far away. The Gobi Desert. Mars. Seriously, how did she find it?"

"Like I said, I truly have no idea."

"You truly didn't ask."

"All I can tell you is that she said she 'stole it back.' Is it stealing when you take something that was stolen from you?"

He looked stymied. "I think I'd let a judge decide that one."

She got up to make him more coffee of the everyday variety. "Good luck to anyone who takes on Mrs. A. So, what did your mother's card say?"

At the end of the trail ride, when they were riding side by side for a few minutes, Jim had told her he'd recommended that Spence just open it. If he was going to take any advice, it would be from Jim.

The look on his face told her he'd done it. She knew how momentous that was, what an important moment it had to be. A potentially life-changing moment, in fact. "Spence?"

"It's probably easier to let you read it."

He got up and went into the bedroom and came back just as the coffee was sputtering into the carafe. The image on the outside of the card—the kind of card you could buy at any drugstore—was a single flower.

"It's nothing," he said as she opened it.

It wasn't nothing.

Three words, but not the ones everyone wanted to hear. It didn't say *I love you*.

But it did say *I'm so sorry*.

He poured a cup of coffee. "I don't know her well enough to believe her, so does it matter? Most people offer up regrets to make themselves feel better. Fine. She's sorry. Good for her."

There was a hint of that abandoned nine-year-old boy in there, despite the sexy morning stubble on his jaw. Despite the way he dwarfed the chair he was sprawled in so carelessly.

She wasn't sure how far she should press the issue. She loved him, so it would be inaccurate to say it wasn't her business, but in the end how he chose to handle it was up to him. She just pointed out, "There's a phone number."

He said over the rim of his cup, "Nice of her to put the ball in my court, isn't it? Please tell me there's another of those Danishes."

Subject closed. She got up and retrieved the box and pushed it toward him. "If you hadn't come out here at such a strategic time, I was going to hide it, but now I suppose I have to share."

He took a man-sized piece and frowned at Harley. "Wipe that hopeful look off your face, mutt. You know the rules. There's people food and there's dog food."

Melody wasn't about to confess that she might have given him the tiniest nibble. To deflect any pastry questions, she asked, "So Mrs. A. said you had the robbery situation under control. What does that mean?"

"Thanks to you going to Junie, and Junie talking to her cousin, we caught Mary Allen, aka Marilyn Artois, at the post office picking up her mail, just like the law-abiding citizen she isn't. How Mrs. A. figured out her address is beyond me, but several law-enforcement agencies are working on arresting her accomplices. Jim used that sword, the one I told you about last night, as bait. Then he set up one of those cameras on his back deck, the kind you can use to take pictures of animals prowling around your house. They're activated by movement, so we have pictures of them actually breaking in."

"You thought the thefts were personal."

"Well, yes. I'm embarrassed to say that Mary—I mean Marilyn—thought she and I had more of a connection than we did. She resented my breaking up with her, and she resented you when she figured out who you were—the woman I was interested in. So to that extent, they *were* personal. The fact that you were also a jewelry maker fit perfectly with her vendetta. I found all of this out from Junie, by the way. Marilyn, uh, shared some of this with the cop who arrested her, who then shared it with Junie."

"So that's also why she trashed my place and yours the way she did."

"Yup. She's got quite the hate-on for me."

"Why would she admit what she'd done?"

"Basically to make me look incompetent. Which she did," he said wryly.

Melody started to defend him, but he shook his head. "Hey, it doesn't make any difference. We got her in the end, despite the fact that her fingerprints didn't appear in any state or federal database—that's how good she was. I actually thought for some time that she was operating on her own." He shrugged. "That was quite the enterprise she ran—the number of aliases she had, the accomplices, the way they built up the level of crime, from less serious ones, like stealing Ross Hayden's trolling motor and antique tools to the Pierce diamond."

"What a waste of ability. With those kinds of skills, she could have been the CEO of a major company."

"She might not have moral fiber," he agreed, "but she's smart."

"Is that what attracted you to her?"

"I like intelligent women, yes, but can we remember I went out with her only a few times? She wasn't you. End of story. Same with every woman I've even looked at during the past nine years."

The man had his moments. Melody said, "You can have the rest of the Danish. I find I'm in a generous mood."

THERE WAS SOME chagrin involved in having a crime ring broken up by everyone but the one person who was supposed to be in charge. The consolation was that other law enforcement hadn't succeeded before now, either. Spence even had to speak at a press conference, and that didn't make him very happy. A press conference was unprecedented, as far as he knew, in the history of Mustang Creek.

He'd much rather be on Reb at a full-out gallop, clean air in his lungs, Harley running alongside them.

And better yet, another rider with him, her blond hair blowing in the wind.

Tripp asked, "What do you think? Is she a beauty or what?"

The palomino mare had a gentle look in her eyes,

and she took the carrot he produced like a well-mannered lady. "That's an understatement."

Melody was going to love her. His throat tightened.

"Her former owner was transferred for her job and couldn't find property that didn't involve boarding her somewhere. So she put her up for sale, saddle and bridle included. I have some very specific instructions on how she likes to be brushed and so forth." Tripp gave an exasperated sigh. "Like I'd never brushed down a horse before. But I understand. The only reason I won the bid was that I told the owner about Melody before the auction. And the only reason I knew about this *horse* was Tate. He's thinking about starting a bloodstock business. His father's an investment banker, and if Tate can deliver a profit, his dad will front the setup costs. He's been to every auction in this area, and he's done a lot of research. He said this horse was worth snapping up for a special lady. Mel qualifies."

She sure did.

"I owe both you and him." Spence stroked the mare's silky mane. "This is a perfect wedding gift."

"Hadleigh's pregnant."

Spence turned and rested an arm on the fence rail. "Am I supposed to be surprised? I'm pretty sure I know what you do together in your spare time. Just sayin'. Congratulations."

Tripp grinned. "Thanks."

He didn't mention that he'd seen the charm Melody was working on, the mare with a foal, and had immediately guessed who it was for.

After writing Tripp a check, he loaded the mare in the trailer he'd brought and took her home. She and Reb greeted each other with caution at first, but quickly came to an understanding. A muzzle touch and some communal grazing went a long way.

What he wanted to do was craft the perfect evening. He wasn't sure how to do that, so he just sent Melody a text.

How do you feel about running out to the ranch? Harley misses you.

If nothing else, she was a sucker for the dog. Why not shamelessly exploit that weakness?

She sent back

See you in a few. I've got a couple of deliveries to make.

Casual dress code tonight. Jeans and boots.

He hoped that didn't give too much away, but he was really looking forward to an evening ride, and occasionally Melody wore shorts or a sundress to show off those long legs he admired.

Especially when they were wrapped around him, he thought with an inner smile.

He sat on the front porch and called his aunt while he waited. "I'm engaged, Aunt Libby."

"Spence, this is Mustang Creek. I've been waiting for you to tell me, but if you think I didn't already know, think again. About time if you ask me. How does she like the horse?"

"How did…" He trailed off with a sigh. "I'm giving the mare to her this evening. I sure hope everyone isn't as well-informed as you are. I was planning a surprise."

"I ran into Pauline at the grocery. No one will tell Melody. Don't worry."

"My mother sent me a card." It was a terse declaration. "Out of the blue."

"That I did not know." There was a brief silence before she asked, "What did it say?"

"That she was sorry. She included a phone number."

"Interesting."

"That's all you have to say?"

"Spence, I haven't seen her or talked to her in twenty-seven years, either. I always wondered if she'd have regrets. But there's one thing I can tell you for sure—I don't. Even when you were your most cantankerous teenage self, raising you was my greatest joy. I got a little frustrated now and then, make no mistake, but you turned out to be a fine man, and I'm proud of you." She paused. "Are you going to call her?"

There was a reason he loved this woman so much.

"I haven't decided."

"Either way, you have my support. I hear Lettie Arbuckle is going to plan your wedding."

He barely managed to contain a groan. Gossip in Mustang Creek really caught fire if there was anything to talk about; he figured that between the thefts and his engagement, he'd given them lots. "Well, I'll leave that to her and Mel."

They were *definitely* eloping.

Just as he ended the call, he saw Melody's little yellow car pull into the long drive, and if he hadn't, Harley would have alerted him, leaping up and barking excitedly.

She didn't make it to the house, braking to an abrupt halt by the pasture. In two seconds flat she was out of the car and leaning over the fence. She'd put the car in Park, but had neglected to turn the engine off, so he bent and did that for her.

The look on her face was priceless. He didn't have to say a word.

The mare trotted over, just as inquisitive, and of course, Reb followed.

"Spence." Melody's eyes were alight. "She's so beautiful."

"You suit each other," he said softly.

"What's her name?"

"That's for you to decide. Her former owner has separation anxiety. She didn't want to say. She wanted the mare to have a brand-new start with a brand-new name."

"That's easy. Charm."

He approved, but again, it wasn't his call.

"Boots and jeans. I wondered about that." She rubbed the palomino's velvet nose. "Can we go for a ride?"

"That's the general idea. I'll saddle the horses. Meanwhile, you'd better pet Harley. He's feeling neglected."

Half an hour later, they were in the meadow by the stream, walking the horses. The trail ride had helped, since Melody seemed more comfortable in the saddle now. And the mare had the smooth gait and gentle disposition Tate had promised, which helped, too.

Velvet blue sky, darkening above. Warm breeze.

He pulled up Reb, and the mare halted on cue as Melody sent him an inquiring look. "Do you see that grassy bank right there?" he asked in a teasing tone.

"I was just wondering, if…well, it's a nice night, and the horses could graze…"

"Outside?"

"Could there be a better setting?"

SPENCE HAD A valid point.

He dismounted and then lifted her out of the saddle. Melody didn't object as he placed her on the grass and eased off her boots then unbuttoned her blouse, unhooking her lacy bra to expose her breasts. She made an involuntary sound as he took a taut nipple in his mouth, and he settled comfortably over her, his weight braced.

He tasted every inch of her, from head to toe, finally moving to her most intimate part, the pleasure so intense she shuddered. She would have cried out except that the sound was locked in her throat. She couldn't breathe enough to let it escape.

Then he did it again.

Not until she was utterly limp did he move inside her, sliding in fully, his eyes half-closed as he exhaled.

There was only so much a girl could take, she thought later, lost in a haze of sensual pleasure, the tickle of grass at her back.

He proved her wrong. Twice.

* * * * *

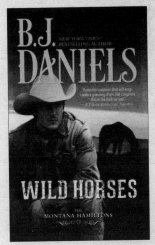

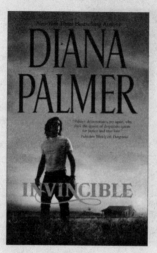

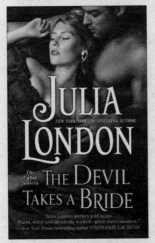

REQUEST YOUR
FREE BOOKS!

2 FREE NOVELS
FROM THE ROMANCE COLLECTION
PLUS 2 FREE GIFTS!

YES! Please send me 2 FREE novels from the Romance Collection and my 2 FREE gifts (gifts are worth about $10). After receiving them, if I don't wish to receive any more books, I can return the shipping statement marked "cancel." If I don't cancel, I will receive 4 brand-new novels every month and be billed just $6.24 per book in the U.S. or $6.74 per book in Canada. That's a savings of at least 22% off the cover price. It's quite a bargain! Shipping and handling is just 50¢ per book in the U.S. and 75¢ per book in Canada.* I understand that accepting the 2 free books and gifts places me under no obligation to buy anything. I can always return a shipment and cancel at any time. Even if I never buy another book, the two free books and gifts are mine to keep forever.

194/394 MDN F4XY

Name _____ (PLEASE PRINT) _____

Address _____ Apt. # _____

City _____ State/Prov. _____ Zip/Postal Code _____

Signature (if under 18, a parent or guardian must sign)

Mail to the Harlequin® Reader Service:
IN U.S.A.: P.O. Box 1867, Buffalo, NY 14240-1867
IN CANADA: P.O. Box 609, Fort Erie, Ontario L2A 5X3

Want to try two free books from another line?
Call 1-800-873-8635 or visit www.ReaderService.com.

* Terms and prices subject to change without notice. Prices do not include applicable taxes. Sales tax applicable in N.Y. Canadian residents will be charged applicable taxes. Offer not valid in Quebec. This offer is limited to one order per household. Not valid for current subscribers to the Romance Collection or the Romance/Suspense Collection. All orders subject to credit approval. Credit or debit balances in a customer's account(s) may be offset by any other outstanding balance owed by or to the customer. Please allow 4 to 6 weeks for delivery. Offer available while quantities last.

Your Privacy—The Harlequin® Reader Service is committed to protecting your privacy. Our Privacy Policy is available online at www.ReaderService.com or upon request from the Harlequin Reader Service.

We make a portion of our mailing list available to reputable third parties that offer products we believe may interest you. If you prefer that we not exchange your name with third parties, or if you wish to clarify or modify your communication preferences, please visit us at www.ReaderService.com/consumerchoice or write to us at Harlequin Reader Service Preference Service, P.O. Box 9062, Buffalo, NY 14269. Include your complete name and address.

ROM13R